Black Love, White Lies 2:

A BWWM Romance

Black Love, White Lies 2:

A BWWM Romance

Genesis Woods

www.urbanbooks.net

Urban Books, LLC
300 Farmingdale Road, NY-Route 109
Farmingdale, NY 11735

Black Love, White Lies 2: A BWWM Romance

ISBN 13: 978-1-62286-599-4
ISBN 10: 1-62286-599-5

First Mass Market Printing June 2017
Printed in the United States of America

10 9 8 7 6 5 4 3 2

Distributed by Kensington Publishing Corp.
Submit Orders to:
Customer Service
400 Hahn Road
Westminster, MD 21157-4627
Phone: 1-800-733-3000
Fax: 1-800-659-2436

Black Love, White Lies 2:

A BWWM Romance

by

Genesis Woods

This book, as well as all of my other books, is dedicated to my mother,
Ms. Jennie Williams.

One day, I'm going to make you proud of me.
Thank you for everything! Without you, I don't know where I'd be!

Thank You!

To everyone who has ever purchased a book by me, whether you liked it or not, I just wanna say thank you. Although my goal is to make you love me and my work, I don't do this for any reader or nonbeliever. I do this to show my cubs that, regardless of what people say or how people may feel about you, your talents, or your beliefs, never become discouraged.

A lot of you don't know my story, but I come from an upper-middle-class family where I was given any- and everything I ever wished for or wanted. As I got older and started to feel myself, I began to make choices that my family didn't agree with. And, just like any young, dumb, and full-of-cum adolescent, I thought my ways of living and thinking were right.

Fast-forward fifteen years: I'd finally experienced life in the lowest form. Not only did I marry a man I knew wasn't right for me, I ended up having two babies by him and ultimately ended up homeless and living in a motel with my two cubs, trying to prove to everybody else but myself that they were wrong about our union.

Thank You!

I almost gave up my dream of being an author because my life changed for the worse when I thought it was just starting to look up. If it weren't for people like JM Hart, Jessica Wren, my BFF Nickey Mallory, my cousin and BFF Tia Alexander, Tavon Alexander, Brittney DeJohnette, Rollin Holt, Candace Mumford, Geraldine Grady, Patriece A'zayler Watts, Jamal Harget, Gerard Beard, and my readers (I can't remember all of your names, but you know who you are) who believed in, reached out to, and kept me in their prayers regardless of knowing my situation, I wholeheartedly thank all of you! At one point in time, my mental wasn't where it should've been, and it was because of you I didn't jump off of that cliff. At this moment, I'm still down, but my focus is only to keep moving up! One day someone, somewhere, is going to read one of my books and my career will take off from there. I'm already claiming it, believing in it, and pleading the blood of Jesus over it. Continue to keep me in your prayers as I will continue to keep you in mine.

—Genesis

A special thank-you to Mr. Blake Karrington. Thank you for this opportunity and for all you've done for me! I appreciate you.

CHAPTER 1

CAIRO

"She's having whose baby?" Alex screamed over my head as I knelt down next to Audri. I was so concerned with making sure that she was okay I totally forgot that Alex was standing there.

"Audrielle, I need you to breathe, okay? Take a deep breath. That's it. Hold it for a few seconds. Now release it. We need a bus now, or she's going to deliver the baby right here!" the doctor turned and yelled over her shoulder.

"Aaaaarrrrrrrggghhh," Audri screamed as another pain shot through her body. "I feel like I have to push."

"No, no, no, no! Not yet, Audri. Don't push right now. Try to hold it for a minute. The paramedics are coming through the door now."

I looked up just in time to see four uniformed men rushing through the double glass doors of the medical office. Two had big yellow boxes in their hands, while the other two pushed in a gurney. I focused my sight back to a now crying Audri. From the look on her face, I could tell that she was going through an inexplicable amount of pain. Since I wasn't able to take any of it on for her like I wanted to, I wiped the tears from her eyes and gave her a reassuring smile to tell her that everything would be okay.

A light tap on my shoulder had me feeling a little more than irritated. When I turned around, I came face to face with a pissed-off Alex. The scowl on her face was so deep that you could see all of the worry lines she tried to hide with Botox injections forming in the corner of her eyes. "Um, Cai, we can leave now? The paramedics are here to take her to the hospital. I'm sure whoever she's pregnant by will meet her at the hospital. We have an appointment in an hour with the people at the hall where we are going to have the baby shower, and we can't be late."

I shook my head and turned my attention back to Audri, who quickly averted her eyes from mine and started to look at everything in the lobby but me. When the EMTs finally made it to where we were, they had everyone including myself back away from Audri as they checked her vitals then lifted her onto the gurney.

After confirming what hospital they were about to take her to, I turned on my heels and was headed to my car. Before I could even get a foot out of the door, Alex was running behind me crying and screaming at the top of her lungs. I couldn't understand a word she was saying because her words were sounding like a bunch of gibberish. I didn't have time for her or her shenanigans, so I kept walking. I was almost to my car when one of the nurses ran out behind me and said something about my pregnant girl-friend falling. Thinking those EMTs mistakenly dropped Audri, I ran full speed back into the medical building. When I got there, however, it wasn't Audri who was on the floor.

"Ma'am, we need you to breathe, okay? It's not healthy for you or the baby to be under all this stress."

Alex looked up at me with sad eyes. "Honey, you came back."

Ignoring her, I walked over to the paramedic standing next to her and asked what happened. After telling me that she fell out chasing after me and that she would be okay, I gave Alex the keys and hopped in the back of the ambulance with Audri.

The whole way to the hospital, I was a big bottle of nerves because I didn't know what to do. I wanted to call Mama Faye but changed my mind. Although she'd be happy to finally have a grandchild from me, this was some news that would be better told face to face than over the phone. I looked at Audri's beautiful face squinted up in pain. Besides holding her hand and trying to feed her ice chips, there wasn't really too much more that I could do to make her feel any type of comfort.

When we made it to the hospital, a team of nurses was waiting in the bay for us to pull in. As soon as they wheeled Audri from the back of the ambulance, the team rushed her to the awaiting doors. I hopped out of the back of the ambulance right behind them but stopped just before I entered through the ER. It seemed as if, in that moment, the reality of everything that was about to happen hit me like a ton of bricks and I needed a few minutes to get my mind right for what was about to go down. I was about to become a father, someone responsible for a life other than my own, and I was feeling some type of way about that.

Pulling my phone out of my pocket, I decided to call the one person I knew would help me make sense of what was going on.

"What up, bruh?" Ness asked as he answered the phone. I could hear my nephew and Ari in the background laughing, and I felt kinda bad for interrupting their little family moment, but I had to.

"Ay, Ness, I need you to stop whatever you got going and get to the hospital now."

"Hospital? Why? Is something wrong with Mama Faye?"

"Naw, Mama Faye is good." I wiped my hand down my face and blew out a breath. "She's about to have my baby, man."

I could hear the shock in his voice. "Who? Alex? She shouldn't be due for another couple months, right?"

I had to laugh to keep from going crazy. "Yeah, Alex is cool, but I'm not talking about her." I paused for a second. "I'm talking about Audri."

"Wait, what the hell are you talking about, man? Now, what's wrong with Audri?" By this time, I could hear Ari in the background asking the same question. At some point, she snatched the phone from Ness's hand because the next voice I heard through the speaker was hers.

"Cairo, what have you let that crazy bitch do to my sister? I swear fo' God if she hurt Audri, I'ma kill that psycho chick."

"Man, Ari, calm down. Alex hasn't done anything to Audri. I wouldn't let her, or anyone else for that matter, lay a hand on her."

"Then what's the matter with my sister? Why is she at the hospital?" I could tell that she was walking around the house gathering up things to head this way because her voice started to go in and out.

"Well, apparently she's pregnant with my baby and about to give birth to your niece or nephew at any minute."

"Wait! She's what?"

"Yo, Cai. Ay, Cai, man. What's the matter? What's going on?"

Ness was talking real loud on the phone, and I was hearing everything he was saying, but for some reason, I couldn't take my eyes off of Audri. Standing in the doorway of her hospital room, I couldn't stop looking at her. Lying peacefully in her bed with wires coming from her belly, chest, and hands, she was still a sight to see. Even with the ugly hospital gown on, her hair all over the place, and her makeup smeared all over her face, she was still the most beautiful woman to me.

"Earth to Cai. Dude, I know you hear me."

"Yeah, I'm here, Ness. Just got caught up for a minute," I responded, moving farther into the room. "The doctor came and gave Audri an epidural about ten minutes ago, and she's been going in and out of sleep ever since."

"Okay, well, Ari and I are on the way. We're going to drop Cas off with Mama Faye first. Then we'll be up there in about twenty minutes. You're at St. Mary's, right?"

I nodded my head as if he could see me.

"Cai?"

"Yeah, yeah. We're at St. Mary's, in the maternity ward. The nurse said she's already eight centimeters, so hopefully you guys get here before she delivers."

Ness laughed. "I can't believe Audri is about to have a baby. How do you go a full nine months and not know you had another human being growing inside of you? I know Alex has to be shitting bricks right now. I'm surprised she didn't go into premature labor her damn self trying to have her baby first."

I laughed because I was just as surprised as Ness. Especially after the way Alex rolled around and acted when Audri told me the news while we were standing in the ob-gyn's office. She cried and screamed so much that she became lightheaded and fell. The same EMTs who came to get Audri had to check her out too. Once they said that she was good to go, I sent her ass on. There was no way in the world I was going to let her snide remarks—about needing a DNA test or Audri tricking me into getting pregnant for my money—ruin us welcoming our child into this world. Besides, I didn't need a piece of paper to tell me what I already was feeling in my heart. This was my baby, and I was just happy Audri would be the first to give me a son.

Yeah, you heard right, Audri was getting ready to give birth to my first son. We found out about an hour ago when the nurse came in and did an ultrasound. To say I was elated would be an understatement. I was beyond ecstatically happy, and I couldn't wipe the smile off of my face.

"Aaarrrggghhh," Audri screamed hunched over in the bed as a contraction hit her again. She'd been dozing off for at least five minutes before one would hit; now it seemed like they were coming every two minutes.

"Ms. Freeman, it seems like your contractions are coming back to back," the nurse who'd been coming in and out since we got here stated. "Let's check to see if you're ready to bring your little prince into the world."

After the last contraction had subsided, I helped the nurse prop Audri's legs up as she inspected her cervix.

"Okay, Dad, it's show time. I'm going to page the doctor now. The next time she has a contraction, we're going to start pushing."

"Wait. No," Audri screamed. She looked from the nurse than to me. "Where's Rima? Where's Ari? Where's Nana? I can't have this baby withouuuuut aaaaarrrrrgggggh."

The minute that the last contraction hit, everything seemed to move as if I was pressing the fast-forward button on the Blu-ray remote. The doctor came in shouting for Audri to push while a handful of nurses and other staff moved around the room with everything needed to ensure that my son came into this world healthy, alert, clean, and weighing a nice amount of pounds.

"Ms. Freeman, on the count of three, I need you to push, okay?"

Audri hesitantly nodded her head as her eyes connected with mine. She began to slowly push the breath she was holding out of her mouth as she raised her hand and motioned for me to grab it. "I'm in all this pain because of you. The least you can do is come and hold my hand and stop standing there looking as if you're going to pass out."

I smiled and walked to her side, grabbing a hold of her sweaty hand. Looking down into her face, I wanted to kiss her on her dry lips and tell her that everything was going to be all right, but when I bent down to capture her mouth, an ear-piercing scream came from it while my hand started to fall asleep from the lack of blood circulating through it. Audri was squeezing the hell out of my hand. I made a mental note never to get on her bad side.

"Okay, Ms. Freeman, after this push, we're going to take a break for ten seconds, but then I need you to give me another big push, all right?"

"I feel like I have to use the bathroom."

"That's how it's supposed to feel, honey."

"Noooooo, I feel like I have to do number two."

"Again, sweetie, that's how it's supposed to feel. Even if you do use the bathroom, it's okay. It's not going to harm your baby at all."

Audri nodded her head, then started to squeeze my hand. I could tell by the kung fu grip she had this time that this contraction was a big one.

"Ms. Freeman, I see the head crowning right now. Just give me a few good pushes on my count and your baby boy will be celebrating his birthday in a minute. Daddy, if you want to record the birth or anything, you're more than welcome to come stand behind me."

I shook my head no and opted out of that option. I knew I would probably regret it later but, for some reason, I didn't want to have the image in my head of Audri's pussy stretching to the size of a basketball. So, from the spot where I was standing, I watched as the older version of Padma Lakshmi positioned herself a little lower between Audri's thighs, bracing herself for what was about to happen with the next push.

"That's it, Ms. Freeman, his head is out. Just one more good push and he'll be here."

Audri lowered her chin to her chest, took a big breath, then started to scream at the top of her lungs as she pushed with all of her might.

"Oh, my God! This shit hurts! I fucking hate you, Cai. I hate you for doing this to me. Aaaargh!"

I knew she was talking only out of pure pain, so I didn't respond or take heed of what she was saying. Audri may not have liked me right now, but I knew she didn't hate me.

"That's it. That's it. Don't push anymore, Ms. Freeman. Your son . . . Oh. I mean, your daughter is out," the doctor said with a confused look on her face. "Happy birthday, little cutie. Would you like to cut the cord, Daddy?"

She handed me the scissors as the nurses around her cleaned our daughter off. A huge shot of pride swelled up in my chest and had my heart beating like crazy. When they told me that I was having a son earlier, I was happy as hell; but, knowing now that our he was actually a she, words couldn't express how I was feeling right now. Gladly accepting the weird-looking tool from the doctor, I looked down at the small creation of ours. Even with her eyes closed, I could already see some of the features she inherited from her mother. That round face, cute button nose, and cute elf-shaped ears were all Audri, while that sun-kissed tan skin and curly dark blond hair was all me.

After they had finished weighing her, cleaning her, and wrapping her in one of those pink birthing blankets, the nurse handed the little bundle of joy over to me first. I instantly fell in love the minute she was placed in my arms, and I didn't want to let her go. I held my breath and stared into her precious sleeping face for what felt like hours before I started to breathe again. When she finally opened her eyes, I fell even more in love when those bluish green irises identical to mine stared up into my face.

"She's perfect, Audri," I said, leaning over toward her so that she could see our daughter's face. When I didn't get a response, I figured she'd probably dozed off again, until I heard a groan escape from her lips.

"Something's not right, Cai," she said, shaking her head from side to side. "I feel like I need to push again."

"Oh, honey, that's just the afterbirth getting ready to come out. Sometimes it takes a little longer for it to pass," one of the nurses said.

She shook her head. "No, it feels like I need to push and go to the bathroom agaaaarrrgggggh."

I jumped from my seat with my daughter still in my arms. "What's wrong with her? Is she okay? Where's Dr. Rushdie?"

"I gotta push. I'm about to push, Cai. I can't hold it in. Aaaaarrrrrgh," Audri screamed.

By this time, everyone who was still in the room started to scramble around. One of the nurses came and took the baby from me and took her to the nursery while the others started hooking the monitors and wires back up to Audri.

"What's going on? Why does she still need to push?"

"I think she might be in labor again."

Labor again? I said to myself. This hospital was really tripping. First they told us the wrong sex; now they were saying Audri was about to have another baby.

Dr. Rushdie ran into the room and went right to checking things out. She lifted the sheet covering Audri's legs and gasped. "Oh, my Lord. Ms. Freeman, I don't know how this wasn't seen on the ultrasound, but you're about to have another baby."

"Another baby!" Audri and I shouted at the same time.

"Yes, another baby. The head is already out. I'm holding it right now. When you started pushing earlier, the baby was already in the birthing canal. I don't know how they could've missed this. Maybe that's why the nurses thought you were having a boy earlier. This little one's foot probably looked like a small penis since he or she was hiding behind their big sister. On this next contraction, Ms. Freeman, just give me one more big push, and you'll be ready to meet your second baby."

The color in Audri's face was completely drained. I didn't know if it was a good or bad thing. When I tried to make eye contact with her to gauge how she was feeling, she wouldn't return my stare. Needless to say, two minutes later, Audri gave birth to another bundle of joy who came out looking identical to our princess who was just born seven minutes ago.

"This time, it's a boy!" the doctor happily screamed as she handed me the scissors to cut his cord. "Congratulations, Mommy and Daddy. Twins."

"You sure it's not triplets?" Audri asked in a drowsy voice. "My stomach is still hurting."

"No, dear, you're good now. That's just the afterbirth. I made sure to check myself. Once they get you and the little guy cleaned up and checked out, the nurse will bring both babies back into the room. On behalf of the hospital, I want to apologize about the misinformation earlier and again say congratulations to the both of you." She patted Audri's leg, shook my hand, and then left.

I stood lost in my own thoughts. Twins. I mean, I knew it was possible, but I never thought that it would happen, at least not today. Not only did the woman I love give me a daughter, but she gave me a son as well and all on the same day. Whatever Audri and I were going through before this didn't even matter right now. If she thought she was gon' just walk away from me that easy, she definitely had another think coming. If the love we shared couldn't help us weather this storm, at least the two gifts she just blessed me with would have me in her life for the next eighteen years.

CHAPTER 2

AUDRIELLE

Before your love, baby, I was muddy
So deep with pain 'til you took it from me
You showered me with a new beginning
Now I'm clean

I didn't know if it was the feel of being a new mother or the hormones that were still acting up inside of me, but I couldn't help the tears that were falling down my face as I looked into the greenish blue eyes of my baby boy and in the direction of a proud Cairo cuddling our precious baby girl. The scene before me had my tear ducts working overtime as Monica's voice played from my cell phone sitting on the stand next to my bed. For some strange reason, the R&B playlist I had playing helped with keeping both babies quiet at the same time.

Looking down at my prince, I didn't know how I ever went nine full months without knowing I was pregnant with not one but two babies. I didn't feel any kicking, moving around, or anything. It was like they were cool with being in the comforting warmth of my womb just relaxing. I thought since I didn't take any prenatal pills, and indulged in more than a few drinks during the time that I was pregnant, there would be some problems. But, to my surprise, both of my babies came out healthy and with every limb intact. They were both a pound or two under for their weight but, after observing them overnight, the doctor advised they were good to go.

"So what do you want to name them?" Cairo asked as he came and sat next to me. I was so caught up inhaling the fresh baby scent of my son that I never noticed Cairo move from his spot in front of the big bay window.

"Do you have any names in mind?"

He shrugged his shoulders. "Well, I was thinking for this little angel, we name her Egypt. Egypt Amari Broussard."

Our eyes connected and I bit my bottom lip as a surge shot through my body and went directly to my clit. Even after just giving birth to two babies, the way this man looked at me had me wanting to skip the six-week thing and take his ass right here on this hospital bed.

"What you think about that one?"

"I like it. Since you gave her a whole name, I think it's only right that I give him his," I said, nodding toward our son who was holding my pinky finger as he dozed off. "I figured since we're going with this whole Cairo, Egypt thing, we can name him Nyles, with a Y, not an I."

Cairo nodded and smiled.

"Nyles Amon Broussard. What about that?"

"Egypt and Nyles. I love them both," Cai said as he gently placed Egypt in her bassinet. Once he made sure she was safe and comfy, he stood up and took a knocked-out Nyles from my arms, kissed him on his forehead, then laid him next to his sister.

Although I was missing the fragrant new baby scent wafting up my nose, I was kind of thankful for the little break Cairo had just given me. I hadn't been to sleep since I had the babies, and I was more than a little bit tired at this point. I sat up straight in my bed, yawned, and stretched my arms wide before lying back on my pillows. I was just about to turn over and catch a few minutes of sleep when Cairo grabbed my hand, turned it over, and kissed my wrist. Because of all the blankets covering my legs, I know he couldn't see the way I was squeezing my thighs together to stop the wild thumping my pearl was doing; however, I knew he heard the soft moan that escaped my lips because he smirked after I opened my eyes and looked at him.

"Audri, I just wanted to say thank you for giving me those two precious jewels over there." He looked over his shoulder, then returned his gaze to me. It was so funny how Egypt's eyes were the same color as his. For a second, I wondered where Nyles's eye color came from, but then Cairo reminded me that his twin Toby had those greenish blue irises that I couldn't get enough of. Besides their eye colors, curly dark blond hair, and light skin they inherited from Cai, our babies looked exactly like me. Slanted eyes, round chubby face, cute little nose, and all. "Regardless of where we're at, Audri, I just want you to know that I will be here for you and our kids. Whatever they need, whatever you need, just let me know, and I'm there."

I completely understood and accepted the double entendre he gave me when he said: "whatever you need." Yeah, I knew the night of the grand opening for Shoe Kicks 2 I told Cai that he and I could never be, but something in me changed the minute I delivered Egypt and saw the way Cai cradled her in his arm as if he never wanted to let her go. The way he looked at her with all the love he had in him was the same way he would look at me whenever we were in the same vicinity or near each other, and I didn't think that I could go on living without experiencing that feeling in my life.

Cairo kissed the corner of my mouth and then my forehead before he got up to go stand over our babies again and watch them sleep. In that second, my mind was completely made up. If Cai was willing to fight for our relationship through all the bullshit that Alex was putting him through, then I would do the same to make sure our little family stayed together. Ms. Alex and everybody else had another think coming if they thought that I was gon' continue to sit back and let them dictate my life. They were all in for a rude awakening because there was a new and improved Audri in town.

"Let me see my great-grandbabies," Nana said as she walked into the room followed by my mother, father, Ari, and Ness. Everyone had excited looks on their faces except for my mother. I couldn't really tell what she was feeling. The expression she was wearing right now was one I'd never seen before.

Sill a little drowsy from the nap I just had, I pushed the button on the side of my bed so that I could be sitting up straight. I was hoping by doing that that I wouldn't fall back to sleep again while I had all this company in my room.

I watched as Nana walked over to Cairo, who had both babies in his arms, and gently picked up Egypt. Ari was next taking Nyles from the comfort of his father's warm and strong embrace. You'd think that this was the first time Nana and Ari had ever held a baby with the way Cairo kept hovering around them and coaching them on what to do like he was an expert himself. We all shared a laugh, including my mother when Nana swatted his hand away and told him to go sit his ass down somewhere.

"So how are you feeling, honeybee?" my father asked as he kissed me on my cheek. He looked over at his grandkids. "I can't believe my baby has babies," he said with misty eyes.

"Aw, Daddy, it was bound to happen one day. Just so happens that this day snuck up on us."

"And how in the fu . . . I mean, hell did that happen?" Ness asked, correcting himself in front of my parents.

I shrugged my shoulders and looked at Cai. "I don't know; it just did."

My mother scoffed. "Not knowing you're pregnant for nine months doesn't just happen, Audrielle. Are you even sure Cairo is the father?

How much did these babies weigh? They are a little small. Is the doctor sure they're not preemies? These might be Eli's babies. You two have been getting close in more ways than one these last few months."

The whole room went silent as all eyes turned toward my mother. Leave it to her miserable ass to mess up this joyous occasion.

"Diana," my father started, but Nana cut him off with a touch to his arm and nodding her head toward me. The way her perfectly arched eyebrows raised up to me told me what she was pushing me to do. A couple weeks ago, after we made a second attempt at her trying to show me how to make another one of her famous cakes, we had a deep conversation about Cairo, the new store, and, of course, both of our love/hate relationships with Mrs. Diana Freeman.

"So, Nana, what's the deal with you and my mama? You guys always played nicely in front of Ari and me when we were younger, but now it's like you guys hardly speak. You're civil to one another, yeah, but y'all don't have that mother/daughter-in-law relationship. Never have."

Nana grabbed a couple of dessert plates from my cabinet, along with some forks and napkins, then set them on the table in front of me. I watched as she walked back over to the coffee maker in her pink Adidas yoga outfit and poured us both a cup of coffee. Her long light and dark gray tresses, which were up in a messy bun, gave off a small glimpse of her real age while the youthful look of her makeup-free face contradicted that notion. After cutting both of us a big slice of the pecan toffee cake, she sat down and answered my question.

"Audri, your mother and I have never gotten along. From the beginning, I never cared too much for Diana. She's one of those women who like to look down on people like she came from money, when in fact she didn't. That little money she got from her aunt's insurance policy was small potatoes in comparison to what our family made. But your father, being the prideful man we raised him to be, didn't want to be a disappointment to your Paw Paw and me, so he made a deal with the devil." She shook her head. "Worst decision he could've ever made. Had he come to us and told us what had happened, we could've easily fixed the situation and gotten everyone who he took money from their money back. But no, that little harlot sank her teeth, claws, and pocketbook into Aaron's dumb ass so deep, he didn't know which way was up. Your mama came in, saved the day, and like a dummy, your dad's ass agreed to her terms of marriage and being a part of the new company, even though he knew he didn't love her in that way."

"If that was the case, why didn't he just get the marriage annulled after he got the money?" I asked, confused. "Did she have him sign a contract or something?" I couldn't help but think how my father's and Cairo's situations were kind of similar. Both of them married for money. Maybe that's why they got along the way they did after their first encounter with each other at the family dinner when Ari introduced Ness to our parents.

Nana cut me another slice of cake, but I declined. Although it was moist and good as hell, the combined taste of the cake, toffee, and caramel sauce was too rich for me. Then the fact that I could only drink my coffee with a lot of cream and sugar played another factor into it. I wasn't really watching my weight like that, but that was a lot of sugar to be consuming in one sitting.

"No, they didn't have a contract drawn up or anything. Quiet as kept, your father did leave your mom at one point. About two years into the marriage, they actually separated for a few months, but when Diana found out that she was *pregnant with you, your father went back to try to work things out. A few years after you popped up on them, Ariana came along. By then, your father just decided to stick it out for the sake of your family and to make sure that you and Ari grew up like he did in a two-parent household."*

Hmmm, that was something I didn't know. I made a mental note to ask my father about that little break the next time I saw him. Until then, I'd just get as much information as I could from Nana.

"So, had it not been for Ari and me, you and my mother would've more than likely come to blows at a family dinner or picnic, huh?" I asked with a laugh.

"Child, hush." Nana waved me off. "I may come from money now because of all of your Paw Paw's hard work back in the day, but please believe me when I say your mama wouldn't have wanted to see me. I was and still am that same chick from Bed-Stuy Brooklyn, born and raised. That will never change." We shared a laugh.

"So what was it about my mother that seemed to rub you the wrong way?"

She seemed like she was deep in thought for a second before she placed her fork on her empty *plate then looked at me. "Diana has always been a major bitch to anyone and everyone. Then, on top of that, she's always been so disrespectful with that slick mouth of hers. When Aaron first started bringing her around, she used to get real reckless with that thing. Cussing any- and everybody out who had something to say about the way that she and your father got married. Her ruining our family functions with her bad attitude went on for a while, until I had to cuss her ass out one time and bring her back down from that high horse she seemed to think she was the only one sitting on. I went from Hollywood to Bed-Stuy in three seconds on her ass and, ever since that day, she keeps her mouth closed when I'm around."*

Nana wasn't lying on that part at all. I knew that was true first-hand because my mom always used to talk about my weight and things when I was little, more than the kids at my school. However, those three months during the year that Nana would come to stay with us, she didn't say a word about my food intake, my outfits that she felt were not flattering on my body, or my lack of exercise. She was mum with her words until the day Nana left to return to her home.

Nana grabbed my hand and looked at me in my eyes. "Audri, baby, I know your mother loves you, and she only wants what's best for you, despite her approach to the shit being way off. Your father tells me about some of the things she says to you behind closed doors and even in public. I know you don't normally say anything because you were taught to respect your mother and not talk back; however, baby girl, you are a grown woman now. There are ways to check your mother without being all-out disrespectful. You hear me?"

I nodded my head, and she grabbed my chin. "If you want her to stop talking to you the way that she does or trying to run your life on who you should love and be with, you gotta open that pretty mouth of yours and let her have it a good time or two. Until then, she's going to continue to do what she does. You understand?"

"I understand, Nana," I said, smiling at her.

The little speech she gave me was all the push I needed in having the courage to set my mom straight about her reckless mouth. Because I hadn't been around her the last couple of weeks, I hadn't had the chance; but, now, with her in my room, being not only disrespectful to me but to Cairo and our kids, I wasn't about to let the moment my Nana had just given me be in vain.

"Mom." I shifted in my bed and sat up a little straighter when her gaze turned to me. I needed to make sure she heard everything I was about to say. "If that's the shit you're about to be on in front of my kids and their father, then you can turn your ass right around and wait for Daddy in the waiting room or in the car. I really don't care where you end up, but I do know you will be getting the fuck up out of here disrespecting me"—I looked at Cairo—"and our family."

"Audri!" She gasped, grabbing at her pearl necklace. "How dare you talk to me like that? I am your mother."

"Are you? Because now that I'm a mother, I don't think I could ever fix my mouth to say to my son, let alone my daughter, half of the shit you've said to me. Do you even know how bad you hurt me with some of the things you've said?"

Before she could answer, the nurse who had been checking on the twins walked into the room. Her head was down looking at some charts, but I knew she felt the tension as soon as she stopped next to my bed and looked up at the expressions on everyone's face. "Is everything okay?" she hesitantly asked.

"Do you mind taking the twins to the nursery for a minute? I'll call when we want them to be brought back to us."

She looked at Cairo and nodded her head and took our babies out.

"I think you and your mom need a minute to talk in private." He looked at everyone in the room. "We'll all be outside when you're done, okay?"

I nodded my head.

"We about to bounce, Cai," Ness said, pointing to himself and Ari. "I know Cassius is probably running Mama Faye crazy right now." They did a brotherly hug. "I'll be up here later on or tomorrow after I get off, all right? Congrats again on locking my bro down, Audri." Ness laughed as he kissed me on my forehead.

"I'ma go drop him and the baby off, and then I'll be back up here, okay, sissy?"

"Okay, Ari."

I watched as she, Cairo, Ness, and my dad, who kissed me on my forehead again, walked out of the room, leaving my mother behind. Nana was the last one to leave, but not before looking at me with a reassuring look and nodding her head. As soon as the door closed behind her, my mother and I sat there for a few moments in an uncomfortable silence. If it weren't for the TV playing a muted episode of *Being Mary Jane,* I might've gone crazy just sitting in this room with my mom and nothing else to distract my attention.

"Audri, if it's any consolation to you, I'm only trying to help you when I do the things I do and say the things I say."

I laughed. "You know the funny part about what you just said?" I didn't wait for her to answer. "You probably believe that bullshit you're trying to feed me. You have never said or done anything to help me in my entire life. If you weren't talking mad shit about me and my weight to anybody who would listen, you were plotting diet regimens with my doctors behind my back, or making me special dinners laced with diet supplements in them. Then, if that weren't enough, you went so low as to hire a man to pretend that he liked me just to 'help' me with my self-esteem. How well do you think that worked out? Did you think me catching him with your ho-ass sister would make me feel better about myself?"

"Audri, you . . . you are such a drama queen," she said, sitting down in the chair next to my bed. She crossed her legs, clad in black slacks, then sat back. The baby pink ruffled blouse she had on complemented her smooth brown skin and matched her lipstick and blush. Her hair, which didn't have a strand out of place, sat in a low bun at the back of her head. The pearl necklace around her neck was intertwined with her freshly manicured nails as she stared at me. "Everything I've done was only to help you. From pushing you about your weight to trying to have a hand in the man you fell in love with." She sighed and looked down at her other hand, which was in her lap. "Audri, you just have to understand—"

"I don't have to understand shit coming from you that's pertaining to my life," I said, cutting her off. "Newsflash, Mom: I'm a grown woman now with my own house, car, career, and money. My life shouldn't even be a concern of yours anymore, especially after a few hours ago I just became the mother of the two cutest, most adorable little beings I have ever seen. Your first grandchildren. Right now, your main focus should be on becoming a better grandmother for them than you were a mother to me."

She looked up at me with shocked eyes. "Audri, now you're going a little too far now, sweetie. I was a great mother to you."

"In what world? Where do you see anywhere on my timeline on this earth when you were a great mother to me? Did you provide? Yes, but with the help of my father. Were you a shoulder to cry on when the kids would tease me at school? No, because you were right there with them talking shit. Do you know how miserable I was when your precious Eli broke my heart? Nope, because you were too busy trying to tell me how my weight was what made him leave. Anytime I was going through something in my life where I needed you to be my mother, you were too busy trying to be my dietician, stylist, or madam. If you ask me, I was raised by my father and my wicked stepmother, because there ain't no way in hell you can sit here and tell me that you treated me with a mother's love."

We sat for a few seconds just staring at each other as she took in everything I just said. She slowly stood up and started to head for the door. "I'm sorry you feel that way, Audri. To me, I thought I was being a good mother by trying to make sure you never experienced the same things I did when it came to your peers and love. I know how it feels to be talked about by the people you thought were your friends, as well as to be in love with someone who's meant to be with someone else. My way of trying to show you that may not have been the best, but it was all I knew how to do. With you being a new mother to my grandchildren, you will now have a first-hand look at what I'm talking about. Hopefully, you do a 'better job' than I did."

And with that, she walked out of my room, gently closing the door behind her. I didn't know if I was seeing things, but it looked as if her eyes were a little glossy as she left. *Diana Freeman crying about something, hmmm.* That would be that day. Then again, maybe I was a little too hard on her. I probably could've worded some of the things I said in a different way. *Naw,* I thought as Cairo walked back into the room with our two blessings in his arms. I'd never treat my kids the way she did me when it came to the way they looked or who they wanted to love. Even if I was trying to protect them from something, I would still shower them with some motherly love. Anything to let them know that I was here for them regardless. Something my mother never did for me.

CHAPTER 3

ALEXANDRIA

"Excuse me, but you can't just walk into Mr. Tate's office without an appointment, ma'am."

I rolled my eyes at my father's receptionist. Well, most likely, his newest play toy, Tippy; it was just another lawsuit in the making. Just looking at the Britney Spears look-alike already told me my father was up to his old tricks again. The reason the company was about to go bankrupt now was because he couldn't seem to keep his dick from pointing at every young, ditzy blond bitch in a skirt. With the ten sexual harassment suits against him and the blackmailing scheme from Laura's tramp ass, you would think he'd slow down and keep his extracurricular activities strictly outside of the office. Unfortunately, that was a task too farfetched for him.

"Ma'am, if you just give me your name and have a seat in the waiting area, I can see if Mr. Tate is done with his conference call and buzz you right in."

I continued to ignore her ass as I made my way down the long, narrow hallway toward my father's office. The thick cherry wood double doors being closed was an indication that he just might be on a conference call. However, when I looked down at the watch on my wrist and noted the time, I knew it was too late in the evening for my father to be handling any type of real work. If I were in the office today, he'd be gone right now doing God only knows what, while it would be me staying after hours and making last-minute calls to clients and investors, trying to keep their business. Ever since I found out I was pregnant, I'd been spending a lot of time outside of the office trying to make sure everything with Cairo and that inheritance money was going smoothly. Now that I thought about it, that may not have been a very good idea, especially after hearing what Audrielle told Cai at the doctor's office earlier.

I stopped in front of my father's door and rubbed my small belly. Because my normal ob-gyn was out of the office today, Cairo and I had the pleasure of meeting with Dr. Patricia

Lowe. I almost rescheduled my appointment when the little nurse told me I would have a sub doctor today, but with Cairo standing next to me with curious eyes and me having no legitimate reason to reschedule, I had no other choice but to sign in and give up that twenty-five dollar co-pay. After waiting about fifteen minutes, my name was called, and we headed straight to the back.

When Dr. Lowe came in and did the ultra-sound, I knew she would have a question or two about my pregnancy. Especially after expressing how surprised she was at how big my little princess was already. "Are you sure your last period was seven months ago?" she'd asked after doing a few measurements and turning the machine off. "Because if what I'm looking at on the screen is correct, you're a little further along than that. From the size and weight of the baby, you should be a little over eight months right now. Dr. Greene, being your normal ob-gyn, has never expressed that concern to you?"

I could feel Cairo's ass staring daggers into the side of my head waiting for me to answer her question. I was hoping whoever he'd been texting since we got here continued to keep his attention off of what was being discussed but, unfortunately for me, that wasn't the case. From the corner of my eye, I could see the wheels turning in his head, and I needed to do something that would stop the ticking of his brain. So, instead of trying to answer the question with a lie, I did the first thing that came to mind and played like I was having some sort of dizzy spell.

Grabbing my head and wincing in pain, I rose up from lying down and bent over the table a little, making a hissing sound and rubbing my belly. Of course, the doctor was the first to become alert, which caused the whole line of questioning to shift to, "Alexandria, what's wrong? Alexandria, are you okay? Alexandria, are you hurt?" I'd smiled on the inside at my Golden Globe performance. After the doctor took my blood pressure and temperature again, then brought me some aspirin and water to take for my sudden migraine, Cairo and I left the room without another thought as to how far along I really was.

Little Miss Toxic was hot on my trail. She bumped right into me as I stood in front of my father's office, causing me to slightly hit the door. I turned around with the meanest glare I could muster up and just stared at the little cunt. I could tell by the way that she started to shift from side to side that she was becoming a little uncomfortable, but ask me if I gave a fuck.

"Do you mind? I need to talk to my father about some very important family business. We won't need your services right now. The front of the office might, though."

"Your father?"

I smirked at her question. I stuck out my hand for her to shake. "Alexandria Tate-Broussard; and you are?"

Embarrassment was laced all over her spray-tanned face. "Oh, I'm so sorry, Miss. Tate, I thought you were one of his little . . ." She trailed off.

"That would be nasty, don't you think? My father and I are close, but not that close, sweetheart. For you to even assume that I was here to see him on that level only lets me know that—"

She cut me off as she backed away, shaking her head. "I'm truly sorry for misjudging who you are, Ms. Tate. Please accept my apology." I could tell by the way her cheeks were becoming a darker shade of red that she was still agitated. "I'm just going to head back to my desk and continue taking calls."

"Yeah, you do that." Without another word, I turned around and entered my father's office without knocking. As soon as my eyes started to really focus on the scene before me, I almost threw up the contents of my late lunch. The sharp intake of breath that I took had me gagging behind my hand clasping my mouth and caused my father's eyes to shoot open and look directly at me.

"Alexandria!" he yelled as he pushed a head full of blond hair off of his lap. At that point, the lobster bisque and smoked turkey and gouda sandwich I ate earlier finally decided to make its grand appearance all over my father's polished hardwood floor. It was one thing to see my father getting serviced by one of his blond whores, but to see his bright pink penis covered in saliva and sticking straight up made my stomach turn.

"Alexandria, what the hell are you doing just barging into my office without knocking! Where is Tippy? Why didn't she call and announce that you were here?"

After throwing up one more time and dry heaving for about five minutes, I finally made my way over to one of the red Eileen Gray Bibendum armchairs in front of my father's desk. The blonde, who I thought hightailed it out of the office after my father's outburst, was still on the floor with her face turned away from me. I found it odd that she was still here. Most women would've been gone, but this one, she stayed. Something about her seemed familiar, but I couldn't quite put my finger on it. Every time I tried to get a look at her she would turn her head and shake it lightly so that her hair would cover more of her face.

"Alexandria, what is it? Could this not have waited until I got home?"

I plucked a few pieces of tissue from the box sitting on his desk and wiped the corners of my mouth. "No, it couldn't have waited. I've been calling your cell for two hours straight." I cut my eyes at the woman still hiding her face. "Now I see why you weren't picking up."

"That has nothing to do with me not answering my cell. I left it at home this morning when I left for work. Besides, Marjorie only got here like twenty minutes before you did."

At the sudden realization of his loose lips, my father closed his eyes and shook his head. Marjorie, whose head snapped as soon as my father mentioned her name, finally decided to get up from the floor and face me. She ran her fingers through her hair, flipping it out of her face, and bit her bottom lip as she looked at me. The red lipstick that was once on her lips was smeared all around her mouth. The dark blue eye shadow and heavily lined eyes made her look like a trailer park Dina Lohan. If it wasn't for the black Zac Posen duchess dress she had on, I would've never thought she came from money.

"Alexandria, dear, how are you this evening? You look beautiful as always."

"I'm fine, and thank you, Marjorie, but you can cut the bullshit. Like I told you before, I already knew about my father's . . . extracurricular activities with you when my mother is passed out drunk at home and Mr. Wright is at work making sure you can stay wearing those $2,400 dresses you wear for special occasions like giving head."

She opened her mouth then closed it, not sure what to say or how to come back. I raised one of my perfectly arched eyebrows and smirked, daring her to say anything. I was pretty sure Mr. Wright was aware of her little drug habit, but this stepping out on him with his oldest and dearest friend was a little faux pas she most definitely wouldn't want to get out.

Grabbing her purse off of the floor, she turned around to my father. "Um, I think I'm going to go. Let me just use the restroom real quick then I'll be on my way."

My father wanted to object but, after I had cleared my throat, he nodded his head, unwillingly dismissing her. I watched as she hurried into the bathroom in my father's office and quickly closed the door.

"You're getting too comfortable with your little sexcapades, aren't you? What if it was Mother who walked in instead of me?"

My father waved me off. "You know as well as I do that your mother is on the chaise longue in the sunroom passed out right now." He looked at his watch. "In about an hour, she'll be up for her pre-dinner drink, then back out again once she puts something in her stomach and have a few more after-dinner cocktails."

He was right, but that still didn't make what he was doing right, especially after witnessing what I just saw. *He needs to stick to his little hotel romps from now on. I might go into actual labor the next time I walk in on some nasty shit like that.*

"So what's the big emergency, Alex? What was the reason for you calling my cell all day as you said?" He got up from his desk and walked around until he was in front of me. Bending over, he placed both of his hands on my protruding belly and rubbed it. "Is everything okay with our little golden ticket in here?"

"Yes, and no."

He stood back to his full height with a look of confusion on his face. "How so?"

I took a deep breath, then broke down everything that had happened in the last couple of days, from the doctor almost slipping up about my actual due date, to Audri claiming to be pregnant by Cairo, then giving birth to his supposed babies on the same day. Once I finished telling my father everything that went down, all of the color had drained from his face. I really couldn't tell what the look on his face was, but I knew it wasn't good.

"Dad!" I snapped, gaining his attention. "What are we going to do now? If the baby actually turns out to be Cairo's, we can kiss all of this"—I waved my hands around his office—"good-bye. That little five million he gave me won't be enough to save you, me, or the business." I bit my bottom lip and damn near drew blood. "That fat cow having his firstborn not only knocks us out of the running for the extra fifty million we asked for, but it gives Cai all the ammunition he needs to go through with the divorce he's been asking for."

"So what if he divorces you? You're acting as if that wouldn't be a good thing. There was no real prenup signed. So even if he goes through with the divorce or finds out that the baby you're carrying isn't really his, we can still get a hold of some of that money he has." My father looked at me with a questioning glare. "You act like you really love the guy or something."

I held my head down to avoid looking into his eyes. My father could always tell when I was lying, and I didn't want him to know that I was really and still in love with Cai. Yeah, I married him for the money, but I was hoping that somehow, somewhere down the line he'd remember all of the good times we had and start to love me again like he did before. Even after our rocky start, I figured we'd eventually get it together as time passed. But now I saw that would never happen, especially with him being so in love with that oversized Pop-Tart.

"Alexandria, please don't start to deviate from the plan again. That's how you failed the first time. Had you kept your head in the game and your heart out of it, you and Cairo would've probably been married by now with the money being as good as yours already."

"I know, Dad."

He grunted and sat back down behind his desk. "For the sake of this company and the way that we love to live, I hope you do. Now, while we're sitting here, either we need to come up with a plan to have Cairo pay you a large sum of money to get out of this marriage, or we need to somehow make the baby's DNA come back as a match to his, since he's asking for a test."

"I doubt he'll pay me any money because I did sign that paper that only entitled me to the five million, and I know he'll pay any amount of money to make sure I don't get my hands on anything else. And, seeing as we don't have the money for the same cutthroat lawyers he may hire, I doubt that would be a good idea."

"What about Sarah and her husband's firm?"

I shook my head. "That wouldn't be a good idea. I kind of pissed Sarah off, and right about now I don't think she'll budge even if I threaten her with the blackmail like I normally do."

My father and I were so into our conversation that we forgot all about Marjorie being in the office bathroom until the door opened and she came out looking like her normal self. The trashy trailer-looking chick who was here a few minutes ago was gone. I shook my head and laughed. During the time that she was in the bathroom, she must've removed the previous makeup and reapplied her usual light look. Her hair was now in a loose ponytail with a side part bang hanging loosely over her eye. Her jewelry, which included a heart pendant necklace, a diamond tennis bracelet, and that fat-ass wedding ring and band, was back in place like it was just there. Before me now stood the Mrs. Wright my mother would sometimes have over for high tea or Sunday brunch. The Mrs. Wright who had a little drug problem, but was still an upstanding citizen in our little rich community. The Mrs. Wright who was happily married to the heir of the Wright Oil Company. I shook my head. If they only knew what I knew.

"You know, I can help you guys out if you like," she said, walking back into the office and taking a seat next to me, crossing her legs. She opened the little plastic bag in her hand and dumped a few pills in her hand, then swallowed them back without water. "I have a few friends who owe me favors I can reach out to with regard to DNA testing." She snorted and wiped at her nose. "If that doesn't work, I have an idea that will, for sure, have my dear ol' stepson giving up a lot of that money."

I looked at my father, who looked at Marjorie then at me. We sat and stared at one another, silently asking if we should trust the whore and junkie to my right. When my father gave a quick nod and crossed his fingers over his stomach, I redirected my attention to Marjorie. That little move he just did was something we would do when we had business dealings with some of our crooked investors. We would go along with their plan but at the same time make sure we covered our tracks so that if things didn't go right, neither my father nor I would be in the mix. The same would go for Marjorie if her so-called plan didn't go right. I would make sure that all fingers pointed at her if we were ever to get caught.

"What do you have in mind?" I asked as I sat back in my seat and listened to her plan as I rubbed my belly.

CHAPTER 4

CAIRO

I sat back in my chair at the Baltaire Steakhouse and yawned. This meeting I had with Chasin and Roderick couldn't be held off any longer. I had some questions about a few things, and I knew those two were going to be the ones to help me with the answers. Yawning yet again, I looked with drowsy eyes at the time on my watch, and I shook my head. I knew Roderick's ass was probably going to be late, but I expected Chasin to be here on time seeing as his law office was right down the street.

"Are you ready to order, sir?" the waitress asked me again for the third time. I'd been sitting in the little upscale steak and burger joint for about thirty minutes now and hadn't ordered a thing. Honestly speaking, I was too tired to eat anyway. I hadn't had a decent ounce of sleep since the twins were born and it was finally starting to catch up with me.

Audri's ass thought I was playing when I told her that I wanted to help her out and experience every second of raising our kids together. I'd been at her house since the morning she was discharged from the hospital, and I hadn't left since. Of course, I would go to the gym during the twins' four a.m. naptime, and even sneak in a few hours of work when Audri would take them with her to handle business at the shoe stores; but, other than that, I'd been up changing diapers, and feeding, bathing, bonding with, and getting to know the two different personalities of my pretty princess Egypt and handsome prince Nyles.

"I'm actually waiting for a couple of colleagues to show up before I order anything. How about you bring me a double shot of apple Crown Royal and a small cranberry juice on the side?"

After nodding to my order, the waitress turned away from me with a smile on her face and walked toward the bar.

Taking out my phone, I smiled at the picture on my home screen of a sleeping Audri with the twins nestled under her arm. The candid shot was so adorable that I just had to take it. I knew she'd probably kill me because you could see the little trail a drool going down her cheek and against the pillow, but I didn't care. I loved it and would have it blown up and shown to the world without any shame.

I'd just hit Audri with a text letting her know that I'd be back to her house in an hour when my phone started ringing. Thinking that the blocked number may have been Chasin calling from his office, I answered without a second thought. "Where you at, man?"

"Cai?" A soft, feminine voice asked.

Silence.

"Cai, I know you hear me talking to you. I've been calling you for weeks. When are you coming home?"

I rolled my eyes and inwardly groaned. "What do you want, Alex?"

"So you just forgot about me and the baby we have growing inside my belly, right?"

I swallowed in one shot the whole glass of apple Crown Royal the waitress just placed in front of me. If I was going to entertain Alex and her temper tantrum for the minute, I needed some sort of distraction to level me out. Placing the empty tumbler back down on the table, I motioned for the waitress to bring me another round. "What can I help you with, Alex?"

"Why are you doing this to me, to us, Cai?" She actually sounded sad. "You don't think we can be a family? What about our son?"

"I see you're still trying to come at me from that angle, huh?" I said, ready to knock back another round. The line got so quiet for a second that I had to look at the screen to make sure Alex was still on the phone. "Hello?"

"What is that supposed to mean?"

"You'll find out soon enough, Alex."

"I'll find out soon enough?" She paused for a second. "I bet you don't treat your other babies' mother this way."

And there she was. Just when I thought she may have changed a little bit, crazy, evil Alex was back. I could tell by her tone that she was about to start yelling and screaming, so I needed to end this call soon.

"Have you even gotten a paternity test like I told you to, Cairo? How can you be so sure that the babies even belong—"

"Why haven't you signed those papers yet, Alex?" I cut her off at that moment because there was no denying that Egypt and Nyles belonged to me. Alex hadn't seen a picture of my kids yet to be making that type of assumption about their paternity anyway. She almost had me for a second, but I wasn't about to fall for this bullshit again. Instead of entertaining anything she just said, I hit her with some shit that I knew would shut her up. "I sent a set to your house, your job, your parents' house, and even the apartment you didn't think I knew anything about. All of them sent certified through the mail and signed for, yet I haven't received one copy back."

Silence.

I laughed. "Now you don't have anything to say, huh? Where's all that shit talking you were doing a few seconds ago?" I saw movement from the side of my eye. When I looked up, Chasin was pulling out a chair, getting ready to sit down. The waitress came back with my second round of Crown. She took Chasin's drink order, and another for me, to the bar. "Look, Alex, I'm about to handle some business real quick so I can go back to bonding with my babies. Hit my line when you've sent the papers back, all right?" Without giving her a chance to say anything else, I ended the call and turned my phone off.

"Alex still tripping, I see," Chasin said, laughing as he unfastened the top button on his navy tonal windowpane Brioni suit.

"Man, you don't know the half. She calls my phone so much that I've changed my number three times. The funny thing is, every time I change it, she always seems to get the new one."

Chasin shrugged his shoulders. "You know this is all your fault, though, right?" I cut my eyes at him, and he held his arms up in surrender. The sparkle of his Bulgari cufflinks danced across my face. "Don't get mad at me, man. I'm just trying to keep it real with you. I wouldn't be a true friend if I didn't tell you when you fucked up."

The waitress returned to our table with our drinks and placed them in front of us, silencing our conversation. "Y'all ready to order yet?"

Chasin looked at his watch. "I'm not waiting for Roderick's ass. I have a meeting in about forty-five minutes, and I wanna eat before I head back to my office." He picked up and opened the menu that was sitting in the middle of the table. "I'm going to go with the bone-in rib-eye, medium, olive oil whipped potatoes, lobster mac and cheese, and some of those lollipop lamb chops for the appetizer."

The waitress turned to me. "And what about you, sir?"

I looked over the menu and couldn't make up my mind. "I'll take the . . ."

"Just give him the same thing I just ordered, beautiful," Chasin stepped in and said. "You'll thank me later. I come to this place all the time with clients and what I just ordered is the best thing on the menu."

I shrugged my shoulders. "I'ma just take it home and give to Audri anyway. This the type of food she eats."

"Growing up eating all of that Jamaican food done messed with your taste buds and head I see. If you would have grown up as Thaddeus, I bet this would be the type of food you were used to."

I couldn't do anything but laugh. "You're probably right, but I bet you this place ain't fucking with Mama Faye's curried goat or rum jerk chicken."

"Of course not. No one's food comes close to Ms. Fayetta's, but this place isn't that bad. Shit, for as much as the bill's going to be when you get it, it'll be worth it."

After a little while, the waitress placed our appetizers in the middle of the table. "Now what's going on? What did we need to talk about?"

With Chasin being a lawyer, I knew he would be able to get certain information pertaining to Alex and her father's company without anyone asking questions. Something about the way her father was so gung-ho about Alex marrying me in order to get my inheritance money started to make me question his eagerness behind it. Then the fact that he was acting as if we were a real married couple and needed to do real married couple things like having sex and kids had me thinking as well. Then there was the talk I had with my biological father and Toby the night of the dinner when Audri ran out crying. I learned that Alex and her father's company was in a lot of debt, way over five million dollars' worth, and they had everybody from the IRS to previous clients to ex-employees coming after them.

"So, once I find out all of this information, what do you want me to do with it?" Chasin asked, just as our steaks and sides were placed in front of us. I'm not going to lie, everything looked and smelled so good, especially the lobster mac and cheese, but I wasn't in the mood to eat, so I pushed my plates a little to the side. Chasin cut into his steak and placed a big chunk in his mouth.

"Man, Chase, whatever you dig up, I want to make sure we can come up with some sort of charge or plan where Alex can't get her hands on any more of my money other than the five million she was promised."

He chewed his steak then swallowed. "I can do that, but what about the baby? If that baby happens to turn out to be yours, he or she will be entitled to that additional fifty mil just like Egypt and Nyles."

I looked at Chasin like he was crazy. "Dude, I already told you that I don't believe that baby is mine. I mean, at first, I thought maybe it could've been after the night she and her father drugged me, and we ended up having sex, but like I told you, a lot of shit ain't adding up. I mean, I'm not no baby doctor or anything, but I do know that Alex's stomach is way bigger than what it's supposed to be at seven months pregnant. Then, I told you about what the doctor said at the doctor's visit that day. That just further heightened my suspicion."

Chasin nodded after taking a few more bites of his food then wiping the corners of his mouth with his napkin. "But still, Cai, there is that small chance that Alex actually did get pregnant by you and is just blowing up bigger than normal. I know you want to ride off into the sunset and forget about everything else other than Audri and the heir and spare she blessed you with, but as much as you can't stand Alex, it wouldn't be right for you to punish her child just because you don't like the mother. Not only will you regret it in the long run, but that child will too."

That was my boy Chasin for you. Ever since we were younger growing up in the neighborhood, he'd always been the one to see the logic in everything. Although he liked to clown around and keep you laughing out loud, he had a good head on his shoulders, despite his dysfunctional background. That's why when this inheritance shit first started coming up he was the first person I called. Graduating summa cum laude from USC and at the top of his class from USC's Gould School of Law, I knew he'd steer me in the right direction professionally, and when I needed to be checked on something coming from the personal side of things, he wouldn't have a problem doing that, either. So yeah, I understood everything he just said, but that didn't mean I had to believe it. Audri even said something similar, but I could feel in my heart that this baby Alex was carrying was not mine.

Just as we were getting deeper into our conversation and what I needed Chasin to look into, Roderick finally decided to grace us with his presence. "What's up, fellas?" he said as he dapped up both of us. "Sorry I'm late, but I got caught up with Ri . . . I mean, a case I've been working on."

Chasin and I gave each other a knowing look, then busted out laughing at Roderick's little slip-up then lie.

"Rod, man, you don't have to lie to us. If that little fine Blaxican *mami* had you climbing the walls, by all means, don't deny that fact, brother," Chasin said, causing me to laugh and Roderick to shake his head.

"Her name is Rima and watch what you say and how you look at my girl."

"Damn, your girl, Rod? Aw, shit, Chase, I think we got another one down."

"You should be the one to talk, Cai. Your ass so far up Audri's ass, I bet you don't care that she's got you walking around that house with blue balls twenty-four-seven. Yeah, man, don't even try to deny it. Rima already told me you've been staying there since y'all took the twins home, and Audri hasn't even let you sniff the pussy. And I know it's gotta be hard as hell, because when I ran into her the other day at Rima's house, my dick twitched a bit with how good her ass was looking. If she was into that freaky shit like Rima, I probably would've been had her try to hook up a threesome or something."

I bit my bottom lip and balled up my fist. See, this was the exact reason why I said I couldn't really kick it with this dude. His mouth was just too much sometimes. Although he was right about me walking around with blue balls every night, I didn't wanna hear about his li'l smoky reacting to Audri or him thinking about touching her in any kind of way.

"Calm down, Cai man. I was only joking. Well, about the threesome part, but everything else was true." Roderick and Chasin laughed again then stopped when they saw that I wasn't about to keep playing with the Audri sex jokes. "So what's up, man? Why did you want to meet up?"

The waitress came back to our table to ask Roderick if he wanted to order any food, but he declined. After going over everything I needed Roderick to look into for me, we sat and had another round of drinks, shot a little bit of shit, then got up to leave.

"Thanks for the lunch, Cai. I'll have that info for you in about two weeks tops," Chasin said, giving his ticket to the valet attendant. "And don't forget to have Alex sign those papers. The sooner the better because I know you're getting tired of paying that $350 for each set."

"That fool can afford them. Hell, he can send a set every day for the rest of the year and still have some money to splurge with," Roderick added. "You'd think he'd step his dress game up a little, but the nigga dresses like he still broke."

I looked down at the Hudson Ryder fleece leather joggers on my legs and the matching black hoodie with leather pockets that I had on. Yeah, this fit wasn't high-end retail like the suits he and Chasin had on, but it went good with the all-red Salvatore Ferragamo high-top sneakers I was rocking.

"Leave my boy alone, Rod. Some people don't want to run through their money buying all of that dumb shit. Cairo has a family to think about who's going to be here long after he's gone, and if wants them to still be living well when that time comes, he has to be smart with his money now."

"Thank you, Chase. Please school the detective," I said to my childhood friend, giving him a brotherly hug.

"No doubt. But let me get going. I'll get at you later, Cai, and tell Audri I said what's up."

"I'll do that."

"I'm out too, man. I need to get back on these cases. I'll call you when I find out about that other stuff," Roderick threw over his shoulder as he headed down the street toward his car.

Grabbing the to-go bag off of the bench I was sitting on, I got up and retrieved my keys from the valet then got into my car. Turning my phone back on, I noticed I had a few voicemails and missed calls from Alex and some text messages from Ness and Audri.

My heartbeat: Just got home. About to try to put the babies down for a nap. Wish me luck!

I laughed at her text, then threw my phone onto the passenger seat. If both of the twins were sleeping by the time I made it back to Audri's house, I was going to throw caution to the wind and do what I'd been wanting to do since the last time my dick slid between those luscious thighs in the front seat of my car. She couldn't deny the sexual tension between us if she wanted to, and I knew if I was walking around her house with blue balls, she was walking around with a backed-up kitty. There was only one way for us to rid ourselves of our problems, and tonight I wasn't going to beat around the bush anymore or take no for an answer.

CHAPTER 5

AUDRIELLE

"Mmmmmm," I moaned as I finally sat my tired body down in my Jacuzzi tub. The twins had been running me crazy all day, and I was finally able to put them both to sleep at the same time. After making sure I placed the baby monitor next to the sink, I lay back in the hot water and closed my eyes. It had been a hectic six weeks, and this was the first time, since I gave birth, that I had a quiet moment to myself. If I wasn't at one of the stores making sure things were going smoothly in my absences, and handling payroll, I was at home being a full-time mother to two of the most beautiful beings on earth. Trying to be a super mom and a super businesswoman was starting to become a task in itself but, honestly speaking, I wouldn't trade either job for anything in the world.

The light scents of chamomile, rose, and lavender had my senses at ease and my body in a relaxed mood. I grabbed my bath sponge from the soap bowl and began to squeeze the bath crystal–scented water down my neck and onto my chest. All I needed now was a glass of red Moscato and some chocolate-dipped strawberries, and I would be in heaven.

Sinking my body farther down into the water, my eyes started to become heavy. I was almost on my way to la-la land but sat straight up and on alert when Egypt's "I'm hungry again" howl wailed through the baby monitor, filling the whole bathroom with her soprano cry. With half of my body now out of the water, I slowly started to rise from my aqua sanctuary, but froze when I heard a deep, smooth tenor voice start to sing:

> *Remember, someone loves you, honey.*
> *No matter what.*

"You can continue with your bath, Audri. I got her," Cairo said just above a whisper before he started to hum the rest of the June Lodge song.

I sat frozen, staring at the monitor as a shock wave of goose bumps decorated my body. Hearing his voice wasn't unexpected because Cairo had been staying at my house since the day we brought the twins home; but, for some reason, it felt as if I could feel those beautiful greenish blue eyes staring at me at that precise moment, looking over my body from head to toe with lustful eyes as he licked his full lips, and silently commanded me to lie down and open my legs wide to get ready for—

"Audri!" I heard Nana's voice call out, interrupting me from the sexual release I was just about to give myself. "Audri, honey, Rima's down in the living room waiting for you. I made you a Mandarin chicken salad and put it in the fridge. I'm going to run to the store real quick to pick up some things for dinner. Don't keep that girl waiting."

"Thank you, Nana," I said through the door. I laughed to myself because Nana thought her ass was slick. I didn't know why she kept telling these little fibs about going out, just to meet up with her little playmates. She must've forgotten about the list of things she gave Cairo this morning to get from the grocery store for dinner. He brought back everything she needed to make one of my favorite meals: buttermilk-fried chicken, mashed red potatoes with chicken gravy, fresh string beans, which I myself snapped earlier, homemade biscuits, and a coconut cream pie. I swore I was gonna miss my Nana when she went back home. Until then, as long as she was back in my house by six to start dinner, she could go and do whatever the hell she wanted.

With no further distractions, I sat back down in the tub. I knew Rima was downstairs waiting for me, but I had to take this free time for all it was worth. I soaked in my relaxing bathwater for another thirty minutes, then finally got out and dried myself off. Walking into my room completely nude, I wasn't expecting a shirtless Cai to be lying across my bed totally knocked out. He must've been real tired and gotten my room confused with the guest room he normally went to sleep in, because in the six weeks he'd been here, not once had he ever come into my room without being asked.

His dreads were up in that sexy man bun that I loved at the top of his head. The scruffy facial hair on his face gave him an edgier look that made him look like one of those foreign Calvin Klein models. I didn't know where he was still finding the time to work out, between helping me take care of the twins and going to work, but whatever he was doing had every inch of his body looking right. My eyes scanned his very toned stomach and chest then went to the colorful tattoos that decorated both of his tanned and muscular arms.

Admiring the large bulge straining against his black joggers, I unconsciously licked my lips at the sight. The thumping going on between my legs intensified, causing me to clamp my thighs together, which only added more pressure to my sensitive nub. I didn't know how long I was standing there, willing myself not to cum just off of the memory of what this man's dick felt like inside of me, because when my eyes drifted back up to Cairo's face, they connected with those greenish blue irises I couldn't get enough of.

My throat became dry after inhaling the big gulp of air I took when I noticed his heated gaze roam over my exposed body in appreciation. He lowered his arm from his face and placed it on the straining print between his legs. He licked his lips as he eyed my heavy breasts and he started to stroke himself through his pants, trying to decide if he should pull his third leg out. As much as my head was telling me to stop anything before it could happen, my heart wouldn't let me move from the very spot I stood in. Did I really trust Cairo enough to give him another chance? Rima was right: my mind, body, and soul yearned to take him back. I'd been fighting with myself about these very feelings for weeks. My heart wanted one thing, but my mind knew there were still some things that could go wrong.

So into my thoughts, I never noticed Cairo remove himself from my bed and walk over to me. His sexy frame towered over mine. I wanted to speak, to say something to make him stop, but the words seemed to have slipped my mind. I opened my mouth to try to say something again, but I was gifted with his sweet-tasting tongue instead. Cairo's arms were wrapped around my waist, pulling me closer to his body. On instinct, my arms wound around his neck, pulling him farther into me, causing my aching breasts to crash against his solid chest. My nipples were so sensitive to the touch that I could feel curvy welts across his skin.

Breaking from our kiss to look at his chest, my eyes widened in shock once they focused on the fancy artwork in front of me. "When did you get this?" I asked, amazed. I didn't know how I missed it when I was idolizing his body a few seconds ago.

As if he couldn't go another second without my mouth against his, he gently kissed my lips then pressed his forehead to mine. "I went and had it done the day after you blessed me with our two angels." Taking one of my hands from around his neck, Cairo moved my fingers across the three names tattooed across the left side of his chest. "My heart will always belong to them, and you, Audri, until the day I take my last breath. I love you and our kids more than life itself, and I will do anything in my power to make sure you guys never want for anything. Just give me another chance to make everything right, and I promise you won't regret it."

That was it. In a matter of seconds, everything boggling my mind about Cai and me was cleared up with a few simple words. My heart was not about to fight with my head anymore. Cairo's declaration of love for me and our kids was all I needed to finally stop running from the one thing I'd known ever since the first time I laid eyes on his ass. I was unequivocally and hopelessly in love with Cairo, and I was not about to let Alex, or anyone else for that matter, push me away from the man I now felt was created for me.

I reached my hands up and took off the twistie holding his hair up, causing his dreads to fall and hang all around his face. The intoxicating smell of the mango and shea butter lotion he used wafted in my nose. I cupped his cheek inside my hand and just looked into the eyes of the man I wanted to spend the rest of my life with. My smooth caramel-colored skin blended well with his bronzed tawny beige hue. I knew that there were still some things we needed to talk about, but the conversation between his fingers and my bare flesh was the most important discussion at the moment.

"Lie down," breathlessly came from between his lips. His cool breath hitting my face caused my nipples to become hard as diamonds, and my pussy walls start to tremble. I stepped over a few feet to my king-sized bed and lay down on top of the purple duvet I'd just bought. "Open up," was my next instruction as soon as my back hit the 1200-count cover. Opening my legs, I couldn't help the way my body shuddered in anticipation of what was to come next. Cairo positioned himself between my legs and placed his hands on both sides of my hips caging them in. When he dropped his head, I could feel the light strokes of his dreads brushing against my body. As he lowered his lips to my stomach, the light kisses from his lips caused tiny bolts of electricity to shoot through my body. Every stretch mark, every wrinkle of fat was gently tended to before he used his tongue to leave a wet trail down to my palpitating nub.

"Your scent drives me crazy, Audri. I'd never get tired of it." He moaned as he nibbled on my hooded prize. I swear the minute his mouth latched on to me, I could feel my juices rolling down the crack of my ass and onto my bed. The moist spot under my ass got bigger and bigger the more he twisted and made figure eights with his tongue. I arched my back and let out a low moan when Cairo moved to sucking on my hairless lips and using the same kissing technique he did when he was ravishing my mouth.

"Fuuuuuuck, Cai." I moaned, biting my bottom lip. I was trying my hardest to suppress the loud scream that was stuck at the back of my throat, but Cairo was making it harder and harder for me to stay quiet. "You're gonna make me get too loud and wake the babies up. Stoooooooooop," I said, pushing at his head but not really moving him out of the way. Instead of stopping his famished attack on my pussy, he continued to dine as if he was on death row and this was his last meal.

When he moaned against my clit, I knew he'd just finished gulping down the lady juice I'd just shot into his mouth. Releasing my now weak and noodle-like legs, Cairo didn't waste any time lying down next to me on the bed then pulling me over to straddle his lap. I didn't have a second to adjust myself or get my breathing in order before his dick was sinking deeper and deeper into me with every upward thrust he made.

"Fuck!" we both yelled in complete and utter amazement. I didn't know what it was, but it felt as if Cairo's thick, long, and curved dick was molded just to fit comfortably into my tight, wet, and cushioned walls. I enjoyed and accepted both the pleasure and pain when his shit stayed knocking again my cervix and sometimes pushing it into my throat.

"Ride your dick, baby, and give me all of my pussy," was all of the hype I needed to hear. Placing my hands on his tattooed chest, I sank farther down on his dick, then started to move my hips back and forth. I leaned forward so that I could lift my hips higher and I pushed down on his chest every time I slammed down on his shit.

"Fuck, Audri. Ride that shit," he screamed. When I looked into his eyes, I couldn't see anything but the love he'd always had for me. Even with marrying that bitch Alex, there was no dimming the light he had in his heart for me. "You gon' make me cum if you keep doing that shit."

Cairo moaned as he tried to grab my hips to slow me down, but I wasn't having it. I'd been backed up since the last time we had sex, and I needed to get a release. I heard soft knocking on my bedroom door, but I didn't care. Whoever it was would have to wait until we were finished. I didn't hear the twins crying through the monitors, so I knew that they were good.

"Shit, Audri. Slow down." Cairo moaned again. I wasn't trying to hear that, though, so I took his mouth into mine and stuck my tongue down his throat. I felt my pussy getting wetter and his dick throbbing against my walls, so I knew that he was almost there, but just when I was about to slam down again and milk his dick for every last drop of cum he had, Cairo placed his arms underneath my thighs and flipped me onto my back and started drilling into me unmercifully.

"You wanna play, right?" he growled in my ear. "Didn't I tell your ass to slow down?" he said with a smirk on his face. My eyes rolled to the back of my head. "Uh huh. Look who can't talk now," he said as he buried his face into my neck and gripped my thighs tighter. "I love you, Audri, and I promise with everything in me I'm going to keep you happy. You are my life and my heartbeat, and I will never do anything to hurt you again. You ready to give me what I want?"

I moaned and grabbed a handful of his dreads.

"I didn't hear you, baby. You ready to give me what I want?"

I was so high off of the dick down he was giving me that I couldn't speak coherently, so I just nodded. Cairo saw the small nod then started to circle his hips and dig deeper into what was always his.

"Give it to me then, baby," he said with bated breath and, just like that, I gave him what he wanted: the biggest orgasm I'd ever had. My body was shaking so bad that I pushed Cairo out of me a couple times. By the time the tremors started to slow down, Cai had reached his peak and let out a loud roar-like sound as he filled me up with all of his liquid pearls.

He stayed entwined with me for what seemed like forever before he fell over to the side and pulled me into his arms. Before either one of us could drift off to that good sleep calling our names, a chorus of cries echoed from the bathroom and into my bedroom.

"I got them, baby. You just get some rest, because the next time it's all on you," Cairo said as he kissed my cheek and patted my ass.

Too tired to even move a muscle in my neck, I just closed my eyes and let the sleep take over that I'd been holding off on. I had a few hours of slumber to enjoy before I'd be back up to feed and change Egypt and Nyles then go for another round with their daddy.

CHAPTER 6

CAIRO

"Yuh did a good job with mi grands. Mi proud of yuh, boi," Mama Faye said as she held a sleeping Nyles. "And ain't no denying dem yuh blood, either. Dem two da spitting image of yuh. That funny-colored hair and crazy-colored eyes. It like you carried dem instead of der mama."

"Yeah, that's what everybody says. But how are you doing, Ma? I know it's been a minute since we've talked and you've been to the doctor a couple times. How did your last appointment go? Everything still good?"

Mama Faye waved me off and said something under her breath. I could tell she was hiding something from me by the way she kept rolling her eyes, but I knew she'd never tell me. For the most part, though, I was just glad that whatever it was didn't have her beautiful, rich mocha skin ashy, or her thick, natural hair thinning again.

Since she wanted to be so tight-lipped about what was going on with her, I made a mental note to reach out to Eli's bitch ass to see if he'd tell me if there was anything wrong.

"Mi doing jus' fine, Cairo. So don't chu go poking that nose in mi business nah. Da doctor said to live mi life as any normal day, and that's what mi been doing. Especially since mi and Nana started hanging tahgather. That woman is a craaaazy gayl, but she keeps mi enjoying mi life."

I smiled at what she said. Since the night of her welcome home party, Mama Faye and Nana had become the best of friends and spent almost every day together doing some sort of activity. Whether going out to lunch, getting their hair done, or going shopping for their new grandkids, those two were always on the go. I loved seeing my mom getting out and being social with people her age now. I thought all the laughing she'd been doing had been helping her with her health a little bit, too. Finesse swore Mama Faye's new attitude was because Nana had been hooking her up with some of that young dick she was used to getting, but I doubted it. Could you imagine Mama Faye dealing with someone my age or younger than me? Shit, I couldn't. I didn't think she'd be able to differentiate between him being her lover or her son.

"What chu ova der tinkin' about? Mi been talkin' to chu for de last two minutes with no answa. What's got chu mind all jumbled, boi?"

I shrugged my shoulders. "Nothing really."

She looked at me over the rim of her glasses. "Chu must not rememba mi knows when chu not tellin' de truth, ay?" Mama Faye stood up from the dining room table, walked over to me, and took a fussing Egypt from my arms. When she sat down in her rocking chair, I tried to hand her a bottle, but she swatted my hand away and shook her head.

"Don't feed de baby every time dem cry. Chu gon' make dem chubby and fat. Mi neva gave you and Ness a bottle more than tree times a day. Breakfast, lunch, and dinna. Not'ing more, not'ing less, until chu two were old enough to eat rice, bean, and all that other tings growing boys need. All chu have to do to get this beautiful angel to quiet down is rub her back and hum in her ear."

The minute Mama Faye started rubbing circles up and down Egypt's small back and humming the lyrics to Bob Marley's "Three Little Birds," she was out like a light. "See, boi, mi told chu," was all she said as she continued to rock my baby into a deeper sleep. "Now, tell mi what's da matter wit' chu."

I sat for a second trying to decide where to start with my problems, and I decided to go with the most recent thing going on in my life. "Well, for starters, Audri and I are trying to make our relationship work again."

The corners of her lips curled up a bit. When she didn't respond, I kept on going. "I mean, I think this time I'll get it right and make her mine for the rest of my life. The only problem I'm having is Alex."

Mama Faye sucked her teeth and rolled her eyes. She'd never been a fan of Alex's, so I wasn't tripping off of the response she gave.

"Alex ain't trying to let this charade of a marriage go for some reason. I've sent her multiple copies of the divorce papers and she has yet to sign and return them. When she's not blowing up my phone every second of the day, she's driving by Audri's house and leaving dumb shit like ultrasound pictures, baby catalogs with certain items she wants circled, and romantic cards begging me not to go through with the divorce. I've been doing a good job of keeping it from Audri, but I know sooner or later, once she starts to become more desperate, she'll probably take these little stunts of hers to a different level."

Mama Faye sat Egypt in her bouncer then sat back down. "So whatchu gon' do about it?"

"That's the thing. I don't know what to do. I got Chasin and Roderick looking into a few things for me, but other than that . . ." I shrugged my shoulders. "Right about now, I'm not opposed to going to her house, holding a gun to her head, and making her sign those divorce papers today. Especially if it means I could be that much closer to being with the person I should have married in the first place. I'm willing to do a few months in jail to ensure that Audri and my kids are a permanent fixture in my life. I let Alex talk me into fucking up what Audri and I had the first time. I won't let her do it again."

I pulled my vibrating phone from out of my pocket. When I looked at the screen, I couldn't help the way my eyes rolled to the back of my head. "See what I'm talking about?" I turned the phone toward Mama Faye. "Fifty missed calls, twenty voicemails, and fifteen text messages. All from Alex."

"Well, what do dem say?"

"Same shit they say every day. 'Why are you doing this to us? We can make this work. Don't you care about our baby?' And, last but not least, 'Can we meet somewhere and talk?' Like, right now, she just sent a text message asking if we can meet for lunch today at Crustaceans in an hour."

Mama Faye bit her full bottom lip then pushed her glasses up on her nose. I didn't notice until right now how the purple frames of her glasses and the purple polish on her nails matched the purple flower in the floral-print sleeveless dress she had on. A far cry from the muumuus and Jamaican-colored pieces she usually wore. Although it was a change I wasn't too much used to, it looked good on her.

"Mi tink chu should go meet with de gayl and see what she has ta say."

"Alex ain't got shit—"

She held her hand and cut me off. "That may be true, Cairo, but, chu neva underestimate de powa of a pissed-off woman. Chu may not want to hear what she has ta say, but chu need to hear it. Rememba, de mouf of a canon is safer den de mouf of a woman scorned."

"Audri would kill me if she knew I had the twins around her."

"Don't worry about dem babies. I will watch dem until chu get back. Go hear what de gayl has to say. Maybe chu can talk her into signing de papers face to face, yeah?"

I nodded my head. "Maybe." I really didn't want to meet up with Alex, but if Mama Faye thought this was a good idea, then I'd try it.

I pulled my phone back out of my pocket and sent Alex a text. It was already one fifteen, and I was pretty sure I'd be running into some light traffic on the way to Beverly Hills.

Me: I'll be there in an hour.

She texted back immediately, as if she had been holding her phone in her hand, hoping that I'd text her back.

Alex: I'll be in the back in the corner booth. I'll order an appetizer and a round of drinks.

Me: I'm good. I already ate. Just coming to talk.

She already got me once with drugging my drink. Her ass wasn't about to get me again.

After making sure the twins were still asleep, I kissed Mama Faye on her forehead, grabbed my keys, then headed to the restaurant. I sent Audri a text letting her know that I'd be back to her house around five and that I'd be bringing dinner. I knew I needed to butter her up with some food from her favorite restaurant before I told her about this little meeting with Alex.

It took me about an hour to get from Mama Faye's house to Crustaceans because of the horrible Los Angeles traffic. Other than the lane closing because of unnecessary road construction going on, I thought the Lakers' opening game tonight was another reason why it took so long. By the time I pulled up to the valet, I was more than irritated and pretty sure Alex was about to make it ten times worse. I sat in my new 2016 Ford Bronco for a few minutes, trying to get my mind right and back on chill mode. J Cole's "No Role Models" was playing through the Beats by Dre speakers I had recently installed. I rapped along to with the words to about the middle of the song, then decided to get out and head into the restaurant.

Bypassing the reservations line, I was literally walking on water as the bottom of my custom Desert Storm Air Jordan 1s I got from Audri's store last week glided across the fish aquarium that was built inside of the floor. As soon as I reached the back of the restaurant, I spotted a very pregnant Alex stuffing her face. Alternating between the big piece of crispy noodle in one hand and some dumpling-looking thing in the other, Alex didn't notice my arrival until I pulled the chair out from under the table and sat down.

"Cai!" she tried to say with a stuffed mouth. "I tried to wait for you, but CJ was not having it."

CJ? Alex's ass was really trying to see this pregnancy all the way through with claiming me as the father. Too bad for her I already knew the truth. Well, at least, I felt it in my heart.

"So what's up, Alex? What did we need to talk about?"

She stuffed another dumpling in her mouth then took a sip of her tea. "You sure you don't want anything to eat?"

I shook my head.

"What about to drink? I can have the waitress bring you—"

I cut her off. "Alex, you have five minutes to say what you need to say; then I'm out of here. I have to go get my kids from Mama Faye then go home."

"Your kids?" she asked with a confused look on her face. I grabbed my keys and started to rise up from my seat. "Okay, okay, okay, Cai, please don't leave."

I sat back down without another word. She had one more time to get off topic and I was out of here.

Dabbing the corners of her mouth with the linen napkin, she chewed the last of the food in her mouth, then cleared her throat.

"Okay, so the reason I wanted to meet up with you is so that we could talk about our baby and the portion of inheritance money that he will be entitled to." I opened my mouth to cut her off, but she raised her hand silencing me and kept going. "Before you start to speak, just hear me out. I know when we were at the lawyer's office, I said some things that were out of line and threatened to take you to court for the whole amount, but I've had a change of heart. Because I want our marriage to work, I'm willing to just settle for fifteen million, on the condition that you agree to go to marriage counseling with me and stop this silly divorce nonsense."

"How about you sign those papers and just call me after you have this baby so we can get the DNA test out of the way?"

"How about you just cut me a check for that fifteen million now and I'll happily sign the papers today? As far as the baby goes, I'll just give him my last name and act as if his father doesn't exist."

As tempting as that offer sounded, I couldn't agree to it. If the baby Alex was carrying did turn out to be mine and I chose to purposely stay out of his life, I wouldn't be any better than my biological father. I always promised myself that if I ever had a kid, I would never do him or her the way that my father and mother did me. As much as I hated Alex right now and wanted to make Audri happy, I wouldn't be able to live with myself if I did.

I watched Alex as she ate a few more dumplings then finished the rest of her tea. My phone vibrated in my hand, and I smiled at the text and picture message Audri had just sent me. I guessed she got the surprise I had Nana help me plan. Seeing that gorgeous smile on her face was what I lived for and would surely die trying to keep. I just hoped that she'd still be smiling after I told her about this little impromptu meeting.

After chewing a few of the ice cubes that were left over in her cup, Alex covered her mouth and belched, then started to rub her belly. "I don't think he liked those seafood dumplings at all. I'm starting to feel a little nauseous," she said as she belched again. Her eyes opened wide in embarrassment as the couple sitting next to us looked over at our table with a disgusted look. "Excuse me for a minute, Cai. I need to use the restroom."

Not waiting for me to say anything else, she got up from the table and made a beeline to the back of the restaurant.

Looking at the picture Audri sent me again, I set it as her new contact photo then sent her a text back. While waiting for Alex to come back from the restroom, I ordered a glass of water from the waitress then looked around the packed restaurant. People of all shapes, sizes, colors, and backgrounds sat around in the modern interpretation of a Vietnamese

club-restaurant during the French colonial
period, having a great time and enjoying the
mouthwatering food.

Scanning the large and jubilant crowd one
more time, my eyes stopped on a couple sitting
to the left of the bar. They weren't trying to
be discrete, but if they wanted to, they could
have. I didn't know what it was, but the back
of the woman sitting with this handsome older
gentleman looked familiar. Her hair was in loose
flowing curls, and she was twirling a pearl necklace in one hand while the other was being held
by her date. As he whispered something in her
ear, her head fell back exposing her slim neck,
and she laughed. After bumping her suitor with
her elbow then laying her head on his shoulder,
I couldn't shake the feeling that kept telling me
that I knew this woman from somewhere. As if
she felt my eyes staring at her, I saw when her
back stiffened, and she slowly turned her head in
my direction.

I swallowed the large lump in my throat when
Audri's mother's eyes connected with mine. The
way her eyes opened in shock told me I was the
last person she was expecting to see. Her eyes
traveled to the empty chair in front of me, and
then back up to me. The dude who obviously
wasn't Mr. Freeman wrapped his arm around
the back of her chair, then said something into

her ear and smiled. When she didn't respond to whatever it is that he said, he glanced up at her face then followed her line of sight. Before his eyes got a chance to connect with mine, Alex returned to the table and stood in front of me.

"All right, I'm back. Now where were we?" she asked, finally taking her seat. "Oh, yeah, you were about to cut me a check for fifteen million to sign the divorce papers and forget about you being my baby daddy."

When I looked back over at Audri's mother's table, I couldn't describe the look on her face. Whatever it was, it didn't look to pleasing, especially after she saw who I was sitting with at the table.

"Um, earth to Cai," Alex snapped. "Are you going to write a check now or would you just like to wire it to my account?"

With my eyes still focused on Mrs. Freeman, I responded to Alex, "I'm not about to write you a check today, tomorrow, or any other day, for that matter. I paid you the money we agreed to, and that was it." I finally focused my eyes back on Alex. "I'm tired of playing these games with you, Alexandria. Either you sign those papers by the end of this week, or you will be sorry you ever decided to hit me with your sick, twisted proposition in the first place. I don't love you.

Never have, never will. My heart has been with Audrielle since the first time I saw her, and that's where it's going to stay. Now either we are going to do this the easy way or we can do this the hard way. You already know how Chasin gets down. He's already looking into your and your father's backgrounds, so whatever secrets or scams you two are trying to pull will most definitely come up if you decide to do something stupid like take me to court. Now I told you once the baby is born to give me a call. Then and only then will I come to the hospital, but only to take a paternity test. If the baby comes back as mine, I won't have no problem providing for him, but if the test comes back and says that he's not mine, which I honestly believe it will say, I want you to leave me, Audri, and anyone else associated with us alone. I don't want you to contact me, stop by any of her stores unannounced, or even send another bouquet of flowers to her house ever again."

She swallowed the knot in her throat and nervously looked around.

"Oh, you thought Audri wasn't going to tell me about all the shit you keep having delivered to her house for our 'supposed' babies, or the lies you've been trying to make her believe about you and me being together when I was away from her. Regardless of what you think, Audri is a strong, confident, and smart woman. Your little games didn't and don't faze her one bit."

I stood up from the table and grabbed my keys and phone. "You have one week, Alex, to have those papers signed and delivered, or I'ma let Chasin loose on your ass with no remorse or any kind of sparing of your feelings."

I reached into my wallet and dropped two one-hundred dollar bills on the table. "It's only right that I pay for our last meal as husband and wife. Have a nice life, Alex, and tell your mother I said hi."

Not waiting for her to respond, I left her sitting there with the dumbest look on her face. She didn't know whether to say something or just keep quiet. I glanced at Mrs. Freeman's table one more time before finally turning around to leave. Not only did I have to tell Audri about this meeting between Alex and me, I had to tell her about her mother possibly having an affair on her father; and if I knew Audri, neither one of my confessions was going to sit well with her, regardless of the who, what, when, where, and why.

CHAPTER 7

AUDRIELLE

"Mmmmm," I moaned out in complete satisfaction as I ate the last piece of banana cheesecake I'd made earlier with Nana. That woman was determined to get me to make a few things in the kitchen before she left and, so far, I'd been on a roll. For the last couple of nights, with Mama's Faye's recipes and some supervision from Nana, of course, I was able to make Cai a few of his favorite Jamaican dishes for dinner: fried plantains, easy; jerk chicken, no problem; rice and beans, simple. However, the curried goat, conch fritters, oxtails, and beef patties I tried to make didn't come out so well. Cai still ate his entire plate every time I placed one in front of him, but I could tell by his forced smile after so many bites, and his many trips to the bathroom during the night, that I still had some work to do.

Switching the channel on the TV back to HBO to finish watching the marathon of *Ballers,* I placed my empty plate on the nightstand next to my bed and snuggled deeper under my covers. Today was the first day of my birthday week, and I was about to take full advantage of it. Well, for a few hours at least. Cairo took the twins with him to run some errands and to see Mama Faye while Ariana was going to be taking care of everything at both stores during my week-long vacation.

I'd just got into a comfortable position when my phone started to go off. I could tell by the ringtone that it was Rima calling, but I didn't feel like getting out of my bed to go grab it off of the dresser. Her ass called back to back about five times before she finally decided to leave a few text messages. Whatever it was wasn't too important, because if it were, she would've called my house phone instead.

After watching the fifth episode of The Rock and Denzel's fine-ass son John David Washington trying to get shit together, I decided it was time to press pause and go for a bathroom break. Lazily kicking back my comforter, I got up, grabbed my phone from its spot, and headed to handle my business.

Going through my call log and e-mails, I sent back a few responses then checked my text messages. Of course, the majority of them were from Rima, but I also had a few from Cai, Ariana and, surprisingly, my mother. My palms started to become sweaty when I crossed Ari's name again, so I decided to open her message first. I knew if anything was really wrong, she would've called, but that still didn't stop me from thinking the worst.

Sissy, just wanted you to know that everything is going good at both stores, so stop tripping! Enjoy your vacation and kiss my nephew and niece for me. I'll see you later on in the week.

Whew! I thought as I read her message again. Although she just assured me that everything was going great, I still made a mental note to pop up on her ass later on in the week. I knew Ari was capable of handling both stores, but because her interest had been more focused on opening up that small cafe she'd been talking about, I just wanted to make sure everything was on the up and up.

Bypassing Rima's texts, which ranged from Wya! to Pick up your phone! I ignored them all and tapped on Cai's name. As soon as his message opened, I couldn't do anything but smile.

A selfie of the twins and their father smiling warmed my heart to the fullest. Three pairs of hypnotizing eyes stared back at me with nothing but pure love in them. It was amazing how in a matter of a few months both Egypt and Nyles were starting to look more and more like their father and less like me. The curly dark sandy blond locks, sun-kissed skin, beautiful eyes, and pouty pink lips screamed Cairo Broussard all day. Even Mama Faye mentioned a time or two in her thick Jamaican accent how it seemed as if Cai had those babies and not me.

My lifeline: Just wanted to say that we love you and will see you later on this evening. We're at Mama Faye's now. We need to talk when I get back, too. Until then, enjoy the rest of your time off and your surprise!

"My surprise?" As soon as the question slipped from my mouth, there was a knock on my bedroom door. "Just a second!" I yelled out as I tried to wipe myself with one hand and not drop my phone with the other. Once I flushed the toilet and washed my hands, I headed back into my room.

"Surprise!" Rima and Nana screamed, pushing their way into my room, followed by this tall, muscular, fine-ass chocolate dude with all black on.

My hands flew to my head in embarrassment. A couple hours ago, I'd watched a video on YouTube and put some Bantu Knots in my hair, so I was looking all sorts of crazy. Not only that, but I had some purple boy shorts on with a white wife beater and no bra or panties, so my titties and ass was just swangin' everywhere. Then, don't let me get started on the pooch above my coochie area that made its return thanks to the twins and that damn Nana with all of her cakes, pies, and cookies. My face, which was makeup free, didn't take away from my beauty, but I was pretty sure that the dabs of toothpaste on the three pimples that I unwittingly woke up with this morning probably did.

"Ummmm, what is all of this?" I asked no one in particular as I eased my way back toward my bathroom. My terry-cloth robe was hanging on the other side of the door, and I needed to put it on if I wanted to get the chocolate Adonis standing in my room to stop staring at my body lustfully and licking his lips.

"It's a pamper party. Courtesy of your baby daddy," Rima offered. "If you would've answered your phone or my text messages, you would've known."

"Cai didn't mention any of this."

"Hence, us shouting 'surprise' when you opened the door," Nana added. "Come on, Audri, you aren't that slow. It is your birthday week, right?"

"Yeah, but what does that mean? I have a birthday week every year."

"That's true, but this is the first year you've had it with a man who damn near worships the ground you walk on."

"A man who is willing to do any- and everything to make sure you enjoy your birthday week to the fullest," Rima said as she plopped down on my bed.

I walked into my bathroom and wrapped my robe around my body then took a towel to wipe the toothpaste off of my face. I thought about taking my hair down but changed my mind. I wanted my curls to be extra tight tomorrow when Cai and I went to breakfast with my father.

Walking back out of the bathroom, I noticed a few more people standing in my room. Like chocolate Adonis, they had on all black as well, except their shirts had a small logo that said WONDERHANDS in the top right corner while he had on a black long-sleeved button-up that hugged his body and every single muscle in his arms just right. Had I not been so in love with Cai and respectful of what we were trying to build, I would've definitely given ol' boy the opportunity to get it.

"Allow me to introduce myself," he said with an outstretched hand and the sexiest grin on his face. "My name is Wayman Jones, and I own the massage company that will be catering to you this afternoon. We have some masseuses downstairs setting up and waiting to give you full-body massages, nail techs ready to give you manicures and pedicures, as well as a few estheticians that will be providing facials and whatever other skin treatments you may want."

I exhaled the breath that was caught in my throat and looked at Rima and Nana then back to Wayman. "Are you serious?"

"As a heart attack. I'm also a trained chef, so while you and the rest of your beautiful entourage are enjoying your pampering, I will be in the kitchen making a few things for you to snack on as well as a few signature drinks that I think you may enjoy."

"Wow. Well, let's get started if there's nothing else."

One of the girls standing behind him handed him three gift bags, which he then handed to Rima, Nana, and me.

"Inside you will find everything necessary to change into, as well as little something extra for you in your bag," Wayman said, pointing to me. "We will be downstairs waiting for you when you're ready. Take your time. We've been paid for three hours of service, so there's no rush." And with that, Wayman and his employees walked out of the room, closing the door behind them.

"Giiiiiirl, I don't know about you, but I'd be in here doing monkey flips on Cai's ass the minute he gets back. I'll take the twins home with me tonight if you want."

"Nonsense. My great-grandbabies can be right downstairs with me while their parents are up here having sex on the ceiling."

"Nana!" I shouted, laughing. "What do you know about having sex on the ceiling?"

"Child, you know the age range of the men I mess with, so hush. Some of them like to listen to that music you all like while we're handling business. Just so happens that the young man I'm seeing right now has that song on a playlist he likes to play whenever we get together."

Rima stuck out her tongue and snaked her body around. "Heeeeeeeeeeey, Nana! Let her know."

I threw one of my decorative pillows at Rima's head and hit her dead in the face. I was all for Nana doing her thang, but that didn't mean I wanted to hear about it. Reaching into our bags simultaneously, we all pulled out the plush white Turkish cotton bathrobes that had our names engraved in gold on the front of each one. The matching house-shoe slippers also had our initials across the top.

"Tell bro-in-law I said thank you when he comes home tonight, Audri. I needed a new robe. Cassius little ass spit up something on my old one that will not come out for nothing."

Turning my robe around, goose bumps instantly decorated my body when I saw the big gold crown on the back with the words MY QUEEN etched underneath. The multicolored jewels on the crown were Swarovski crystals that shone whenever the light hit them.

My eyes became misty as I wrapped the new robe around my body and slid my feet into the slippers. Grabbing my phone from the bed, I dialed Cairo's number and waited for him to pick up. When he didn't answer, I shot him a quick text.

Me: Babe! Thank you soooo much for my surprise. I love it and you!

My lifeline: NP. You deserve it and more. Especially with what I've put you through. I told you I'ma spend the rest of my life making it up to you. Enjoy your day and I'll see you in a few.

After sending another thank-you text and a selfie of me in my new robe, I slid my phone into my pocket and headed for the door.

"All right, ladies, let's go get beautified. We have a few hours before Cai comes home and I need to get these muscles relaxed for what I'm about to do to him tonight."

"Your ass gon' be pregnant again, watch," Rima joked, getting up. Her dark hair was pulled up into a slick, messy bun, which allowed her exotic features to show a little more. Her light honey-colored eyes were lined to perfection as always. The fake lashes she had on made the shape of her eyes look tighter than they actually were. She almost looked as if she were mixed with Chinese rather than Puerto Rican. I couldn't help but notice the way her hips were spreading out a little more than normal, too. Yeah, she still had that baby weight from Cassius, making her petite frame thicker than a snicker, but those hips were poking out something crazy.

"I know your ass ain't talking. With the way them hips are spreading, it looks like Roderick's ass done put something up in your belly already."

She rolled her eyes. "If I were pregnant again, what makes you think Roderick is the one who did it?"

Nana stood up from her spot on the bed. Her long silver tresses were pulled to one side of her head and hanging loosely over her shoulder. "Girl, please. Anybody with eyes can see that you can't get enough of that man. If that isn't a tell-all sign, that fifty thousand you dropped on his ass at the auction was."

"I must say, bestie, fifty thousand dollars is a lot of money. Roderick must have a bronzed dick."

"As if you should be the one to talk. At five hundred thousand dollars, your shit must be made out of nothing but pure gold seeing as Cai didn't have one problem dropping half a mil for just one night to spend with you."

We all shared a laugh as we walked down the stairs.

"I'm not trying to brag or anything, but my girl sometimes has that fool speaking in tongues."

"That's right baby. Golden pussy runs in the family, so I know exactly what you're talking about. How do you think I snagged your grand-father?" Nana added, giving me a high five.

When we got to my living room, I looked around the area in complete awe. The whole room was changed into a mini spa with three different pampering stations. Portable black massage tables sat in the middle of the room while the spa pedicure chairs were lined perfectly in front of the sliding doors and the facial beds were against the wall where my TV usually sat. Each section had their designated workers with smiles on their faces ready to get to work.

"Your drinks, ladies," Wayman said, holding a tray with three sugar-rimmed martini glasses filled with a pink drink topped with a strawberry. We all took a sip and moaned.

"What is the name of this drink?" I asked as the fruity flavors and smooth taste of Pinnacle vodka assaulted my taste buds. I'd stopped breastfeeding the twins a couple weeks ago, so I was about to enjoy every drink that was brought out to us.

"It's a sweet and juicy little drink I like to call Silver Fox," he replied as he licked his lips and eyed my Nana. Rima and I looked at each other then back at these two. "Most of my signature drinks are in some way inspired by a sexy woman I'm seeing or have had the pleasure of seeing. You all go ahead and start at whichever station you want, and I'll be back with the second round of drinks as well as your first course of finger foods." When he turned away, I couldn't help but notice the song he started whistling.

"Was he just whistling 'Sex on the Ceiling'?" Rima asked before I could.

"Nana, is he the dude you've been sneaking around—"

Nana raised her hand up to cut me off. "I'm seventy-five years old, darling, and don't have to lie or sneak around to do anything I want to do." She sat on the massage table and crossed her legs. "Not that it's any of your business, but Wayman and I know each other professionally and personally. Have for a couple years now. He's done a few of my parties and get-togethers here and in New York. When Cai asked me to get this little surprise for you together, Wayzie was the first person I thought of." She shrugged her shoulders. "The fact that he and I mess around sometimes didn't have anything to do with him being here today. Although once I put the twins to sleep later, I might have to duck out for a few."

"Check you out, Nana. Calling the man by a nickname and shit already."

"Yeah, and let's not forget the big-ass smile on your face when he said 'Silver Fox.'" Rima's voice dropped a few octaves as she tried her best to imitate the sexy vibrato of Wayman's tone.

Nana laughed. "Uh-huh. But it's the same way you start daydreaming when someone mentions Roderick." She pointed at Rima. "And the same way you just lose all sense of time whenever someone brings up Cairo." She nodded her head at me.

"I guess we're all on the same love boat, huh?"

"Honey, he'd have to do way more than naming a drink after me to get my love."

"What would he have to do for it then, Nana?"

She thought for a few seconds. "Be willing to drop fifty or five hundred thousand dollars just to have one date with me would be a start."

I couldn't do anything but shake my head and laugh at my Nana. Leave it up to her to say some shit like that and be the one out of all three of us to be fucking the young, sexy business owner who could cook and make one hell of an alcoholic beverage. If the next round of drinks was anything like the first one, I knew Cairo would be getting more than monkey flips later on tonight. With the way I was feeling right now, his ass was liable to get a whole zoo worth of sexual tricks.

"You love me?"

"Fuuuuuck, Audri! Hell yeah, you know I love you."

"How much?"

"A lot."

I slowed my assault on Cai's dick down to a medium pace. With my back curved on top of the exercise ball that sat between his legs, I rolled my hips in a side-to-side motion. We'd been going at our second round for about two hours now. Not only was I getting some of that good dick, but I was getting my work out on as well.

"How much is a lot?" I asked. My eyes were closed, and my mind was drifting in and out of pure ecstasy. My pussy may have been golden to him, but his dick was for sure platinum to me. Dropping my hips, I sank down a few inches more onto Cai love muscle, causing that thick mushroom head to tickle my stomach from the inside. "How much is a lot, baby?"

Cai grabbed my hips and pulled me down on the remaining two inches I purposely left out. A small grunt escaped my lips the minute he thrust up into me and wiggled his hips. Reaching for his dreads, I took a handful in each hand and sat upright. With my feet now planted flat on his sides, I started to bounce a little bit. I knew with my bad knees I'd regret this position in the morning, but I had to show out right now and properly thank him for my surprise earlier.

Pulling his head back by his dreads, I bit his bottom lip and sucked on it. When his tongue darted out, I grabbed it with my teeth then pulled it into my mouth. As soon as my taste buds were rewarded with the faint flavor of my own juices on his tongue, my body went into a frenzy. Before I knew it, I was bouncing feverishly on his dick and cumming at the same time as he released another load of his seeds into my body. His frame shook for a few seconds before his grip released from my hips and his hands moved to slowly stroke the middle of my back.

"I'd take a bullet for you."

Removing my face from the crook of his neck, I pulled my body back, putting all of my weight on his thighs and looked him in the face. "What did you say?"

Tracing the features of my face with his fingertips, Cairo leaned up and kissed me softly on my lips. "You asked me how much is a lot. A lot for me means my life. I'd take a bullet for you to show you how much I love you."

I became speechless at his admission of how much he loved me, and as I looked into his eyes, I could tell that he meant every word.

"I'd take a bullet for you too," I said in return, resting my forehead against his. We sat like that for a few minutes, staring into each other's eyes, and breathing in each other's breath. We were so lost in each other's love high that we didn't hear Nana knocking on the door until her light knocks started to turn into loud bangs.

"Yes, Nana!" I yelled out, not taking my eyes off of Cai's.

"I just put the babies in their beds. They should sleep for the whole night but, just in case, turn the monitor on in your room. I already plugged the one up in their bedroom."

"Thank you, Nana," Cai and I both said at the same time.

When I finally stood up, my legs were wobbling so much that I almost fell back down, but just like with any other aspect of my life, Cai was there to catch me.

"I should be the one with the weak legs as hard as your ass was bouncing on my shit."

"Shut up, fool."

He kissed me on my forehead then smacked me on my ass before he walked into the bathroom. My eyes followed his backside as he strolled out of the bedroom without a care in the world. His shoulders were tight, and his back muscles were firm and finely sculpted. A passage from Paulo Coelho was tattooed between his shoulder blades in the most beautiful handwriting I'd ever seen.

It's one thing to feel that you are on the right path, but it's another to think that yours is the only path.

"Why did you get that specific quote tattooed on your back, babe?" I asked Cai as he came and wiped between my legs with a warm towel.

He shrugged his shoulders. "It was something Mama Faye used to always say to me when I was younger. I would get mad when she wouldn't tell me about my biological parents sometimes, and I'd tell her how much I hated them. I always made a point to say how whenever I became a father that I would never do what mine did to me. Instead of talking bad about them, she'd just recite that passage to me all the time."

After he had finished cleaning me off, he threw the towel in the dirty clothes hamper then came and got into the bed with me. Pulling me into his chest, I could feel his heart beating at the same rhythm as mine.

"I just wanted to say thank you again for earlier. We really enjoyed ourselves."

"No problem. That was just the first of your many surprises this week," he said against the back of my neck. His breath touching my skin caused the goose bumps to rise and my nipples to get hard. I could feel Cai smile against my neck. "We tapping out tonight, baby. I can't go no more. You've drained my dick dry, and we need to get at least a few hours of sleep before we meet up with your pops tomorrow for breakfast."

I'd almost forgotten all about our breakfast date with my father. Normally it would be me, Ari, and our parents, but since Ari was handling the stores and I told my father not to bring my mom, it would just be the three of us and the twins.

Thinking about the text Cai sent earlier, I asked him about the talk he mentioned we needed to have.

"Man, I almost forgot I told you that. You had my head so gone after that thank-you sex I lost all train of thought. Anyway, I wanted to be the first to tell you before it got back to you like I was on some sneaky-type shit, but I met up with Alex earlier."

I could feel my blood start to boil, and I rose up from my comfortable position in his arms. *Did he just say he met up with Alex earlier? I could've sworn he said he was at Mama Faye's house when he texted me earlier.* I had to slowly count to ten to get my attitude in check before I asked this next question. If he gave me any other answer than what I was hoping for, we were going to have a big problem in here tonight.

"Uhhh, Cai, where the hell were my kids at when you went to meet up with this bitch?" I closed my eyes waiting for his answer. If this fool even fixed his lips to say that he had our kids with him, all hell was about to break loose. Something about that chick didn't sit right with me, and I hoped he wasn't dumb enough to take our kids around her.

Grabbing me back into his arms and pulling me closer to his chest, Cai kissed my bare shoulder then the middle of my back. "Mama Faye watched them for me. I was only gone for about an hour. When I left the restaurant, I went right back to her house, picked the twins up, then came straight here."

I blew out a slow breath, then said a small prayer thanking the Lord for not sending me to jail tonight. Once he could feel the tension that was in my body start to fade, Cai went on and told me everything that was said during the meeting with his little pregnant, delusional, and thirsty-ass wife. To say I wasn't surprised by her proposition would be a bald-faced lie. The bitch basically did the same thing with this fake-ass marriage, and now that that was about to be over, she had to find something else to try to get more money out of Cai.

"So what are you going to do?"

"I'm not going to do anything. Her and her greedy-ass father can both go to hell. She already got paid the money I promised her and her ass isn't going to get a dime more. Besides, I'm damn near broke again anyway. I took that other fifty million and opened a trust and college fund for Egypt and Nyles, as well as made a few silent investments in some businesses. If she does try to take me to court, I made sure the money that I do have left over won't be able to go to her. Besides, I have a feeling that once this baby is born, along with the info that Roderick and Chasin are looking into, we won't have to worry about Alex or her father anymore."

Although I was able to breathe a sigh of relief about Alex not getting any of Cairo's money, the question of her child's paternity still rang in my head. "Do you . . . do you think the baby is yours?"

"Honestly, no. I don't remember much of that night because of the drug, but I do remember pushing Alex off of me before I came. Once my body realized it wasn't these thick caramel thighs straddled across my waist, it reacted."

We lay in silence for a few minutes, lost in our own thoughts, him probably wishing like hell Alex's baby didn't come out as his and me wondering if I could stay with Cairo if it was. Shaking those negative thoughts from my mind, I silently made the decision that if the baby was, in fact, Cai's, I would love it as if it were my own.

I already let Alex's conniving ass break us up once, and I wasn't about to let her do it again. If Ari was able to accept Cassius for the man she loved, I should have been able to do the same.

"Oh, one more thing. I saw your mom at the restaurant today while I was up there."

"Crustaceans is one of her favorite places to go. My father usually takes her once a week just to shut her up about them going out on dates."

Cai shifted on his side of the bed a little and moved his head on the same pillow as me. The mango scent of his dreads filled my nose and had me licking my lips. If he wanted to get at least a few hours of sleep, his ass needed to stop moving, breathing on my neck, and touching me the way he was. He had one more time to make my pussy tingle before I jumped back on his dick.

"The thing is, she wasn't with your father. She was with some Richard Webber–looking cat, and they were looking pretty cozy."

"Pretty cozy how?"

"Like they were on a romantic date. They were sitting on the same side of the table rubbing shoulders. They kept holding each other's hands and smiling at each other with dreamy eyes. Then it seemed like . . ." He trailed off as if he didn't want to finish what he was saying.

"Seemed like what?"

"At one point it seemed as if they were going to kiss, but your mother must've felt me staring at her because she turned around. When her eyes connected with mine, she looked as if she'd seen a ghost. At the time, Alex had excused herself to the restroom, so I'm assuming your mom thought I was sitting at the table with you, but when Alex came back, your mother gave me a weird look then turned her attention back to the man she was with."

My mother cheating on my father? Naw, it couldn't be. Even with her evil ways, anybody with eyes could tell that she was head over heels in love with Aaron Freeman. Maybe Cairo was just mistaking their friendly lunch date for something it wasn't.

But he said they were about to kiss? Naw, he said it seemed like they were about to kiss. Maybe she was about to blow something out of his eye. All I knew was that I was going to get to the bottom of this. Mother or not, she wasn't about to be out here having my father looking stupid, whether we were talking or not.

"You okay, babe? I didn't tell you that to try to add more fire between y'all."

"No, I'm good. I'm sure it was nothing." *At least, for her sake I hope it wasn't.*

"All right, well, I'm about to try to get some sleep. The twins will be up for their feeding and diaper change in a couple of hours. I'll get the first round, but the next one is all you," he said, kissing me on my shoulder again.

"Thanks, babe. I love you."

Even with my eyes being as heavy as they were, I knew sleep wasn't about to come to me anytime soon. I needed to find out who this mystery man was, and I needed to find out soon. Until then, I was going to just lie here and enjoy being wrapped in Cairo's warm embrace.

Pulling me more into his chest with his left arm, Cai wrapped his other arm around my waist. After kissing the sensitive part behind my ear, he positioned his head at the back of mine and finally closed his eyes, but not before whispering softly, "I'll take a bullet for you."

CHAPTER 8

ALEXANDRIA

When I walked into my house after a long day of appointments, shopping, and avoiding my father's annoyingly consistent phone calls, I knew something was off. Not only were the sliding doors that led to the pool in the backyard open, but my very expensive bottle of 1978 Montrachet had been uncorked and sampled.

A part of me told myself to drop all of the bags in my hand, then to quietly turn around and run; however, the side of me that wanted the unknown intruder to be Cairo coming to apologize for embarrassing me at the restaurant a couple days ago and begging for a happily ever after had me walking toward the open door.

Once I stepped out of the doorway and down the three little steps that led to my pool, my eyes scanned the backyard for Cairo's sexy frame.

When I came up with nothing but the beautiful Hawaiian landscaping I'd had constructed when I first bought the place, I walked along the flowered pathway that led to the side of my house.

"Maybe I forgot to close the door," I said as I searched the side of my home and came up with the same results. I shrugged my shoulders and gave up on my search for Cairo. Like I said, maybe I didn't lock the door after I was out here this morning but, with that possibly being true, that still didn't explain the open bottle of wine on my table.

I walked back into my house, making sure I closed and locked the sliding doors behind me this time. When I turned around to gather up my purse and bags, I damn near pissed on myself when I saw a slender figure sitting on one of my barstools, pouring another round of wine into the crystal tumbler she got from behind my bar.

Because her back was turned to me, I really couldn't see the full features of her face, but from the side profile, I knew that I'd seen her somewhere before. I just couldn't remember from where. My eyes shifted to the Florentine antique gold mirrored jewelry box that was sitting on the console table behind my velvet white Chesterfield couch. If I could just make my way over there, I could grab the Tiffany-blue Ruger LCP my father bought for me a couple years ago. He knew that I didn't like guns, but with me staying in this big house by myself, he figured I should have a little protection just in case anything ever happened. The thing wasn't even loaded, but I wasn't going to tell her that. I just needed to scare off whoever the fuck she was and get her out of my house.

After watching her take a few quick sips of the wine and savor the taste in her mouth, she spun around on the barstool to face me. "I already took that pretty little gun you had in that jewelry box over there and put it somewhere else, so you can forget the little idea you had swimming in that pretty little head of yours."

"Who are you and what do you want?" I asked with all of the confidence I could muster up. If I couldn't scare her with my gun, hopefully I'd make her think I wasn't about to take no shit from her with my take-charge attitude. Although I was shaking like a leaf on the inside, I was about to act like I wasn't scared at all.

She smirked and stood up. I took in her curvy figure and blemish-free brown skin. Her hair, which obviously was a wig, was in loose Farrah Fawcett flips that perfectly framed her face. The jet-black color of the synthetic hair contrasted with her light skin but went perfectly with the all-black bodysuit she had on. I watched as she slid her gloved hand across my counter and picked up the tumbler again. "You have great taste in wine, you know that?"

"I do," I stated confidently.

Her perfectly arched eyebrow lifted. "Twenty-four thousand dollars a bottle and you have over ten more in your wine collection downstairs. You must be rolling in money, huh?"

"Not that it's any of your business, but my family and I are doing well." I took this opportunity to bargain with her even though I really didn't know what she wanted. I figured if she knew how much a bottle of 1978 Montrachet was, she'd robbed a few wealthy families who had some, or she came from money. Either way, I knew me offering her some large amount of money in exchange for her to leave would go better than me trying to physically remove her in my condition. "If it's money that this is about, how much are you asking for? Just give me a number and I'll see what I can do. I'm pretty sure you have a couple other homes to break into and families to shake down."

She laughed as she sat down on my couch and crossed her legs. "Does it look like I need to rob you or anybody else, Alex? Hell, the outfit I have on is vintage Versace. My shoes"—she raised her leg in the air—"are from Jimmy Choo's new collection, which you should know, seeing as you have the same pair in your closet."

I looked down at the black suede and mesh pointy-toed pumps with crystal rocks she had on and, sure enough, they were the same pair I just bought for myself a few weeks ago.

"As you can see, I'm not here to harm you in any way. I just stopped by to handle this small problem someone I love seems to be having with you."

"Excuse me—"

She held her hand up, cutting me off. "Do you know how annoying your voice is?" I could tell the question was a rhetorical one, so I kept quiet as she continued. "Now, as I was saying. There's a small problem that someone I love is having with you, and although she may feel as if I haven't been the best mother to her throughout the years, everything I've ever done and/or said was my way of trying to help her. I can't change anything that has happened in the past, but I can try to make up for it in our future. Case in point, the reason why I'm here." She reached into the blue Céline bag that was sitting on the floor next to her leg and pulled out a manila envelope. "I believe these were given to you a few weeks ago. However, you have yet to entertain the thought of signing and returning them. Do you mind telling me why that is, Alex?"

Everything she just said to me flew in one ear and right out of the other. I was so engrossed with studying her face, trying to remember it, that I didn't hear a single word she said. I knew I'd seen this woman somewhere before, and it was killing me that I couldn't place her. This pregnancy brain was really taking its toll on me, and I didn't like it one bit.

I watched as she took another sip of wine from my glass then set it on my coffee table without a coaster. For an older woman, her beauty was without question undeniable. Smooth brown skin, high cheekbones that I was sure Tyra Banks would kill for. Slanted mocha-colored eyes that seemed to be turning darker and darker as we sat here in silence. Full lips that even I'd tried to mimic, with Botox of course. With the wig on, she reminded me of a younger Beverly Johnson but, then again, she could pass for a slimmer, older version of . . .

"Audrielle! That's where I know you from." A small smirk appeared on my face after the recognition, and my body started to relax a little bit when she nodded her head. I'd never met the woman before, but I did remember her being in a few pictures the PI gave me that time I had him following Cairo. When I asked him who she was, he informed me that she was Audrielle's mother: an upstanding pillar of the community, a highly educated businesswoman who helped Audri's father start the successful brokerage company he had today, and someone who was against the union of Audri and Cairo just like me. From what I was told by Sarah, the relationship between this woman and her daughter was like water and oil, so her being here right now was interesting to me. If I played my cards right, maybe this little offhand meeting could work out in my favor.

"Now that there is no need for introduction, can we get along with what I came here for?" she asked, sliding the manila envelope across to me.

Bending over the best I could, I picked the envelope up and placed it under my arm. Whatever it was could wait for right now. I needed to see how I could get her on my side. "Would you like another refill on that drink? Like you said earlier, I have quite a few bottles downstairs, and they're just going to waste right now," I said, patting my round belly.

When she didn't respond, I went to the kitchen anyway and got the bottle she already opened. Grabbing a bottled water for myself out of the fridge, I returned to the living room and sat on the couch across from her. I tried to fill her glass again, but when I went to pour, she moved the tumbler out of the way and caused me to spill some of the expensive wine on the coffee table. I tried to control my OCD, but it got the best of me. Returning to the kitchen, I grabbed a few napkins as well as a coaster for her glass.

"So, maybe we should start over," I said, stretching my hand out to her after I cleaned the table off. "As you already know, I'm Alexandria Broussard. Mother-to-be, and wife to Cairo Broussard." Although we didn't shake hands, she still held eye contact with me. "If you are wondering, I am talking about the same Cairo who just had a set of twins with your daughter. Granted, they're two bundles of joy; but we're married, and I find it disrespectful that your daughter is trying to keep me and the father of my child apart."

"From my understanding, you two were never in a marriage for love, just a marriage of, shall I say, certain conveniences."

I had to bite the inside of my cheek to stop from lashing out at this snobby bitch. Her cocky attitude and condescending tone were starting to get under my skin. It was like looking in a mirror, except her shit was a bit more high and mighty than mine.

"We are working on the love part. At least, I hope Cai will concede to. I mean, I tried to get him to agree to marriage counseling when he asked me out to lunch the other day, but he just kept asking for sex." Yeah, I knew I was lying, but I'd say anything that would have her hating Cai more and possibly taking what I said back to Audri.

"You two had lunch?" she asked, uncrossing her left leg, just to cross it with the other.

I took a sip of my water. "Yes. He took me to my favorite restaurant, Crustaceans. We were there for a few hours trying to figure us out."

"And he didn't mention anything about what he and my daughter got going on?"

"I mean, he was telling me how he's been staying at her house some nights because he doesn't trust her to be alone with the kids. Something about her being more concerned about losing weight to compete with me rather than looking after the twins. When I told him that maybe he and I should take a break so that he could get the parenting shit with Audri together, he damn near cut my head off. Everybody in the restaurant started staring at us the minute his voice started getting louder. I was so upset and embarrassed at the way he was yelling at me that I ran to the bathroom to give him a minute to calm down. Once I got back to the table, it was like he was a whole different person: the

Cairo I first met during my sophomore year in college. There wasn't any more yelling or anger, just some apologizing, sweet-talking, and him kissing all over me."

"Kissing all over you?"

"Yes. So much so that the couple at the table next to us turned up, the way he couldn't keep his hands or lips off of me. I wanted to stop him but, what can I say, I'm a hopeless romantic, and I missed feeling my husband's touch."

She nodded her head and finished off the last of her drink. She held the tumbler in her hand for a minute before she placed it back on the coffee table, completely missing the coaster. I thought she was about to leave when she reached for her bag but, instead, she set it next to her and started to rummage through it. What she could've been looking for so long was totally unknown to me, but when she pulled a sleek black pen from her purse and placed it in front of me, I scrunched up my face, then looked back up at her.

"If a pen was what you needed, I have plenty of them on the desk behind you."

"I know you do; however, I know for sure that this pen works, and I don't want to hear any excuse about not having a working pen in this house before you sign those papers."

"Papers? What papers?"

She motioned her manicured finger toward me. "The papers in that envelope you picked up off of this table and placed under your arm."

I looked down to my side and picked up the manila envelope that was stuck between the couch's armrest and cushion. "What's this?"

"Did you not hear anything I said to you earlier?"

I shook my head. She rolled her eyes and lightly smacked her lips. After uncrossing her legs again, she sat up on the edge of the couch and looked me straight in the face. The pleasant smile she'd had on her face this whole time we'd been talking was gone, and a look of hate and sheer annoyance was on her face. "Look, Alexandria, I don't have time to play with you today or any other day of the week." Snatching the envelope out of my hands, she opened it up and took a familiar stack of papers out. "These are the divorce papers you've been playing with for the last few weeks. What you're going to do is go through the entire couple pages of paper and sign everywhere you see your name highlighted in yellow, and initial everywhere you see your name highlighted in pink."

"Wait a minute! How dare you come into my house sticking your nose in bullshit that has nothing to do with you? Here I was thinking we could be allies on breaking Audri and Cairo up for good, but you obviously have other plans in mind." It took me a minute, but I stood up from my seat, wobbled around the coffee table, and got in her face. "What Cairo and I have going on in our marriage doesn't concern you, your adulteress home-wrecking-ass daughter, or those bastard-ass babies she gave birth to!"

Before I even had a chance to blink, the sting of her open hand connecting with my face registered with my brain. Smack! I grabbed my cheek and rubbed the burning spot that I was sure had an outline of her handprint. "Are you crazy! I know you didn't just hit me while I'm pregnant."

"I am crazy sometimes and, yes, I did just hit you while you're pregnant; and I'm going to do it again if you don't sign these papers within the next two minutes."

I moved out of her reach. "I'm not signing shit. I already told you that Cai and I are going to work this marriage out, just as soon as he deals with your fat-ass daughter. After he dumps her and those babies—who, by the way, probably belong to Eli since her slut ass has been fucking him this whole time—we will be the perfect family. Multiple houses with the white picket fence, tons of money to spend, and 1.2 kids. Your typical true American family, living the lavish American dream."

The roar of her laughter had me taken aback for a second. You'd never think a loud and ghetto cackle would ever slip out of this prim, proper, and well put-together woman.

"I see we're going to have to do this the old-school way." Sitting back down on the couch, she went back into her purse and pulled out something shiny. After sitting back and crossing her legs, she placed on her lap what I could now see was a pink and chrome 9 mm. I already had to pee, so it wasn't a surprise at all when I felt the warm liquid slowly moving down my legs.

"I already gave you two minutes, and you didn't take those into consideration. Now, I'm about to give you thirty seconds to start signing and initialing everything I told you to."

Even though I was scared out of my mind, I still had to stand my ground. Yeah, she had a gun on her lap, but how likely was she to use it? "And if I don't? It's not like you'd really shoot me."

She stared at me for a second before she picked the gun up and cocked it. "You wanna chance it?"

"I would've never expected this type of behavior from someone like you," I said, picking up the pen and divorce papers.

"Why? Because of my address now?" She laughed. "Honey, that was your first mistake. Although my husband and I worked our asses off to provide a certain lifestyle and safe environment for ourselves and our children to enjoy, that doesn't take away from the fact that I was born, bred, and raised in Bed-Stuy Brooklyn. I'm one of the fortunate ones who was able to make it out of the hood and make something of myself. When I came here today, I had only one goal in mind, and that was to get you to sign these papers. Neither Cairo nor Audri knows that I'm here or put me up to it. I took this little problem on by myself. Like I said earlier, I haven't been the best mother to Audrielle over the years, but that doesn't take away from the fact that I love her and my grandchildren and I will do anything to make sure that they are happy from this point on." She nodded her head in my direction. "Now that you know my reasoning for this visit today, can you please hurry up and finishing signing those papers? I have a hair appointment in about forty-five minutes, and I'm not about to be late because you can't seem to let go."

"But—"

"But nothing. Girl, just sign the damn papers already," she said, pointing the gun in my direction. I pressed the papers against the wall and signed and initialed every yellow and pink highlighted line I saw. I turned around and gave her the stack of papers and watched as she looked over every one making sure I didn't skip anything.

"Now was that so hard, Alexandria?" she asked in her proper voice. The slight accent she had was totally gone. The gun that was just in her hand was out of sight and replaced by a compact. After fluffing her hair and reapplying her lipstick, she stood up from the couch, grabbed her purse, and headed toward the door.

"It was nice doing business with you, sweetie. I hope we never have to have that little talk again."

By the time she left my house, I was so upset that I became dizzy and had to sit down. This was not the way that things were supposed to go at all. I knew that my daddy was going to blow a gasket when he found out that I failed again. Time was winding down, and this baby was going to be here before we knew it; and, once that happened, there was no way that Cairo was going to give me one cent.

My mind went to the plan that Marjorie came up with that day we were all in my father's office. Because I didn't want to add another charge on top of the already long list of charges I'd have if my ass ever got caught, I'd nixed the idea;

but, now that I didn't have anything to hold over Cairo's head, desperate times called for desperate measures.

Picking up my cell phone, I sent out a group text to everyone we would need to make this thing go through without a hitch.

Me: Meeting at my house tomorrow night at eight. Be there!

CHAPTER 9

RIMA

"So did you want to send her out an invite to the club?" asked Dahlia.

I said, "I think I want to hold off on that right now. I still haven't decided what type of divorced wife she is. Gabriella is having a hard time understanding that her aggressiveness is what caused her marriage to fail. I think if she would have had some sort of outlet to let her get rid of all of that pent-up anger she has inside of her, her marriage might've turned out different."

"But isn't that what the DWC is for, to help women like her?"

"To a point, yes. But with people like Gabriella, you have to get inside of their heads first to see what's really going on. When I started the DWC, it was to help women who I feel would benefit from it. Hence, its exclusivity and potential club members being handpicked by me and only me after they've had a few counseling sessions dealing with why they got divorced. If I don't feel that the person is a fit, man or woman, I won't give them the privilege of indulging in what may be the best days and/or nights of their lives."

I watched as Dahlia nodded and scribbled something on the notepad she held in her hand while she stood in front of my desk. Sitting back in my leather chair, I licked my lips as my eyes outlined the curvy silhouette of her body in the orange, black, and white office dress she had on. A few years younger than me, Dahlia could most definitely give me a run for my money in the looks department. Smooth milk chocolate skin, dark brown almond-shaped eyes, thick and full kissable lips, pretty black hair, and a flawless body. However, Dahlia's submissive nature and neediness was somewhat of a turnoff for me. She'd do anything, and I mean anything, that I would tell her to, just to sample a taste of the goodness between my thighs and be around me all the time.

"Did I receive any messages while I was in my last session?" She looked down at her notepad and flipped a few pages.

"You had a few calls from some new clients that Martell's law office referred, as well as some appointment changes from others. Your mother called but didn't leave a message, and Audrielle called to see if you confirmed the reservations for the spa getaway this weekend."

I could hear the confusion in her voice.

"She advised you made them a few months prior, but when I looked on your personal calendar I didn't see anything scheduled, so I told her that you would call her back with the details later on today."

"Don't worry about that. Her ass is just trying to be nosey and see if I had anything planned for her birthday this weekend." Audri had been hinting to everybody that she wanted another day of relaxation like the one Cairo had done for us at her house a few days ago, except this time she wanted to go to one of those swanky resorts in San Diego. "I'll hit her up later on tonight. What else do I have coming up?"

For the last hour, we'd been going over my appointments for the next few weeks and trying to move some things around to accommodate my overloaded schedule. With the divorce rate in California steadily climbing every day, I was becoming more and more busy with helping divorced wives and, at times, husbands deal with transitioning from being married to being single again. On top of that, I had my outside life that was just as hectic. Cassius's first birthday was coming up, Roderick invited me to some holiday events for his job, and I also had to maintain things at the DWC to make sure everything flowed smoothly and that members weren't abusing the opulent amenities. We went over my schedule for a couple more minutes before Dahlia turned to go back to her desk.

"Oh, I almost forgot," she said, turning back around. "You have that new case coming in today. A Jamiko Kato. She made an appointment a few weeks back, and she's supposed to start her first session in an hour."

I looked at Dahlia as if she had three heads.

"Please don't tell me you forgot. I added this appointment to your phone, laptop, and desktop calendars, Ri . . . I mean, Dr. Vasquez." She knew not to call me by my first name during business hours.

"That may be true, but didn't I tell you yesterday, before I left for the day, to reschedule any appointments I had after twelve? I told you I had a business meeting at one p.m., and then I would be taking the rest of the day off to take care of some personal business."

She rolled her eyes at the mention of me handling "personal business," but I didn't give a fuck. Just because I let her eat my pussy a few times didn't mean that we were together.

"Well, when do you want me to reschedule her? We just sat here and changed around everything for the next couple of weeks and, as busy as you're going to be, I don't think you will be able to squeeze her in until sometime next month."

I looked down at my calendar, and true indeed I was completely booked. "Just call Gabriella and reschedule her appointment from the twenty-first of this month to the fifth of next month, and then give Jamiko Gabriella's original appointment." I stood up from my desk and started to gather my things to leave. "Make sure you call both of them and tell them of the change. After you finish everything you need to do here, you can leave for the rest of the day. Just remember to lock up. I won't be in at all tomorrow, so send all of my calls and messages to my inbox. I'll be back Monday; and please have my coffee ready and on my desk."

We walked out of my office and into the front lobby. To my surprise, Roderick was standing there looking sexy as ever in his navy Armani Collezioni suit and panty-dropping smile. The leather holster that held his gun could be seen a little bit due to the left side of his suit jacket being snagged behind the badge on his hip. The sky blue button-up shirt he had on to match clung to his chiseled chest and ripped abs.

I blushed at the way his heated eyes roamed over my body. Roderick told me a few times before that he loved the way the color green looked against my skin, so I'm pretty sure the India-colored backless jumpsuit I had on was making him feel some type of way.

"What are you doing here?" I finally asked, after returning the same heated gaze he just gave me.

He licked his lips, then closed the distance between us. "Where are you about to go looking and smelling like that?" He skimmed his nose against the area between my shoulder and neck and inhaled my No. 1 for women perfume by Clive Christian. "Fuuuck, Rima," he whispered in my ear. "Let's go back into your office for a few minutes."

My nipples were pressing hard against his chest as my panties were being coated with sticky sweetness. Goose bumps traveled the whole length of my body when his arm snaked around my waist, and his open palm touched my exposed skin.

"As much as I wanna take you up on that offer, baby, I got a meeting with Cai in about forty-five minutes that I can't miss."

His lips hovered above mine. "What kind of meeting y'all got going on?"

"You know Audri's birthday is Saturday and Cai wants to throw her a surprise birthday party slash baby shower since we didn't get to have one before she had the babies."

When he licked his lips again, I felt the softness of his skilled tongue brush against my lips. "I think I remember Ness telling me a little something about that the other day when we hung out." He finally kissed my lips, and I closed my eyes savoring the feel of his mouth against mine. "But I don't think you being thirty minutes late today will stop the party from happening this weekend. Let me take you back in that office and bend your ass over the desk like you know you want me to."

As tempting as the offer sounded and as horny as I was, I had to decline. Cai was going to be renting out this mansion in Hollywood Hills for the party on Saturday, and the owner would be available only today to give us a tour of the inside and outside of the property. Although the place looked nothing short of luxurious from the pictures online, we had to make sure it looked the same in person.

"I'm sorry, baby." Peck. "I can't right now." Peck. "But if you want to come over later"—peck—"you're more than welcome." Sucked his bottom lip, then peck.

"Don't you have your son this week?" he breathlessly asked.

"Cassius has his own room and will be knocked out by the time you get to my house."

He looked as if he was contemplating what he wanted to do. I could tell by the big-ass bulge straining in his pants that he wanted some pussy, but his mind was conflicted. We'd had this discussion countless times before and never came to a resolution. Roderick didn't feel it was right to have our little freak sessions at my house while Cassius was there. Eat together, fine. Netflix and chill, okay. But for some reason, having sex was out of the question. We enjoyed each other sexually either when Cas was with his father and Ari, or whenever Audri wanted to watch him for a few hours to give me a breather.

"How about this? I'll just call you when I'm on my way home and hopefully by then you'll have made up your mind," I said, brushing my hand against the head of his dick. Standing on my tiptoes, I placed my lips to his, then snaked my tongue into his mouth. A low growl rumbled through his chest and onto my tongue, causing me to deepen our kiss. It wasn't until the loud clearing of someone's throat behind us that we stopped going at each other.

"Uh, Dr. Vasquez, don't you have a meeting to get to? You know how you hate being late," Dahlia said with a slight attitude in her voice.

Roderick kissed me one last time, then drew his head back and smirked with that "I told you so" look on his face. Ever since the day I left him here to get finished off by Dahlia when Audri called me hysterically crying that time she met Cai's biological parents, he'd been saying that Dahlia was way more into me than I was into her. It wasn't until hearing the tone in her voice right now that I believed it.

"Thank you for the reminder, Dahlia," I responded with my back to her. "All right, baby, I'll call you on my way home. If my mom stays there instead of at her boyfriend's tonight, I'll ask her to watch Cassius, and I'll come by your place."

He smacked me hard on my ass, and I let out a surprised yelp. "Nigga, what the hell? That hurt."

"I'll make sure to give it some extra attention tonight." He embraced me in a hug, then kissed me on the corner of my mouth. "Nice seeing you again, Delilah."

"It's Dahlia."

He nodded his head with that signature smirk of his then walked out of my office.

"What an arrogant asshole." She thought she said it under her breath, but I heard it. I made a mental note to check her ass on Monday about her professionalism and mouth as I walked out the back of the building and to my car. If she wanted to continue working for me, she needed to adjust that shit ASAP. I didn't have a problem replacing her with a temp until I found someone who was into the same things as I was and wasn't afraid to explore their sexuality when and if the time called for it.

As soon as I pulled out of the parking lot my phone rang. "I'm on my way now, Cai."

"All right. I'm already here with Mama Faye. Nana said she's on her way now. How long will it take for you to get here?"

"I just got on the 110, so I should be there in about thirty, thirty-five minutes."

"Bet."

I disconnected the call and smashed on the gas. The faster I got this done with, the faster I'd get to Roderick's. My pussy thumped just thinking about the hurting it was going to get tonight. But, first, I had to make sure Cairo went all out for my girl's birthday, and that push gift he didn't even know he was going to be buying, too.

CHAPTER 10

AUDRIELLE

I was just about to dig into my Hawaiian pancakes when Egypt thought it would be cute to start yelling at the top of her lungs. My mouth watered in anticipation for the crushed pineapple and buttermilk-batter concoction, and I almost started to place in my mouth the huge chunk I had picked up with my fork; but, with the restaurant being as crowded as it was, I decided to tend to my baby and quiet her down first.

"That girl is spoiled rotten," my father said as he stuffed a pork link in his mouth. "Whenever she's with you, she doesn't do anything but holler. When she's with Cai, she's just as quiet as a mouse. It's that one," he said, pointing at a sleeping Nyles, "who acts up when their daddy has them together."

"Yeah, Egypt's a daddy's girl and Nyles is a mama's boy. That's why whenever we all go out together, Cai deals with her and I deal with him. I promise we can get through a four-course meal without a peep from either one when we do it like that. My baby girl doesn't like to be in her mommy's presence without her daddy somewhere around, for some reason."

"That's how you use to be," my father said, wiping his mouth with a napkin. "You were my little tail when you were younger. Following me everywhere I went. I think that's one of the reasons your mother used to be mad. You used to cry out at the top of your lungs just like that whenever I wasn't around. It would take your mother hours to get you to calm down, just for you to start right back up again when your little brain realized that I was nowhere around."

I laughed at the memory but rolled my eyes at the mention of my mother. Ever since Cai told me that he'd seen her out with some other man, I really started to ignore her calls and texts. She was supposed to come to this breakfast with us this morning, but I threatened to cancel if she did. It was bad enough Cai couldn't make it because he had to handle some things at work. Me being in her presence right now without his support wouldn't have gone well at all.

Bouncing Egypt's loud ass up and down on my shoulder and patting her back was not helping at all. It seemed as if the little heffa was purposely trying to cause a big scene. Just when I was about to stand up and take her to the bathroom to check her diaper and to see if a change of scenery would calm her down, my father reached for her.

"Give me a try at it. I may not have them rope things hanging out of my head like her father, and my skin may be a few shades darker than his, but she has some of my blood running through her and, if she's anything like you, she'll quiet down as soon as you put her in my arms."

With my pancakes still on my mind, I picked up off my lap the pink bootie Egypt had kicked off in her little angry fit, and I put it back on her foot. After giving my father a blanket to put over his shoulder, I handed him his grandbaby. Taking her gently in his arms, my father shushed a quieter Egypt and bounced her on his leg until she was sitting there just chilling and looking right at me. I promise the little look on her face almost had me reach across the table and twist her little ear, but I didn't want to start her up crying again.

"See what I told you? Like mother like daughter. Same exact thing you use to do when your mother and I would go out." My father laughed then made funny faces at his grandbaby. For the first time since Cai left the house this morning, her little ass was just smiling. Showing all gums and sitting on her Paw Paw's lap without a care in the world.

Now with the ability to eat in peace, I devoured my plate of pancakes along with the side of sausage, scrambled eggs with cheese, and breakfast potatoes I also had in front of me.

"Wheeew. I'm full," I said as I rubbed my belly. I wanted to drink the rest of my apple juice, but I didn't have any more room. "Thank you for my birthday week breakfast, Daddy. You know this is my favorite thing to do every year."

"You're welcome, honeybee. I just apologize for having to reschedule. If I had known Cairo had plans today, I would've kept our original date a couple days ago, but your mother was going through some things, and I needed to keep an eye out on her."

I wanted to ask where his eye was when she was at Crustaceans with the next man, but I decided that that would more than likely be a conversation we would need to have in his study with a shot of Johnny Walker Black.

After my father had paid the bill, then watched over Nyles while I went to change Egypt's diaper, we left and headed over to Kick Biz 2. I didn't want to seem like I was checking up on Ari, but I couldn't go a whole week without stepping foot in the store. Besides, I wanted to check out this new manager she took it upon herself to hire without my consent.

"So, honeybee, what do you and Cai have planned for your actual day?" he asked as he pulled out of the restaurant parking lot and into traffic.

"I'm not sure yet. I've been hinting that I wanted to go to a spa, but he hasn't said anything yet."

My father nodded. "I'm pretty sure that if you told him that's what you wanted, he'll make it happen. That boy really loves you and will do anything to let you know just that."

It was me who nodded this time. I believed that Cairo did love me, and I knew that he would do just about anything to show me or, at least, die trying.

We drove the rest of the ride in a comfortable silence. My father even turned the radio off, just so the twins would stay asleep. When we arrived at the shopping center that Kick Biz 2 was in, we had to drive around in circles for a few minutes before we were able to find a parking space close enough to walk to the store while carrying two car seats.

"I should've brought the double stroller. I knew I should have driven my car."

"No. You're good, Audri. You carry the mommy's boy, and I'll carry Paw Paw's baby. That way if they get to yelling, the right person will be right there for the job."

I smiled at my father then unhooked Nyles's car seat. When we walked into the store, Kristinia DeBarge's song "Amnesia" was blaring through the speakers.

There were so many people walking around that I couldn't see the circle of registers in the middle of the store. Young and old customers were either being assisted by a Kick Biz employee or walking the floor and checking out merchandise themselves.

"This place is packed today," my father said, looking around in awe. "I don't see Ariana anywhere."

I felt Nyles start to stir around in my hand. Peeking under the thick blue baby blanket covering his carrier, I smiled in relief seeing he was still asleep. "She's probably in the back office. There's more than enough floor reps out here, so she's probably going through the new shipments that came in today."

As we made our way through the crowd, I took note of every employee I passed in their black khaki pants, black polo shirts, and the custom carbon fiber Air Jordan 1s we gave to each of them when they got hired. Their employee IDs hung from around their necks on the Kick Biz engraved ID holder. Everyone looked ready for work and ready to get paid extra off that commission.

When we reached the back hallway, I punched in the ten-digit code only Ariana and I knew.

"You got it like Fort Knox back here," my father said as he looked down at the keypad and ID scanner. After the store was finished, I had this little device installed for security measures. If an employee needed to get back here, they had to swipe their ID. Once they went through the door, in order to gain access to the shoe area, they had to put their thumbprint on the electronic pad. When the system recognized their print, it would allow them access to the storage area. At the same time, their picture would pop up on the computer screen and would be time stamped and saved in the records just in case I needed to know for sure who was coming in and going out of the back if something came up missing. We had thousands of dollars' worth of merchandise back here, and I wasn't about to take any chances.

Walking into the back office, both my father and I got the shock of our lives when we walked in on Finesse pounding the hell out of Ariana on top of the new shipment of Under Armour sportswear we just received.

"Oh, God, I think I'm going to throw up!" I said to no one in particular.

"Oh, my God! Daddy!"

"Oh, shit." Finesse hissed as he pulled himself out of Ari.

I knew it was wrong for me to look down when he did it, but I couldn't help it. It was like my eyes darted directly there. My eyes bucked, and I lightly gasped when I saw the size of dick Ness was working with. I couldn't believe he was packing all of that into Ariana's small ass. No wonder she didn't have a problem with falling in line and helping him raise Cassius; this bitch's mind, body, and soul were being hypnotized by his dick. There was one thing I knew for sure, though. If you dipped Cai in some milk chocolate, you would probably swear that they were twins from the waist down. Both of them boys were working with monsters.

Ari was still scrambling and wrestling with her clothes when my father turned away and walked back out the way we came.

"Why didn't you call like you always do, Audri? Oh, my God! I can't believe Daddy just caught us fucking."

"Baby, stop tripping. Your pops knows what's up. He was once our age, so I'm pretty sure he was hitting y'all mama just like that back in the day."

I cringed at the thought of my mother and father sleeping together, especially when I couldn't get the image out of my head of my mother kissing all up on the dude Cairo said he saw her with, who looked like the *Grey's Anatomy* chief of staff.

"I'ma come back and pick you up after you close, babe, all right?" Ness told Ari as he kissed her on her forehead. "So call me about thirty minutes before." He then turned his attention to me. "You can stop looking so shocked, sis. I'm pretty sure you and my bro be getting down too." After looking under the blanket at his nephew and smiling, Ness finally left the office.

"Look, before you even start, Audri, I tried to stop him, but ever since we got engaged last night, Finesse has been on a dick me down spree."

"Engaged?" I asked, surprised. She nodded her head feverishly and held up her left hand, showing off the platinum three-carat French-set halo diamond-band engagement ring. "Oh, my God! It's beautiful, Ari. Do Mom and Dad know?"

"I'm sure they do," Finesse said.

"He went to the house and asked Daddy for my hand in marriage a few months after Cassius was born. Had my ring and everything. Said the night I stood up for him at the dinner when Rima went into labor was all the confirmation he needed to know that I was the one for him."

"But that was months ago. Damn near close to a year, right? Because Cassius's birthday is coming up in a couple weeks."

She picked up from the floor the box cutter I was assuming she'd had in her hand earlier, and she started opening up boxes. "Yeah, he said he was going to ask me then, but that was around the time I started tripping and thinking that he and Rima had something going on. We were actually arguing a lot around that time. So much so that I thought we were going to break up; but every time I called myself leaving, he'd tell my ass to go sleep it off in the guest bedroom of our condo and to come back to the master once I got my head right."

Ari talked for about five more minutes before Nyles finally decided he had enough of sitting in his car seat. After changing his diaper and letting him say hello to his auntie, I made a bottle and started to feed him as Ari and I headed back out to the showroom floor in search of our father. I knew he couldn't go far because he had Egypt with him, but you never knew where a man's mind would go when he walked in on one of his daughters having sex.

When we walked back out into the store, there were still quite a few people shopping, but not as many as there were twenty minutes ago. I walked around a display in search of my father, but I couldn't find him anywhere. Nyles had already finished his bottle, and I was now trying to burp him.

"Audri, isn't that Egypt's car seat right there?"

I looked over to the stadium seats that were installed for people to try on their shoes. When I walked up to the car seat, it was empty, with my father nowhere in sight. My heart began to race like crazy in my chest. Where was my daughter? Where was my father? Scanning the crowd for his statuesque frame, I forgot all about burping Nyles. It wasn't until I felt warm regurgitated milk sliding down my cleavage and the front of my plum double-layered cami did I notice he was spitting up.

"Here you go, Audri," Nichelle, one of my employees, said, handing me a big wad of paper towels. "My baby gets me like that all the time.

Especially when I'm so focused on studying for an exam. If you're looking for your dad, he's over there with your princess." She pointed to the section of the store that was dedicated to basketball. I saw his back and the top of his head, but I couldn't see my baby. "I was just over there gushing over how pretty and big your little girl is getting. Those eyes are something else. She's going to be a real heartbreaker when she gets older. All that curly golden hair and those rosy cheeks. Here, let me hold him for you," she offered, reaching her hands out for Nyles. I passed him over to her, then wiped down the front of my cami. Grabbing a half-drunk bottle of water from behind the register, I poured a little onto a new wad of towels and continued to clean my shirt and chest.

"They both are going to break some hearts," Nichelle continued. "Look at you, handsome." And in true Nyles fashion, his ass started flirting back. Blowing spit bubbles and smiling. Then kicking them legs and waving his hands. I watched Nichelle's interaction with Nyles. She was a natural. One of the reasons I hired her was because she was a twenty-two-year-old full-time student at UCLA who had two kids to take care of.

I grabbed my son back from her, then headed toward the basketball area. While I was walking up, I could hear my father laughing at something that he obviously thought was funny. When I was finally an arm's length from where he stood, I could see Ari holding Egypt with a weird look on her face. My father embraced some woman for a long time before he finally released his hold on her. She had petite, slender hands. There was a young man who looked about the same age as Ari or a little younger standing behind the woman looking at some shoes.

"There my baby girl goes," I said to Egypt's mean ass as I pinched her cheek. She was about to start crying, but my father grabbed her from Ari's arms.

"Audri, there is someone I would love for you to meet." When my father stepped to the side, my eyes immediately recognized the woman he was about to introduce me to. She looked the same as if she just stepped out of the picture my father has in his study, just a little older. "Audri, this is an old friend of mine, Mrs. Erika King. Erika, this is my daughter and the mother of the cute little angels that made me a Paw Paw twice in one day." He pointed back and forth between Egypt and Nyles. "Audrielle."

"It's nice to meet you, Audrielle. I've heard so much about you."

The first question that popped into my mind was how did she know so much about me? Because, from my understanding, she and my father lost contact after she caught him cheating years ago.

"Nice to meet you as well," I returned, finally shaking her hand.

"Erika brought her son into the store today to get him some new playing shoes. He's going to be the new point guard for UCLA."

"Congratulations," I said to the young man who was now turned around facing us with a pair of Kobe X Elites in his hands. Studying his face, I couldn't help but to see some similar features to mine. "Are you going to be a freshman?"

"Naw, I'm going to be a senior. I was playing for St. John's in New York, but my father's job transferred him back out here, so I transferred to UCLA."

"That's what's up."

"Darren, are those the shoes you want to go with?" Erika asked her grown-ass son. She turned back to us. "I buy him a pair of shoes every year before the season. Hopefully, this year, we get that championship trophy."

Everything she said went in one ear and out the other as the name she just called her son kept ringing in my head. Not only did he have similar features to mine, but his first name just conveniently happened to rhyme with my father's first name. I looked at Aaron Freeman and tried to read his face to see if he gave off any inkling that he was thinking the same thing as me. When I noticed that he was more into keeping Egypt from crying, the thoughts that were just rolling around in my head vanished.

"Well, it was nice meeting you all. Darren and I have to get going. My husband should be home in a minute, and we have dinner reservations."

"Let me help you at the register," Ari offered. "Any friend of our dad's is most definitely a friend of ours. Now let's go see what we can do about this price."

Darren and Erika followed Ari after waving good-bye again and left my father and me in an awkward silence. Not liking how the atmosphere had changed, I had to break the ice. "Dad, is he your—"

He shook his head no before I could even finish the question. "Not at all, honeybee. Well, at least, I don't think so."

Aww, shit. Just like my mother, it seemed like my father had some explaining to do as well.

CHAPTER 11

CAIRO

"So what do you think?" William asked.

Shrugging my shoulders, I looked at Mama Faye. "What do you think, old lady?"

"Mi tink dis too much for a party. Why not have a little get-tahgetha at mi house or yah house fah free? Mi even cook up a big Jamaican meal if yah want." Her eyes wandered up to the ten-foot ceiling then to the walls of glass and sliding glass pocket doors that allowed natural light and air to fill the rooms with sunshine and lake breezes in this million-dollar home. "How much it cos tah rent a place like dis anyway, Cairo?" She turned her attention back to me. "I bet for da price yah gone pay fah one day, yah can take that gayl on a vacation fah a month instead."

William looked at Mama Faye with a confused look, then back at me. "Uhh, I didn't know you were looking to rent the place for just a day. From our conversation on the phone, I assumed you—"

I cut him off. "It doesn't cost anything to rent this place, Mama Faye. I just have to pay for everything else like decorations, food, drinks, and entertainment. William here is an old friend of Chasin's who's going to do this one favor for me."

William looked as if he was about to say something else, but I subtly nodded, hoping he'd just keep quiet until he and I had a chance to talk some other time.

"There no furniture in de place. Where de guest 'posed tah sit or eat?"

"We're going to have the party outside by the pool. That way everyone can enjoy the panoramic mountain, city, and lake views."

She stared at me for a few seconds with squinted eyes before she started walking over to one of the big bay windows that overlooked the city. Her sleeveless green maxi dress brushed against the polished wood floors with every step. On her left wrist was the gold Citizen watch I'd bought her with my first paycheck from working my summer job as a teen, while the five-carat $14,000 gold and diamond tennis bracelet I gave her as a welcome home gift a couple months ago complemented the studs I'd also given her. "Mi gut tells mi yah up ta somet'ing. What, mi don't know, but regardless mi want yah ta know that mi proud of yah. Make sure that gayl and dem babies want fah not'ing and yah be de best fatha and man mi raised yah ta be."

"I'm trying, Ma. I'm trying," was all I said as I walked up and hugged her from behind.

"Cairo! Where you at?" I heard Rima's voice call out. When I turned around, she and Nana were walking into the living room together.

"This house is nice as hell, Cai. How did you find this place?"

"I told him the same thing when I got here," Nana said. "This place kind of reminds me of my summer home in Cabo San Lucas, with this big living room. And the dining room and family rooms and kitchen all flow right to those sliding glass doors, and then you're outside. Yes, I'd think I was in Mexico right now."

"Yah didn't tell mi yah got a home in Mexico too," Mama Faye said as she embraced Nana in a hug.

"Yeah, girl, I have one there too. Maybe after the twins' christening next month, we can take a week-long vacation from these fools and our precious grandbabies. Try to get you your groove back or, at least, a little two-step back."

Mama Faye blushed and waved Nana off while I cringed at the thought of her getting anything back. For as far back as I can remember, Mama Faye had never had a man around Finesse and me when we were growing up, even when we went off to college and graduated. I'd never seen her with any kind of male company. Whenever I would ask her why she didn't date or have a boyfriend, she would always say that her heart died the day Finesse's pops was born. For a while, I didn't know what she meant by that, until one day I heard her telling someone over the phone that Finesse's pop's father died at the same time she was giving birth to him. He was shot by a dude who tried to rob him on the way to the hospital. Ever since then, she hadn't been able to love another man.

Everyone said their hellos and chatted for a bit before I had William give Rima and Nana a tour of the inside of the house, then take us outside to where the party would be held. The looks on their faces told me that I had made the right choice in picking this place. I knew if the private pool, spa, and patios with a dining arbor and lounge area didn't get them, the chipped-glass fire pit and built-in bench seating would. After pulling William to the side and going over a few things, he handed me the keys to the home and left.

"Cairo, how are we going to pull this off in two days?" Rima asked as she sat in one of the chairs that surrounded the fire pit. Mama Faye and Nana followed suit and joined her.

"Well, that's where I was hoping you lovely ladies came in."

Mama Faye smacked her lips and shook her head. "Mi knew yah was up tah somet'ing."

I smiled and continued with my ideas. "Well, basically we all know that this is supposed to be a surprise birthday party slash baby shower. I was thinking since Audri's favorite movie growing up was *Alice in Wonderland,* we could have a Mad Hatter theme. That way all three of them can basically be celebrated and we won't have to clash two different themes."

"I think that's a brilliant idea, Cai," Rima said, texting on her phone. "And I think we will be able to pull it off by Saturday, too, especially with some help from my girl who's a celebrity party planner. She happens to be free this weekend and just texted back that she can have everything done, decorated, and in order by the time the party starts. All she needs is a budget and the address, and it's done."

"Tell her the budget is unlimited; just make sure it's something Audri will love and never forget."

"Well, go 'head then, brother-in-law." Rima laughed. "I knew I liked you for some reason."

We all shared a laugh.

"What about food, Cai? Did you have a caterer or someone in mind?" Nana asked. "What type of food do you serve at an *Alice in Wonderland* party anyway?"

I still couldn't get over the fact that Nana was seventy-five years old. Standing here looking at her sitting next to Rima in her fitted black jeans, cleavage-showing wrap shirt, and six-inch Dolce & Gabbana black lace pointed-toe pumps, I would've thought that they were sisters or, at least, cousins around the same age. The only thing that gave away her maturity was that beautiful head of gray hair flowing down her back. Even then, it was still kind of hard to tell since I'd seen people of all ages rocking that color in their hairdos now.

"That's actually where you and Mama Faye would come in." I waited for an argument from my Jamaican beauty, but when there wasn't one, I continued. "Since the Mad Hatter is centered around a tea party, I think we should just have some finger foods, nothing too heavy, and a bunch of different desserts. Nana, you can make a variety of cakes, cookies, and pies; while, Mama Faye, I want you to make some codfish fritters, those lamb curry puffs, different types of patties, jerk shrimp, and some jerk party wings. Also, do some regular stuff like deviled eggs and other things for the people who don't like Jamaican food." Mama Faye and Nana both nodded, then went to talking among themselves.

"How many guests are we expecting? And what about invites?" Rima asked.

"Send out around sixty to sixty-five Evites. Out of all of those, maybe only about thirty or forty people might show since it's so last minute. I'm pretty sure you have the e-mail addresses of some of your and Audri's friends, family, and associates. I'll send you a list of mine. Then we'll go from there. If they come they come, if not"—I shrugged my shoulders—"oh, well."

"One last thing, Cai: what are you going to tell Audri to not spoil the surprise?"

I smiled then ran my hands through my dreads. "I'm going to tell her that we're taking some family pictures. Her, me, and the twins. Then, after, I'm going to make it seem as if we are going out of town for a couple days to that spa resort she's been talking about. That way, she won't think nothing's going on when the makeup team and hair stylist I hired to come make her up at the house."

"What about her outfit?"

I looked at Rima with an offended expression.

She shrugged her shoulders. "What kind of best friend would I be if I didn't ask?"

"I got everything under control, trust. Everything we went over today were the only things I needed help with. And, just to ease your mind some more, I touch, feel, and caress Audri's body every chance I'm given, so I know what size to get her and what my baby will shut down the scene in."

"Tell her, grandson-in-law!" Nana shouted, laughing.

"If there's nothing else, I'm about to head out. I have to go handle some things. Everybody knows what their job is. Mama Faye and Nana, just write me a list of everything you need and I'll have it delivered here tomorrow."

"Here?" both Nana and Mama Faye asked.

I pointed at Nana. "Well, we can't have you cooking at Audri's house without her asking questions." I turned to Mama Faye. "And I can't have you cooking at your house because your kitchen isn't that big."

"Well, what do you want us to do? Come here Friday, cook everything, go home, and then come back Saturday morning to reheat it?"

"Not at all. You'll be staying here Friday. That way you'll already be here Saturday. So if you don't want to start making things until early Saturday morning, you can."

"Mi not sleeping on no damn floor, boi. There's no furniture in da house. Yah out yah mind if yah tink mi gon' do that."

I laughed. Mama Faye would not let go of the house not having furniture downstairs.

"I'm going to have some furniture I rented delivered here tomorrow. Everything for you to be comfortable in the kitchen, the living room, family room, and everywhere else in the home, except for the two bedrooms that were locked upstairs. You can sleep in one of the other rooms that was left open."

"Why were those two bedrooms locked anyway?" Rima asked, joining back in the conversation.

I shrugged my shoulders. "I'm not sure. I guess the homeowner doesn't want anyone in those two rooms." Rima and Nana nodded while Mama Faye gave me a side eye. "I really gotta go, though. I have to run some errands and get some last-minute gifts for the twins and Audri."

"Make sure it's something she'll like."

"Don't worry, Nana, I got it," I said, giving each lady a hug and a kiss on the cheek. "I'll see you all on Saturday, and if there are any problems, make sure you all call me. Mama Faye, you need me to drop you off back at home?"

"Nah, mi good. I got mi a ride," she said, nodding over to Nana. I shook my head then turned around to leave. I wasn't the only one about to be up to something.

It was amazing how the last day and a half flew by like it was nothing. It was already Saturday morning and time for me to get this charade on the road. I rolled over to my right and smiled at the beautiful face and figure lying next to me. Looking at the way the sheet clung to her body and enhanced every curve, dip, and bump was even sexier. I was one lucky man to sleep next to and be able to wake up to one of the most beautiful creatures God created, and the fact that I now knew that she was created specifically for me, I wasn't about to let another day go by with her fully belonging to me.

I kissed Audri on both closed eyelids, her nose, then her full lips. Even without being moisturized by that cherry-flavored lip gloss she liked to use, her lips felt as soft as pillows. She stirred in her sleep a bit then went back to snoring lightly next to me. The rise of her plump breasts caught my eye and had my dick rising in anticipation of being soaked by her wetness. Although I wanted to bury myself in the softest place on earth, I had to resist if I wanted to have everything go off without a hitch today.

First things first, I had to run by Audri's parents house for a meeting with her mother. I was more than shocked when she called me last night and left a message on my voicemail that said she wanted to talk to me about something. I wanted to tell Audri about this impromptu showdown, but I didn't want to have her worrying about me instead of enjoying her day of pampering.

Kissing Audri once more before I got out of the bed, I hopped in the shower, brushed my teeth, then got dressed. Because for the birthday girl I'd picked out this badass black lace and leather midi dress I found on the Web site of some plus-size designer, I had to match her fly. Dressed in my all-black Robin jeans and crew-neck T-shirt, red Religion cutter leather biker jacket, and red Giuseppe Zanotti high-tops with the golden metal flames, I was ready to go.

After placing on my side of the bed Audri's first gift, a pair of those red Cruel Summer Giuseppe heels that matched my shoes, and a birthday card, I checked in on the twins, then went and opened the door for Ariana, who was going to help with watching the babies and Audri getting ready.

"What up, Ari? Thanks so much for doing this," I said as I moved to the side of the door and let her in.

"No problem. You know I'd do anything for my sister and brother."

"Speaking of brothers, where's Ness ass at? I know he was all in your ear about leaving this early in the morning."

She set her small overnight bag on the floor, then laid onto the table the outfit fresh from the cleaner's that she had around her arm. "You know his ass was talking shit. Ever since we got engaged, he acts like we have to be glued at the hip. If it weren't for Cassius fussing from the little fever he's coming down with, I don't think he would've ever let me leave."

"What can you say? The man loves you. And congrats again on the engagement. I'm really happy for you guys. You've changed my bro in a good way, and it's a good look. I almost lost all hope for him at one time, but it seemed like after he had got with you, you made him see this relationship thing in a whole different light."

"Kinda like the what you did for Audri."

I opened my mouth to respond but closed it when she held her hand up to stop me. I watched Ari's eyes become a little misty before she closed them and tried to will the wetness away.

She tucked a strand of her wild, curly hair behind her ear before she finally looked up at me again. "Cai, ever since you've come into my sister's life, I've noticed a change in her too. Not only is she more confident on the inside, but she has started to embrace the beautiful outside that we've always seen, including our mother. I've always tried to get Audrielle to see the smart, savvy, and gorgeous woman she is, but it only took one look from you that day you and Ness came into the store for her to finally start to see it. Then, after you gave her the gift of becoming a mother, it's like she's ready to take on the world regardless of what anyone has to say about her past, her size, or what she's been through. With all the things you two had to deal with in the last few months, I truly believe that you guys are ideally suited for one another. Just promise that you'll take care of my sister and cherish that big ol' heart of hers; because if you break it again, I don't know if she will ever come back from that."

No words needed to be spoken after that speech. I hugged Ari and promised to take care of her sister's heart for the rest of my life. After going over everything that was scheduled to happen in the next few hours, I finally left the house and started toward Audri's parents' home.

Pulling up in the circular driveway, any nerves that I had before I got here were gone. My mind was already in a good space, and I wasn't going to let anyone, especially Diana Freeman, mess it up today.

I rang the doorbell and waited for a few minutes before Audri's father finally opened the door. "Cairo! What brings you by this morning, son? I thought we talked about everything we needed to discuss last night in my study."

"We did, sir."

He raised his eyebrow.

"I mean, Aaron. I'm actually here because Di . . . I mean, Mrs. Freeman wanted to speak with me."

He looked over his shoulder with a curious glance, then back at me. The glass of brown liquor he had in his hand lightly shook as he stepped back to let me in. He was two inches taller than me. I stood next to Audri's dad uncomfortably. I could feel his eyes on me as he wondered what was going on.

Before he could ask me anything, Mrs. Freeman made an appearance at the top of the stairs and gracefully started to descend. Her auburn hair was pulled back in a low bun, giving a full view of her beautiful face. With delicately applied makeup, freshly manicured nails, and a slim but curvy frame, Audri's mom was most definitely a sight to see.

"Thanks for coming by on such short notice, Cairo," she said as she finally reached the bottom of the steps. "Honey, have you had your breakfast yet?" she turned and asked Aaron.

He cleared his throat. "Not yet. I was just on my way when the doorbell rang." Audri's father looked at his wife with squinted eyes. "What is this all about, Diana? I already told you about being in Audrielle's business. That's one of the main reasons she won't return any of your calls now. When you need to stay in a mother's place, you refuse to do so."

"What I have to talk to Cairo about is with regard to Audrielle's happiness."

"Cut the bullshit already, Di. Since when have you cared about your own daughter being happy? If you weren't trying to discourage her from doing something she loved, you were most definitely griping about her appearance."

The heated glare the both of them exchanged at each other had me looking down at my watch for the time and slowly backing toward the door. If they were going to have a full-blown argument, I didn't want to have any part of it; plus, I had about forty-five minutes before I needed to get back to the house to set everything in motion for the day.

I looked up at Mrs. Freeman to let her know that I was about to head out and that we could try to have this talk later, but the words at the tip of my tongue rolled back into my throat when I saw a fresh set of tears falling down her face. Never in my life would I have thought I'd be a witness to her vulnerable side. With the way she treated me at the beginning and the way she was toward Audri and sometimes Ariana, I didn't think she had an emotional bone in her. I couldn't help but look at the expression on Aaron's face. He too was shocked and, after gulping down the rest of whatever liquor he had in his cup, like me he waited to see what was about to happen.

"Aaron, I know I fucked up in some aspects of our daughter's life, and I now realize that. That's why I'm trying with everything in me to make things right." She pulled a white envelope out of the pocket of the slacks she had on. "I hope the contents of this envelope are a start to my daughter's and grandchildren's happiness. If I've offended you in any way in the past, Cairo, I want to apologize to you. It was never my intention to hurt you. I just . . . I just wanted to make sure you were really in love with my daughter and, now that I see that, I want to make sure I can help with ensuring her happiness." And with that, she wiped a few more tears from her eyes, then hurried back up the stairs without another word.

I looked at Aaron, who looked back at me with the same shocked expression on his face.

"Well, are you going to open it?" he asked, nodding to the envelope I still had in my hand.

Without another thought, I ripped the letter open and unfolded the stack of papers that were inside. My eyes scanned the documents and grew larger every time I flipped to the next page.

"Well, son, what is it?" I could hear the excitement in Audri's father's voice as he questioned me.

Ignoring him for a few more seconds, I continued to scan every piece of paper until I got to the last page, my heart beating faster and faster. "How in the hell . . ."

"How in the hell what? What do the papers say?"

I looked back at Audri's father. Shock, relief, and surprise were now evident on my face. I held the stack of papers up. "These are the divorce papers I've been sending Alexandria for the last two months. Signed, initialed, and dated."

"Well, that's a good thing, isn't it? Especially with what we talked about last night."

"It's more than good, Aaron. This is great. Listen, I gotta go. I need to make one more stop before I go to pick up Audri and the twins. I'll see you in a couple hours, okay?"

Audri's father patted me on my back and squeezed my shoulder before I rushed out to my car and damn near knocked over their mailbox as I rushed out of the driveway. I had to deliver these papers to Chasin before something happened to them or they mysteriously disappeared. I was finally free from that sham of a marriage to Alex, and ready to begin the rest of my life with the woman I was created for.

CHAPTER 12

AUDRIELLE

The feeling of small hands and feet crawling up and down my body and face caused my eyes to finally open from the few hours of sleep I'd finally caught up with. After sexing Cairo for half the night then getting up to feed and change the twins, I'd dropped down on my pillow and was dead to the world.

"Hey, Mommy's baby," I greeted a smiling Nyles as his small hands grabbed at my nose then my eyes. "How'd you get in here? Did Daddy bring you and your sister in here to wake Mommy up?" Nyles continued to laugh while Egypt slid off of my stomach and rolled over to her dad's side of the bed, and lay on his pillow.

"Spoiled little heffa," I said as I playfully rolled my eyes.

"You need to be the last person calling someone spoiled," I heard from the chair in the corner of my room.

"Ari?" I finally sat up. Grabbing Nyles and sitting him next to his sister, I looked around my room until I spotted Ariana sitting lazily in my favorite chair with the remote in her hand, flipping through channels on the muted TV. "When did you get here? Better yet, why are you here? Where's Cai?"

It was at that minute that I noticed that the scent of the mango conditioner Cairo used for his dreads wasn't as strong as it normally was whenever he was in the room. The faint scent of his Old Spice Fiji body wash was still in the air, so I knew he'd already taken a shower.

"Cai isn't here. He went out to run some last-minute errands before you guys go to the photo shoot, then out of town for your little birthday getaway."

"But he didn't wake me up."

"Hence the reason I'm here. Cai wanted you to get your beauty rest on before the festivities started today, so I volunteered to watch the twins until you woke up and to keep an eye on them while you got ready."

I appreciated my sister being here and all, but I kind of felt some type of way that Cai didn't wish me a happy birthday before he left. Plus, I was looking forward to that early morning birthday sex I knew would bring in this day just right.

Getting up from the bed, I walked into the bathroom and handled my business before brushing my teeth and getting into the shower. Placing my bathrobe on, I walked back out into an empty bedroom. On my way to head downstairs to find my sister and babies, I noticed a beautifully wrapped box sitting on the edge of the bed. Squealing like a pig, butterflies started to flutter in my stomach as I jumped up and down in excitement. Forgetting all about the twins and Ari, I took off toward my bed and bounced back onto the soft mattress, picked up the card lying on top of the box, and I opened it first.

Audrielle,
Although today is your birthday, I'm hoping that it will also be the first day of the start of our new life. Loving you has been a blessing for me because I believe in my heart that God brought us together, regardless of what we've been through. You and our children are my heartbeats and without you three, there is no me. Enjoy your morning, beautiful. Breakfast fit for a queen is downstairs waiting for you, and I'll see you in a few. Happy birthday, baby.
Cairo

I must've read that card about twenty times before I finally picked up the box and tore the wrapping paper open. My mouth literally dropped open when I saw the red Cruel Summer Giuseppe Zanotti heels I'd always wanted staring me right in my face. Because of my not-so-narrow foot, I didn't think they would fit at all, but once I slipped my foot in and buckled both straps on the side comfortably, I was good to go. Slipping on the other heel, I walked over to my full-length mirror and gawked at the beautifully crafted heels gracing my feet. Another ten minutes passed before I finally took the shoes off and pranced my butt downstairs.

True to his word, a breakfast fit for a queen and her royal court was spread out on the kitchen table. Bacon, sausage, scrambled eggs, waffles, banana-nut pancakes, salmon croquettes, smothered potatoes, grits, and everything else to feed a small army. Not knowing where to start first, I grabbed a couple plates and spooned a little bit of everything on them. I was sure to gain back those ten pounds I'd lost, but it was going to be so worth it.

Hearing laughter coming from my dining room, I grabbed both plates as carefully as I could with one arm while holding a wine glass filled with a mimosa in the other.

"There she is!" Rima yelled, getting up from her seat and grabbing one of my plates and giving me a side hug. "Happy birthday, Audrielle! My best friend, my sister, my ride or die, my partner in crime, and my main thang. How you feeling this morning?"

"You already know I'm feeling good!" I couldn't hold my excitement in, even though I didn't know what anyone had planned for the day. "Good morning, Niecey. What are you doing here?"

She pointed toward the kitchen. "Ay, any time there's a breakfast like that on the menu, you know I'm there."

"Your greedy ass is everywhere some food is going to be. You not fooling anybody."

We laughed at my little joke and continued catching up with each other. Since I met Niecey that night at Cairo's parents' house, she and I had been getting close. Whenever our schedules allowed, we would get together to grab a bite to eat or go to have a few drinks at Toby's lounge, the Lotus Bomb.

"Audri, the twins are getting so big and cute," Niecey commented as we watched Egypt and Nyles throw scrambled eggs all over the place. "You know every time Cai sends a picture to Toby his ass gets on my bumper about us having kids."

"Well, what's the holdup?" Rima asked. "It's not like you two aren't engaged. Shit, and as fine as Toby's ass is, I'd give him a baby every nine months if he wanted one."

We fell out laughing at Rima's crazy ass. Leave it to her to say some shit like that.

"You too, Ari." I turned my attention to my sister. "With you and Ness being engaged now, when are you going to bless Cassius with a little sister or brother?"

"You and Finesse got engaged?" Rima asked, her voice filled with happiness and excitement.

Ari sheepishly nodded. A loose curl fell to the front of her face, and she tucked it behind her ear. "Yeah, a few days ago." She lifted her arm up and showed her engagement ring. "We haven't set a date or anything yet, but we're thinking sometime next year. That way we can save a little more money and be able to move into a bigger home and have the big-ass wedding I've always dreamed of."

"You act as if your daddy wouldn't pay for the whole thing if you got married tomorrow."

"And Cai and I would have no problem helping out with things. In fact, the reception will be our gift to you."

"Seriously, Audri?" Ariana asked, jumping from her seat.

"Yeah. I mean, I do have a little money tucked away for a rainy day since someone paid for Kick Biz 2 in full."

"What!" all three of them screamed at the same time, scaring my babies in the process.

I nodded my head. "Someone paid for the whole store. All $250,000 of it." I bit a piece of bacon. "I think it was Daddy, if you ask me, though, because when the bank denied me, I told him about it and he offered to pay for it, but when I declined the offer and told him I wanted to do it by myself, I thought he left it alone. Obviously not, though, because like a week later, the bank called and said that I was approved."

When the noise in the room died down and came to complete silence, I looked up from my plate in confusion. There were five sets of eyes on me, including the twins, with that "are you kidding me" look on their faces.

I placed my fork and knife down and wiped the corner of my mouth with my napkin. "What?"

Niecey was the first one to break the silence. "I'm the newbie here, and I have a pretty good idea that your father wasn't the one who mysteriously paid $250,000 for your new store."

My brow furrowed as I looked at Rima then to Ari. "So what are you trying to say, my daddy wouldn't do that for me?"

"Oh, girl, I know your dad wouldn't have a problem helping you out; from what you told me, that's how you got the first store up. However, your dad doesn't seem like that type who would want to hide helping you out. If he was the one who did it, I'm pretty sure he would've let it slip by now."

"Well, if my daddy didn't do it, who do you think . . ." It was at that moment that it finally hit me. "Oh, my fucking God! Cairo."

"Honey, that man is head over heels in love with you, even more now that you blessed him with his babies," Rima said.

"Yeah, sis, that man has it bad. Wait until you see what he has in store for you today."

My ears pricked up at that little comment. "You know what Cairo has planned for me today?"

I watched as all three of my favorite women looked at each other, silently talking to each other with their eyes.

"Okay, you got us," Rima finally spoke. "The reason we're here is to help you get ready for the family photo shoot Cai set up for you, him and the twins today, then to help you pack for your weekend getaway to Rancho Valencia!"

"What!"

"Yeah, girl. So hurry up and finish your food." Niecey looked at her watch. "You have a whole glam squad coming in about ten minutes to get you all glammed up and beat to the gawds."

Those damned butterflies started to flutter in my stomach again as I finished off the rest of my breakfast and headed back upstairs to my room. While Ari watched her niece and nephew and Rima and Niecey straightened up the kitchen, I went to hop back in the shower one more time and brush my teeth before my own little squad arrived to make me over.

Picking up my phone, I sent Cai a text.

Me: Thank you so much for the breakfast and shoes, babe. I loved it.

As soon as I pulled off my robe, my phone dinged with a return text alert.

My love: Anything for you! Now get ready. I'll be there in about an hour to pick you guys up, okay?

I excitedly threw my phone down on the bed then headed to my bathroom. Before I could step into my steaming hot shower, I heard my phone ding again.

My love: Before you get into the shower, I want you to grab your second gift from the closet.

Not sending a return text, I went straight to my walk-in closet and opened the door. There, in the middle of the floor, was another beautifully wrapped box. Tearing that open, my mouth dropped again, and tears instantly filled my eyes when I saw the lace and leather dress Cairo picked out for me. Another card fell from within the box.

I know you're going to look good in this. Now hurry up and get dressed. The faster we take these pictures, the faster I can rip this dress off of you and start on babies three and four.
Cai

This note didn't have to tell me twice. I placed my beautiful dress next to the heels still on my bed, and I hopped my ass in the shower. As much as I loved the dress, I couldn't wait for Cairo to rip that muthafucka off either.

"Audri, you look beautiful," Rima, Ari, Niecey, and the glam squad all said in at different times when I finally walked out of the makeshift dressing room that was set up in one of my downstairs bedrooms.

"Girl, Cai is going to lose his mind when he sees you."

I walked up to the full-length mirror being held up by one of the hairstylist's assistants, and I looked at myself in awe. The dress Cai picked out for me fit like a glove, and even with my little pooch slightly visible, I still was rocking the hell out of this dress. The red Giuseppes went well with the chunky red necklace and ruby studs Nana gifted me. My makeup was light and natural but beat to perfection. My hair was in a fancy braided hairstyle that I knew I could never do by myself. I looked beautiful. I felt beautiful, and I didn't have nobody to thank but—

"Damn, Audri, you look amazing."

Cairo. I turned from the mirror to face him, and I blushed at the way his eyes roamed my body up and down. I could tell by the way his leg started to shake that he was trying to stop his dick from getting harder and harder by the second.

"You look amazing yourself babe. Trying to match my fly and shit." I heard a few giggles behind me, but I didn't take my eyes off of Cai. Hell, I couldn't take my eyes off of Cai. That all-black fit, red leather jacket, and red Giuseppe sneakers that matched my heels looked sexy as hell on my baby. Then, with his dreads braided into a bun at the top of his head and his face being freshly lined up, I knew I would have to go change my panties before we left.

"Now that the two of you have eye-fucked each other for long enough, why don't y'all

take a look at your little prince and princess,"
Ari said as she and Rima came into the room
with the twins also matching their parents'
fly. Egypt had on a black dress that had tulle
on the bottom and red hearts all over it, while
Nyles had on some little black jeans and a red
button-up shirt that had black hearts all over
it. "You guys are going to be late for the shoot if
you don't leave now. We will catch up with you
later, Audri."

"What about all these people in my house? I
mean, I thank them for glamming your girl up,
but I don't know these people like that."

"Don't worry about it," Rima said, handing
Nyles to me. "We will clean everything up and
clear everyone out. You just go enjoy your day
and your family, and we will see you when you
get back Monday, okay?"

No other words were spoken as Cairo and I
grabbed our kids and left my sister and friends
to look after my home. After buckling the kids
into their car seats, and Cai going back into the
house to grab our overnight bags, we got into
the car and were on our way.

CHAPTER 13

CAIRO

We'd just left the photo shoot and were back in the car and headed to the party. Every few seconds I found myself taking my eyes off of traffic and staring at the side of Audri's breath-taking face. I didn't even have to see the proofs from the shoot to know that the photos were going to be beautiful. I couldn't wait to get them back just to have them blown up, framed, and hung on the walls of our home.

"Why do you keep looking at me like that?"

"Because I can." I looked at her face again and watched as she nodded before looking back out of the window. "Where are we going, Cai? Shouldn't you have jumped on the 101 then the 5?"

"My GPS said there's traffic on the 101 because of construction, so I'm taking an alternate route."

She shrugged her shoulders then continued to look out of the window. For the remainder of the ride, we sat in a comfortable silence, while the twins napped in the back. When we got off the freeway twenty minutes later, I knew Audri would have more questions, seeing as the Rancho Valencia resort was an hour and a half away.

"Where are we going now?" she asked as I read a text that came through on my phone.

"Chasin just texted me and asked if I could stop by to sign a few things before we left. You know if this weren't important, I wouldn't be stopping."

"Are these papers your divorce papers finally?"

"Unfortunately not." She opened her mouth to say something, but I cut her off. "Don't trip, though, it's going to be done sooner than you know it."

She bit her bottom lip, and I knew she wanted to say something else, but she kept quiet. We had driven for a few more minutes before we were pulling up to the four-bedroom, four-and-a-half bath residence in Hollywood Hills.

"Chasin lives here?" Audri asked as she took in the newly constructed million-dollar home.

"Naw, a friend of his. He's here celebrating something and happened to bring the papers with him."

"Cai, I don't wanna walk into these people's home uninvited. That's rude and downright tacky, and Chasin's ass should know that. Call him and tell him to come outside and you can sign the papers out here."

"Girl, it's too hot to be sitting out here in this car. Besides, we need to change the twins' diapers before we get on the road and have to stop again."

Audri mumbled something under her breath before she rolled her eyes then opened the back door to unbuckle Nyles from his car seat. Grabbing my princess, and then the diaper bag, I made sure to lock the car up before we walked to the front door.

After ringing the doorbell a few times, Chasin finally answered the door.

"Hey, guys, come on in," he said as he slapped fives with me and kissed Audri on the cheek. "We were just about to start the celebration in the backyard, so you guys are just in time."

I felt Audri pinch me on my side then give me a warning look to hurry and do what I came to do so that we could leave. Ignoring her, I continued to follow Chasin until we reached the showcased kitchen that featured Caesarstone counters, Italian lacquer cabinets, Miele appliances, a wine fridge, and a center island with a six-seat breakfast bar that opened to the spacious family media room. I looked back at Audri and watched as her eyes lit up at every room and thing we passed.

"So, all I need is for you to sign right here on the dotted line and we're all set, my man."

"Chasin, whose house is this?"

He looked at me then to Audri. "A partner of mines. Pretty nice, huh?"

"It's beautiful."

"I could give you a tour if you like."

She shook her head as she bounced Nyles on her hip. "Oh, no, I'm not about to be snooping through these people's home. It's pretty rude of you to invite us here anyway without introducing us to the owners. I feel like we're sneaking in here."

Chasin laughed as I handed him the signed documents. "Well, if you feel that way, how about I take you to the back so I can introduce you to them?"

"Naw, that's okay. Beside, Cai and I need to get going. We're celebrating my birthday this weekend in San Diego, and I wanna at least spend a few hours in the spa while it's still my day."

"Well, first things first. Happy birthday!" He gave Audri another hug. "But this won't take long. They're just having a little get-together outside by the pool. I'll just introduce you guys then you can be on your way."

I looked back at Audri, who looked at me then shrugged her shoulder. "I guess it's a go then."

We followed Chasin back through the living room and toward the back of the home. All while we were walking, I could hear Audri oohing and aahing at the different pieces of furniture and decorations spread throughout the house.

When we made it to the glass wall at the back of the home and Chasin opened the sliding doors, it was as if we stepped into Disney's vision of Wonderland itself. A twenty-two-foot king demure mahogany dining table sat in the middle of the lawn with everything you could think of for a Mad Hatter's tea party: a white linen tablecloth, a variety of desserts and finger foods on stainless steel serving tiers and trays, antique and colorful tea kettles and cups whimsically placed. Circular and regular floral centerpieces of different calla lily arrangements and partially painted red roses were strategically placed around the table and yard. There were also different scenes from the movie in every corner of the lawn: the Cheshire Cat in his forest, the Queen of Hearts and her cards playing croquet, the six-foot female models dressed in lily, violet, marguerite, snapdragon, and marigold

costumes singing "All in the Golden Afternoon."
There was even a section for the animatronics
Caterpillar and his mushroom patch. Audri was
so fascinated at showing the twins everything
that she didn't notice the people who started to
form around her until we all yelled, "Surprise!"

After being startled then finally focusing her
vision on the faces in front of her, Audri's cheeks
became drenched with tears.

"What . . . what . . . who . . ." She looked up
at me damn near speechless, with her makeup
running and still looking beautiful as ever. I
handed Egypt to Mama Faye while Nana took
Nyles from Audri's arms.

"Since we weren't able to celebrate the arrival
of the twins, I, along with your family and
friends, came up with the idea to throw you a
surprise party and belated baby shower for your
birthday today."

"What!" She was still crying as she looked
around at everybody and smiled.

"Audri, you've been so busy with your businesses, becoming a mother, and dealing with
me and all my bullshit that you haven't had time
to celebrate any of the important milestones in
your life. We just wanted to show you that we
see all of your hard work and determination,
and for that we wanna say congratulations,
happy birthday, and we love you."

Before I could say anything else, Audri grabbed me by the back of my neck and pulled me down until our lips crashed into each other. With my eyes closed, I wrapped my arms around her waist and pulled her farther into me, deepening our kiss.

"Get a room already!" Ness shouted, causing everyone to laugh. I slowly ended my kiss with Audri, but not before I pecked her lips a few times, then whispered in her ear, "I'll take a bullet for you."

She smiled, wiped her lip gloss off of my lips, then turned around to a waiting Ari, Rima, and Niecey, and she started to jump up and down, yelling. While she went to go check out the rest of the party and greet more of her guests, I headed over to one of the patios where the fellas were sitting.

"Aww, here he comes," Kong joked, "the man of the hour. I don't know how you even made it here today. With the way Audri looks in that dress, we would've been ducked off and in somebody's hotel right now going a couple rounds."

"Ay, man, we cool, but we not that cool. You better keep your eyes off my girl."

He held up his arms in mock surrender. "I'm just saying, your girl is beautiful, and has a body to die for. Not only that, but she blessed you with two beautiful kids, and any blind man can see that she's in love with you."

"Okay, so what are you trying to say?"

"What Kong's ass is trying to say is when you gone get rid of that crazy bitch Alex and wife the real woman you love?" Ness asked, causing the group of fellas to laugh again.

"Man, even when Cai divorces that psychotic bitch, she's still going to be a pain in his ass. Did we all forget that she has this man's baby in her belly?"

"Man, Kong, shut your ass up. Everybody knows that baby is not Cai's. I ain't even fucked the girl, and I can feel it in my bones." Chasin stood up with a beer swinging in his hand. "In the case of Cairo Broussard Jr., Cairo Sr., you are not the father! We don't even have to go on *Maury* to see that shit."

We all shared a laugh then refreshed our drinks before just sitting around and catching up with each other. I looked across the lawn at the tea party table and watched as Audri and the girls posed for pictures.

A light vibration rattled in my pocket, and I quickly pulled it out. Thinking that it was Audri sending me a few of her selfies, I unlocked my screen and went right to my texts. What I wasn't expecting was a message from Alex in all caps:

DNA: I'm going into labor right now! OMW to the hospital!

"Ay, yo, Cai, man, what's wrong? You seem like you just saw a ghost."

"Nothing, really. Alex just texted me and said that she was on her way to the hospital."

"For what?" Kong and Chasin asked at the same time.

"Said she just went into labor."

Everybody became quiet.

"What?"

"You don't think you should go? I mean, I understand that you feel like the baby isn't yours, but what if there's a chance that it might be?"

"Kong, I know you're the righteous one of the crew, but I ain't trying to hear that shit. If the baby is mine, we will find out in a couple days when I go to take the paternity test. Until then, I'm going to sit here and enjoy the rest of the day with my girl, my kids, my family, and my friends."

"All right, bruh, but I'm just saying—"

"I'm just saying," I repeated, trying to mock Kong's deep voice. "Look, man, I hear you, but knowing Alex, she probably found out about this party and wants to try anything to ruin it for Audri. I fell for her trick one time, and I'm not about to fall for it again."

"Speaking of tricks . . ." We all turned around at the sound of Roderick's voice. It would be just like his *Ebony* model–looking ass to stroll in here two hours after the time he was supposed to be here. "What's up, fellas?" He turned to me and handed me a bottle of Balvenie single malt Scotch, knowing my ass didn't like this expensive, nasty shit. "First thing first, congratulations, bro."

I nodded.

"And, secondly, I can tell you right now that that baby Alex is carrying is not yours, so don't even waste your time."

"Man, how do you know?" Kong asked.

"Because, as requested, I did a little digging on Cai crazy-ass wife. Let's just say that she was already a little over eight weeks pregnant when she started screaming that Broussard heir shit." Roderick sat down in the seat next to me and took the bottle he'd just given me out of my hand. After cracking it open, he poured himself a shot, then waved the bottle around, asking if anyone else wanted to partake. When everyone declined the drink, he set the bottle down on the table.

"Now, do y'all remember that freaky little nurse I used to mess with a couple years ago named Krytol?" We all nodded in remembrance.

"Come to find out, she started working a couple months ago at that ob-gyn's office Alex goes to. I called her up, invited her out to dinner, and asked her to look into a couple things for me."

"Well, what did she find out?" Ness asked as all eyes turned to Roderick.

"That not only was she lying about the due date but that ob-gyn she had y'all seeing wasn't even a real doctor. Well, not yet. She just happened to be doing her residency there. The day when you and Cairo came and had to see a different doctor was the same day her residency ended."

I was confused. "Well, what does that have to do with her telling Alex how far along she is?"

"It has a lot to do with it when you buried in over fifty thousand dollars of student loan debt. Alex offered to pay off all of her student loans if she went along with the timeline she was trying to get you to believe." He pointed at me.

"Daaaaaaamn," Kong said, sitting back in his seat and shaking his head. "That's some cold-blooded shit. Then females wonder why some men respond the way they do when they pop up all of a sudden pregnant." He shook his head again. "Now I get what you were saying earlier, Cai. I'd be pissed off if I left my girls party, which I paid for, to go to the hospital and see a baby who's not mine be born. Not only would my girl be pissed off at me by the time I got home, but I would have to hear a million 'I told you so's' after I told her the baby wasn't mine." Kong turned to Roderick. "Do you know who the father is?"

Roderick poured him another shot and gulped it down. "Now that bit of information, my dear friend, is the icing on the cake."

"So did you enjoy your birthday party/baby shower?" I asked Audri as we stood on one of the patios watching the cleaning crew I hired start to take everything down. There were still a few guests lingering, but the majority had already left, including Ness and Ariana, who took a sleeping Cassius home, and Audri's parents, who offered to take the twins for the night. I was a bit surprised when Audri agreed, seeing as she and her mother didn't socialize throughout the whole party, but Diana needed to spend some time with her grandkids; she hadn't seen them since the day Audri gave birth.

"I did, babe. Thank you so much. The twins got a lot of things. Some I liked, and some I will have to take back and exchange sometime next week."

I laughed. "I thought all of the gifts were cool. What didn't you like?"

"For one thing, my son will not be wearing any type of floral-print outfit. I don't care if it matches his sister's dress or who makes it. Secondly, I don't want my kids rolling around in anything my mother bought them so that Bugaboo Donkey stroller will be headed right back to the store."

I walked up behind her and circled my hands around her waist. Whatever intoxicating scent she had on drifted to my nose and had my dick slowly waking up. "At some point, you're going to have to talk to your mom again, Audri. It may not be today, it may not be tomorrow, but you gotta do it. Regardless of what you two are going through, she's still Egypt and Nyles's grandmother and has every right to buy them things." She shifted in my grasp, but I wrapped my arms around her tighter. "Just listen to her and see what she has to say. After that, I'm with whatever decision you decide to go with on your mother-daughter relationship."

Audri turned in my embrace then wrapped her arms around her neck. "How you were able to get all of that out with your dick pressing into my ass like that is beyond me." She kissed my lips and laughed. "However, I hear what you're saying, and I'll think about doing just that when I go and pick up the twins from my parents' house tomorrow."

Kissing her soft lips again, and then her neck, I pulled her closer to me. "That's all I'm asking you for, baby." I slid my tongue into her mouth and savored the taste of the buttercream frosting she just ate. That mixed with her plush body pressing against mine and her perfume still lingering in my nose, I was ready to bend her sexy ass over the banister and give everybody who was still in this backyard a show. Audri slowly ended our kiss then pulled back from me.

"Now, since we have the rest of the night baby-free, how 'bout we go back to the house and try to work on babies number three and four? If I remember correctly, you did say you wanted to rip this dress off of me and have your way."

A low growl escaped from my lips as I palmed a generous amount of her ass in my hand. "I did and I will. I just got to give you your gifts before we do."

She squinted her already low eyes and tried to stop them from misting up. "Baby, you didn't have to get me anything. All of this was and is already enough."

"I know, but I still wanted to give you a token of my appreciation and to show you how much I love you," I said as I pulled a small black velvet box from my back pocket. Audri's eyes opened wide as she began to jump up and down.

"Oh, my God. Oh, my God." She fanned her face with both hands. "No, you didn't, Cai. I know this isn't what I think it is."

"Hey, hey, hey! What's all of the commotion going on over here?" Nana asked as she, Mama Faye, that guy Wayman, and some dude who looked similar to him walked over to us. "Why is my grandbaby over here jumping up and down and screaming like she's crazy?"

"Yeah, what's going on?" Rima asked as she and Roderick came from the side of the house, oblivious to their clothes being twisted and wrinkled. But what took the cake were the strands of hair sticking straight up in the middle of Rima's head.

Audri tried to get Rima's attention and tell her what's up by smoothing the top of her hair down with her hands, but Rima's ass just wasn't getting it. Instead, she scrunched her face up and looked around at every eye that was now on her.

"What?" she asked, still lost.

"Yah hair, gayl. Fix yah hair on top of yah head. Yah look like a peacock," Mama Faye said, causing everyone to laugh.

Rima, embarrassed, smoothed her hair down then turned and socked Roderick in his arm for not telling her.

"Now that that out of the way. What's going on?"

Audri took the velvet box that was enveloped between her hands and waved it around. "Cairo got me a gift."

"Well, what cha waitin' fah, gayl? Stop waving it around like yah crazy and open de box."

Everyone waited with bated breath as Audri finally calmed her hyper ass down and cracked the box open a little bit. Her eyes lifted to mine, and I could see the minute more excitement covered her face. She closed her eyes, took another deep breath, then fully opened the box. When her facial expression changed to one of confusion instead of more happiness, I almost laughed.

"What's de matta, gayl? Why yah face turn sour like dat?"

"It's . . . it's a set of keys."

Mama Faye and Nana both shot a heated glare toward me. Rima placed her hands on Audri's drooping shoulders, while Roderick, Wayman, and his friend blew out sighs of relief.

"Wasn't expecting keys, huh?"

"No. Yes. I mean, no. It's just that I thought . . ." She shook her head and huffed. "What are these keys for?"

"Yeah, boi. What de hell is de keys fah?"

"Well, according to your BFF," I said, looking at Rima and nodding, "I had to get you a push gift. For the life of me, I didn't know what type of gift you would give to someone who gave birth to your kids. Then, like a ton of bricks, it hit me. We both have individual houses, but neither of them is our home. Now that you have given me all of the ingredients to fill one, I figured, why not buy you one?"

Tears started to fall from Audri's eyes. "What are you saying, Cai?"

"I'm saying, welcome to our new home."

"Noooooooooooooooo, you didn't. No, you didn't, Cai. Are you telling me that this"—she waved her hands around the space—"is our new home?"

I shrugged. "If you want it to be."

As Audri jumped into my arms, everyone around us cheered and said their congratulations.

"So that whole little scene with Chasin in the house earlier . . ."

"Yeah, that was me signing the papers to make it official. Next week, we will go down to Chasin's office and have you sign your name to all of the paperwork so that your name is on the deed as well."

Audri didn't say anything else as she crashed her lips to mine and kissed me with all the love in her body.

CHAPTER 14

AUDRIELLE

To say I was beyond happy would've totally been an understatement. When we first pulled up to this house, I almost lost my breath at how breathtakingly beautiful it was. Then when we walked inside, I couldn't stop looking at the beautiful furniture and decor that so elegantly went with it. Then to find out that this all belonged to me and my little family had me on cloud nine. Cai really outdid himself and was definitely going to get it as soon as I went back inside.

"Congratulations, baby, you deserve it," Nana said as she gave me a hug and kissed me on my cheek. "Now you get your ass back in this million dollar home and give that fine-ass white man of yours some of that million dollar pussy."

"Nana!" I screamed covering my face in embarrassment. Not only was Mama Faye standing there, but so was Wayman and his equally hand-some business partner, Jonah.

"Nutting tah be ashamed of, gayl. Yah had mi son's babies already."

"I know, but still."

"Still nothing." Nana snapped. "Now us grown folks are about to get out of here. You take your ass in there and go get me another Swiss Miss–colored baby with those beautiful eyes and sandy blond curls."

I gave Nana another hug and kiss, and then turned and did the same to Mama Faye.

"Mi glad Cairo finally got it tahgetha. Mi always knew yah was de one fah him, even when that wicked gayl came around. Yah take care of mi boi ay. He might not get everyt'ing right, but fah yah, he will die trying," she whispered into my ear.

I released her, then nodded my head and watched as they all climbed into Wayman's gray Range Rover. Hitting his horn twice, they finally pulled off and were on their way.

"Yo, your Nana better not be hooking my mom up with that other *Ebony* model–looking, dude Wayman had with him," Cai said as soon as I walked back into our new home.

"Hey, Mama gotta have a life too."

He laughed then shook his head. "That may be true, but it won't be with a cat who's around the same age as me. Now if Wayman would've brought his grandpa or something, then I could see it. But not some dude who looks like she gave birth to him herself."

I just laughed as I walked around one of the couches in the living room and sat down.

"Naw, don't get comfortable just yet. I still got a few more things to show you."

What he needed to show me now was going to be a total mystery to me. We'd just toured the house before Rima and everyone else left. The only two things that I didn't get to see were the two bedrooms that were closed. Needless to say, I stood up and grabbed a hold of Cai's hand and headed back upstairs.

When we reached the top of the stairs, we walked to the first door that was closed. Taking out a key, Cairo unlocked it then turned back to me. "Close your eyes."

"For wh—"

He cut me off. "Just close your eyes, babe."

Doing as I was told, I closed my eyes and listened as Cairo opened the door, then grabbed my hand and pulled me farther into the room. The sound of oceans waves was playing in the background while the scent of baby powder hung in the air. Cairo released my hands, then flicked on a light switch and told me to open my eyes.

"Oh, my God. It's beautiful, Cai," I said, damn near tears. I looked around the bedroom-turned-nursery in complete awe. Two tufted-paneled Beverly cribs sat in each corner of the room while a few dressers, some more baby furniture and toys, and two matching rocking chairs were strategically placed around the room. "Two peas in a pod" was the theme, so forest green and mint were the color scheme. "Baby, this is gorgeous."

I walked around the room, opening drawers, admiring the toys, and even trying out the chairs. My fingers even outlined each letter of the twin's names that were engraved on their cribs. Nyles had small crowns surrounding his while Egypt had sparkly tiaras surrounding hers. Our family portraits from the photo shoot earlier were hanging from the wall as well as the pictures that were taken at the hospital a couple days after I delivered the twins. My favorite, which was the one where Cai held a sleeping Egypt's face in his hand, while I held Nyles in mine, was blown up and enhanced with a sepia filter and it hung in a beautiful frame between the two cribs. By far this was my favorite room in the whole house.

I turned to look at Cai, who was leaning on the doorframe with his arms folded across his chest. His piercing bluish green eyes were staring at me intently. "So I take it that I did a good job?" He finally spoke after staring at me for a while.

"Good? Cai, this is wonderful. I can't wait to bring the twins home tomorrow to see how they react to it." I turned back around looking at everything in the room again. Everything was perfect. All except for these twelve round pea-shaped things I didn't notice going across the dresser before. They were the size of golf balls with nothing pictured or written on them. "Baby, what are these?"

Cai rose up from the doorframe and slowly walked over to me with his hands in his pocket. "Why don't you open them and see?" He motioned with his head.

I didn't know what the hell he was up to, but I decided to just do as told and I reached for the first pea, and I opened it.

I huffed and turned around. "Cai . . ."

He shook his head. "Keep going."

In what felt like twenty seconds, I had all twelve peas open, revealing the contents inside. My hands flew to my mouth as tears started to pour from my eyes.

"Baby, what is this?" I asked between sobs.

Cai walked closer to me and gently took my hands from my face and pressed them to his lips. "This is me telling you that I love you and want to spend the rest of my life with you."

I laughed. "With twelve different engagement rings? Do I get to pick which one I want?"

He shook his head. "No, because those aren't engagement rings." He got down on his knee and pulled another pea box from out of his pocket. "This is."

I started sobbing again when I looked down at the four-carat radiant-cut yellow and white diamond split-shank framed engagement ring Cai had in his hand. "Those rings up there are actually wedding rings. Ranging from one carat, which is in the first box, to twelve carats, which is the size of the ring in the last box. Each representing a year of us being married in wedded bliss. So every year on our anniversary, you switch your rings."

"But you stopped at twelve. Do you only wanna be married to me for twelve years?" I knew he was in the middle of his proposal, but I had to ask.

"I figured after twelve we could switch it up. Start taking trips and shit. The twins will be old enough to where they could basically tend to themselves so we could be gone a little longer than the weekend."

He looked down at the ground, blew out a long breath, then looked back up at me with misty blue eyes. "Anyways, Audri, I want you to know that I have loved you since the first time I laid eyes on you in your store. I don't know what it was or how it happened, but I just couldn't see living this life of mine without you in it. Now I know somewhere along the way I messed up and had you doubting that love, but I want you to know and understand that my heart has always and will always be in your hand. You have the power to destroy it. You have the patience to nurture and care for it. You have the life that it beats for, and you've given me the gifts that it lives for. Without you or our kids, Audri, my heart will die, so I'm asking you right now, in the home we will now be sharing as a family, will you do me the honor of becoming my wife, soul mate, and best friend for the rest of our lives?"

"Yes! Yes! And yes!" I screamed without a hesitant bone in my body, even though my mind kept wondering how long we would have to wait to get married since he was still technically married to Alex. However, I wasn't about to let that crazy, delusional bitch mess up this moment.

Cairo stood up from the floor, slid the ring on my shaky finger, and swooped me up in his arms and hugged me tight. I held my left hand up in the air and admired the ring while still being held in his embrace. A big grin spread across my face because, for once, my life and everything in it was going as planned. Minus the small bullshit with Alex, my love life was now on track, my career was moving full steam ahead, and I was learning to become the best mom in the world. For the first time in my life, I was completely happy and didn't have anyone to thank but Cairo.

"Oh, and before I forget," Cai said, releasing me from his arms, "I don't wanna have this long, drawn-out engagement, seeing as you should've been the one with my last name the first time I said, 'I do.'" He opened one of the drawers and pulled a white envelope out from underneath Nyles's onesies and handed it to me. "I figure with the twins being christened next month, we might as well make it a double celebration and get married on that same day. I want all of us to have the same name before we dedicate our kids to Christ."

"But, Cai, how can we do that when you're—"

He pointed to the envelope in my hand. "Open it."

I looked at him, and then the envelope in my hand. Taking a breath, I ripped the envelope open and unfolded its contents.

"When did this happen?" I asked, finally looking at a smiling Cai. "When did she sign the papers? Better yet, where was I when you went to get these things signed?"

Cai laughed. "Baby, I was just as surprised as you when I got them."

"When you got them? So, what you saying, she signed the papers on her own and mailed them back?"

"Not exactly," Cai said as he walked out of the twins' room and to the other door that had been locked as well. Had I not been so focused on Cai answering my question, I would've noticed the enormous master bedroom that we walked into with the extensive wood paneling and matching custom bed. I would've also noticed the partition wall that housed a fireplace and created a separate sitting area, but my mind was on something else.

I followed Cai over to the small office area that was off to the side next to the door leading to a private balcony. Taking off his shirt, he laid it on top of the cherry wood desk, then took off the rest of his clothes. My breath hitched in my throat as I watched the muscles in his back shift every time he moved. When my eyes started to take in every tattoo that covered his body, I completely forgot about whatever it was we were talking about. He turned around and I damn near fell to the floor at the sight of his long, thick dick pointing straight at me.

"Instead of worrying about how I got the papers, let's just be happy that there signed and there's nothing stopping me from taking you to the justice of the peace and marrying you right now," he said as he started walking toward me with that sexy predatory look he always got when he was about to fuck the shit out of me. "If you don't want me to really rip that dress off of you, I advise you strip out of it right now."

"What fun would that be if you didn't stick to your word?" I breathlessly said.

His eyes narrowed, and he smirked before he licked his lips. "None at all."

Next thing I know, everything, including my bra and panties, was shredded off of my body, and I was thrown on the bed. My pussy was already dripping wet, so it didn't give Cai's dick no resistance as he slid in.

We both hissed and through our heads back. "I've been craving you all day," Cai said into my ear. "I need you to soak my dick in that delicious nectar you're going to be feeding me all night." The second the words left his mouth I was coming all over his dick. "Just like that, Audri. Give me what I want," he said as he started to pound deeper into me. "You're going to marry me next month and becoming mine for the rest of my life, right?"

I nodded.

"Let me hear you say it again, baby."

"Yes."

"Yes, what?"

"Yes, I'm going to marry you next month," I said between breaths. Cai was digging so deep into my pussy that I could feel it in my chest. I screamed out as tears started to spring from my eyes. He kissed my wet cheeks then my lips.

"You're mine, Audri. Mind, body, and soul and will be for the rest of my life." He started hitting my shit faster, so I knew he was about to come. "I'll take a bullet for you and anything else that comes your way," he said into my ear as he finally released every drop of come he had into me.

Cairo dropped on top of me, taking short breaths with his dick still wrapped in my warmth. Lacing his hands with mine, he brought my arms up and raised them above my head. Nuzzling his nose in the crook of my neck, I felt as he pushed up on his elbows a little then started to sway his hips from side to side.

I moaned at the feel of his dick growing wide against my walls and pushing deeper into me.

"Damn, baby. You don't wanna rest for a few more minutes?" I asked, then moaned again.

"Nope." I could feel his smile against my neck.

I took my hands from his and grabbed a handful of his dreads. "Well, if that's the case," I said, rolling us over until I was sitting on top, "let me ride you into this coma right quick. That way I know we'll get a little rest."

Cairo put his hands behind his head then bit his bottom lip. "By all means, Mrs. Broussard, handle your shit."

CHAPTER 15

ALEXANDRIA

It had been a week since I delivered my son and I was still in a funk. Not only did Cairo not show up, but neither did my son's real father. Then to make matters worse, both of the ass-holes were still ignoring my phone calls and texts. I threw my cell down next to me frustrated then bowed my head on my knees and screamed. All of my previous plans would've worked if it weren't for that bitch Audri. It was because of her that Cai and I were now divorced and part of the reason why I believed he couldn't love me like he used to. Had she never come into the picture, I had no doubt in my mind that Cai and I would have still been together.

Slowly raising my head, I combed my fingers through my long hair and took a deep breath. If everything went according to plan in the next two weeks, that same money I tried to take from

Cairo while we were married would be given to me without a problem. The night that Marjorie, my father, and I had that emergency meeting after Audri's mother basically forced me to sign the divorce papers, we came up with a better plan, since the switching DNA plan Marjorie originally came up with wouldn't have worked. Even if we had gone through with that one, just taking one look at my baby Cairo would've known he didn't belong to him.

I listened to my son cry at the top of his lungs as the nanny I hired tended to whatever it was that he wanted. For some reason, that motherly connection most women get right after they give birth totally skipped over me. I mean, I loved my son to death, but I didn't want to be around him. As soon as I pushed Elijah out, I told the nurse to take him straight to the nursery. The doctor tried to tell me that I needed to make skin-to-skin contact so that he could get used to my scent, but I didn't need to do that. My scent was going to be the furthest thing from his senses.

Now that I thought about it, I should've had the nanny in the delivery room with me instead of my drunk mother and cunt-chasing father. Elijah was going to be smelling her way more than me, so it should've been her scent he came into contact with first. I didn't know if it was because I was wishing that he was really Cairo's son or if it was because I just wasn't mother material being the reason why I felt that way. I mean, I'd been pregnant a few times before and aborted every one of those unwanted pregnancies without a problem; but, this time, around, I wanted to keep the baby regardless of the fact that I was using him to bait Cairo along. Something in me stopped me from making that trip to the clinic.

What's funny was, even in saying all of that, it still didn't stop the tear that came from my eye when I finally got to see his mocha-colored face for the first time a few hours later. Big brown eyes, curly black hair, and skin smooth to the touch made my son look more like his father than he did me.

"*Sí*, senorita, the, ah, check you wrote for me did, ah, how you say? Not go through," the nanny said in her broken English.

"Oh, I'm sorry about that. I'll just write you another one."

"Oh, no, no. I, uh, sorry, senorita, but, uh, I take cash now, not check."

I looked through my wallet and only came up with the sixty dollars I always carried with me, just in case whatever place I was at didn't accept credit. "This is all I have," I said to her, showing the three twenties. "I won't have any more until I go to the bank a little later."

She nodded slowly then damn near snatched the money from my hand. Placing Elijah in my lap, she started to gather her things from the floor and couch.

"Where are you going?"

"I come back when you have the rest, yeah?"

"But I need you now." Elijah started to move around wildly in my hand, and my eyes widened in fear. "What am I supposed to do? I'm not sure what he wants, and I've only changed a diaper and made a bottle once. What if I accidently hurt him?"

She looked at me with sympathetic eyes.

"I promise I'll go get the money right now. I'll even pay you for a week in advance. *Cinco* hundred, instead of, *dos* hundred *cinco* zero!" I desperately said. I couldn't describe the look on her face, but I knew her ears recognized $500, even if I didn't say the shit right.

She put her things back down, then nodded at me. "*Sí*, I will stay, senorita."

"Thank you!" I appreciatively said as I handed Elijah back to her. "What's wrong with him?"

She licked her lips. "He needs to take a nap." Cradling my son in her arms, she headed to the back of the house and into the nursery.

I cursed myself out in my head because I didn't know where I was going to get this $500 from.

A couple days before I went into labor, the FBI put a freeze on the company's bank accounts as well as my and my father's personal accounts. Something about an investigation that had been going on for some time now. I knew that my father was fucking off money left and right and doing some small backhanded shit to make more, but I didn't know it was to the extent that the Federal Bureau of Investigation was involved. I could dip into the little bit of mad money I had in a couple of my shoeboxes in my closet, but I knew I would need that to pay my mortgage and other bills if this investigation took longer than it had to.

Picking up my phone again, I tried to call Elijah's father, but just like last time I was sent to voicemail.

"Look, I'm not thrilled about the fact that we have a child together, just like you, but it doesn't mean that you don't still have a responsibility to take care of. Elijah's nanny is threatening to leave if I don't pay her for two weeks of service. Could you please bring me five hundred dollars so that I can pay this lady? I'm pretty sure you've heard about the investigation going on about my father's company, so you know money is tight around here. I'll be at the house all day, so you can drop it off anytime. Thanks."

I hung up the phone and hoped like hell his ass brought that money over to me. If not, he'd have a surprise on his doorstep by the time he got home from work.

Getting up from my comfortable position on the couch, I stretched my arms above my head then went into the kitchen to get something to drink. After grabbing a bottle of Fiji water, I walked down to the nursery to check on the nanny and Elijah. When I reached the door, she was nowhere in sight, but my son was peacefully lying asleep in his crib. The little red choo choo train onesie he had on was way bigger than his body, but he looked comfortable. I walked over to the crib and smoothed my hand over his head. At my touch, a small smile spread across his face, and that one dimple in his cheek dented in.

"Where do you get that from, handsome?" I asked as I stuck my pinky finger in it. When he stirred in his sleep, I quickly moved my hand back to avoid waking him up. After taking one last look at my son, and making sure that he was still asleep, I placed the plush blue elephant I bought next to him in the crib and retreated out of my room. Going back into the living room, I was expecting to see the nanny there since she wasn't in the bathroom or in any of the other rooms I passed on my way back to the front of the house. As I got closer, I could feel something was a little off because the white wool sweater that was once hanging from the back of the high chair at the bar was gone. Upon further inspection, I noticed that all of the bags the nanny usually carried with her were also gone from their normal spots as well as my Alexander McQueen purse that I used as a diaper bag.

"What in the . . ." A small yellow Post-it note sticking to my expensive-ass grandfather clock caught my attention. Plucking it off, I read the chicken scratch handwriting on the paper.

"I quit," was the only thing on the note. I looked around my living room in disbelief. Not only did this bitch leave me alone with my baby, but she had the audacity to take my $1,300 purse. That shit was worth way more than two weeks of babysitting I promised to pay her for.

"Aaaaaaargh!" I let out before I quickly covered my mouth with my hand, remembering that Elijah was still sleeping in the back. "What the fuck am I supposed to do now?"

Picking my phone up, I called Elijah's father again, and just like twenty minutes ago there was still no answer. I started to pace the floor back and forth trying to think of someone to call. I was starting to become so agitated that I had to put my hair in a messy bun and splash a little water on my face. I picked up my phone again and started going down my call log, trying to find at least someone I reach out to.

Skipping over my mother's and father's numbers, my eyes came across a contact I hadn't used in a long time. I grabbed the cordless phone off of the table behind me and dialed her number. I would've used my cell, but after the last time we talked, she added me to her blocked list. I held the landline phone to my ear and listened as her phone rang about five times. Just as I was about to give up all hope, she picked up the phone and said a soft hello.

"Sarah?"

"Yes. Who is this?"

"After all these years you don't know my voice?" I wasn't trying to be nasty, but she got on my nerves sometimes.

"Obviously if I knew who it was, I wouldn't have asked."

This bitch. I put on my big girl panties though and changed my voice back to a pleasant one. "It's Alex, Sarah."

There was a slight pause. "What are you calling me for?" I could hear her rustling through a lot of papers in the background. Whatever it was that she was doing, she stopped and walked away from it, because a few seconds later I couldn't hear it anymore.

"Can I call my old friend?"

"Not when I blocked all of your numbers from calling me. You're lucky I never had this number, or it would've been on the block list too. I told you the last time we talked not to call me no more for anything. Whatever you done got yourself into now, I don't wanna be a part of it. I already lost someone I was real close to because of you, and I'm not going to do it again."

I smacked my lips. "Sarah, you act as if I put a gun to your head and told you . . ." I was just about to let her have it but lost my train of thought when I heard Elijah start to whine. It was then that my reality hit me and told me that, instead of going off on her, I needed to be nice and try to get her to come help me. "Look, Sarah, I apologize for anything I put you through. I'm also sorry for threatening to have you disbarred and telling your husband about what you'd been up to."

It took her a moment, but she finally responded. "What do you want, Alex?"

"I need your help."

"Didn't I just tell you—"

I cut her off. "It's nothing like that. I need your help with Elijah."

"Who's Elijah?"

"My son. I finally had my baby a week ago."

"And let me guess. That maternal knowledge thing hasn't kicked in for you yet? Or is it that you're so focused on robbing Cairo blind that you don't have the time to take care of the baby you had? Where's your nanny? I just know the fabulous Alexandria Tate hired someone other than herself to take care of her baby."

I sat on my end of the line quiet. With her saying things like that, it really made me question if I was really all that bad. Elijah's cries started to become louder, and I knew that I would need her help at least tonight if she didn't wanna come any other day.

"Sarah, please. Can you just come help me real quick? You're right, I did have a nanny, but she just quit on me today because I didn't have the money to pay her for two weeks in advance. You know I can't call my mother because she might slip some vodka in his bottle when I'm not looking, and my father is too busy fucking either Marjorie's old ass or that new little temp he hired at the office."

She got quiet on her end again. "Why did you call me, though, Alex? Out of all people. What even makes you think I would come to help you?"

"Because . . ." I lowered my head.

"Because what?"

"Because Elijah is your nephew."

CHAPTER 16

AUDRIELLE

Today I finally decided to meet my mother for lunch and have this talk she'd been begging me for the last two weeks. If it weren't for Cairo telling me that she was the reason for Alex signing those divorce papers, I probably would've still been dodging her calls. I was avoiding my mother so much that when it came to the twins spending some time with my parents, either I spoke with my father to arrange something or Cai would talk to them. As much as I hated to admit it, though, I kind of missed my mother. Her attitude toward me was fucked up, but at least, when she did it, I could tell it came from some form of love. Wasn't the type of love I wanted, but it was her way of showing it.

"Audri, I'm glad you could make it," my mother said as she got up from the table with her arms open for a hug. I walked into her embrace but didn't hug her back.

"Well, you have Cairo and Nana to thank for that. If it wasn't for them, I probably wouldn't have come."

She ignored what I said. We sat down at the table in the small cafe in Beverly Hills and picked up our menus. "Have you ever been here before?"

I shook my head.

"I've always wanted to come here for their Sunday brunch, but your father would never bring me. He'd always give me some sort of excuse about sports or going golfing with some of his frat brothers. It's amazing he still takes me on our weekly dates to Crustaceans."

I nodded as I scanned the menu. There wasn't anything on here I would really eat, so I understood why my father probably never brought her. He and I sort of had the same taste in food. Give us a good mom-and-pop spot with all the grease and sweat, and you could find us there. My mother, however, always wanted to eat this fancy-ass shit that was nasty, healthy, and stingy with their portions.

"Hello, welcome to Panini Cafe. I'm Shane, and I'll be your waiter today. Can we start you off with something to drink?"

"What white wines do you have?" As he ran off the list of wines for my mother, I continued to scan the menu.

"And for you, miss?"

"Audri!" my mother called. "The young man is talking to you."

I looked up from my menu. "I'm sorry, what did you say?"

"He asked what would you like to order. While you were over there daydreaming or whatever you were doing, I already told the man what I wanted."

I internally rolled my eyes then looked at the menu one more time. "Okay, can I have the Caesar salad with chicken and extra dressing?" I saw my mom's nose twitch, but she didn't say anything.

"Will that be all?"

"No, I would also like to try the turkey melt."

"Great choice. What would you like to drink?"

"Um, I'll take a mimosa."

He nodded, collected our menus, then left to put our orders in. While we waited for our food to come out, my mother and I sat in a somewhat awkward silence. She looked around at the other customers enjoying their meals as I texted back and forth with Cairo and Rima.

"So where are my grandbabies?"

I'd just sent Cairo a picture of my naked body in the bathtub last night when she asked her question.

"They are with their father, uncle, and cousin today. Ness and Cai thought it would be a good idea to take the kids to Chuck E. Cheese's since Cas was with Rima on his birthday."

"Chuck E. Cheese's? Aren't they too young to go there? All of those germs flying around and stuff. Can they even play on anything?"

"They're okay, Mom. There may not be anything for the twins to play on, but Cassius is big enough to ride the rides and play the games. I'm pretty sure that Nyles and Egypt are having just as much fun looking at all of the different colored lights and sounds. Plus, they have that puppet show thing. I'm more than sure they will enjoy that."

My phone buzzed on the table, and I quickly picked it up. My mother took a sip of her water the waiter had brought earlier, and she continued to look around the cafe.

My love: We wish you were here right now.

This was the message Cai sent back with an attachment. Thinking it was a picture of him and the twins enjoying their time with that big-ass rat, I opened it without checking my surroundings.

"Oh, my," I heard the waiter Shane say as he placed my food down in front of me. I quickly lowered my phone. "Don't try to hide it now; you just had it open for the world to see."

"What was it?" my mother asked, leaning up in her chair trying to look at my phone screen.

"Some fine white man," Shane answered. "You're a lucky girl, honey."

"Thank you," I said, embarrassed. I didn't know whether to be mad or feel a little concerned at the fact that this straight-looking black man described Cairo's dick as "some fine white man." Either way, he shouldn't have been privy to seeing it. That big beast belonged all to me, and I wasn't about to share it with anybody. I knew to be more careful next time.

"If you ladies need anything else, just wave for me, and I'll be right over." After placing a few extra napkins on the table, Shane winked at me then went on his way.

"What was all that about?" my mother asked after swallowing a spoonful of her soup.

"I'm not sure." I quickly changed the subject. "So what's going on, Mom? Why did you want to meet me here today?"

"Don't you wanna enjoy your meal before we get into all that?" she asked, now cutting into the stuffed eggplant Parmesan she ordered.

"I can do both."

She chewed her food then wiped the corners of her mouth. "Okay, Audri. I called you here because I wanna know why you've been ignoring all of my phone calls."

I didn't even get to bite into my turkey melt. The sandwich was halfway to my mouth when she said that shit. Dropping the cheesy goodness back onto my plate, I wiped my hands and sat back in my seat. "You really wanna sit here and act like you don't know?"

"I don't know. I mean, you said what you said at the hospital, and that was it. Hell, that's the last time I talked to you."

I sat and stared at my mother as she placed another forkful of eggplant in her mouth. "If you wanna sit here and act like you don't know what the problem is between you and me," I said, pointing between both of us, "then I think I should just take my food to go."

"Don't leave, Audri." There was sadness in her eyes as she placed her fork and knife down on her plate and looked at me. "Whatever is going on between us, I called you here today to make it right."

I finally took a bite of my sandwich. The shit was all right. It needed some more bacon and mayonnaise. Other than that, I'd order it again. "So what is going on between us?"

"This love-hate relationship that we have. Albeit it's more hate than love, but I'm willing to work on it if you are."

"I've never said that I hated you, Mom. I just hated the way you treated me when I was growing up and even now."

"Come on now, Audrielle, I can understand the part when you were younger, but now?" She shook her head. "I haven't said half the things to older Audri that I said to younger Audri."

I took a sip of my mimosa. "You think so?"

She nodded and continued to eat as if what she just said wasn't a load of crap.

"Well, since you want to believe the shit coming from your mouth, there's no need for us to continue this conversation. Thank you for the lunch, Mother, and I guess I'll see you around."

"Audri, please," my mother called out, but it was too late. I was about to leave and continue to live my life as if she didn't exist. I'd never deny her getting to know her grandkids, but as far as me being her daughter, she could forget all of that bullshit.

I stood up from my chair, getting ready to leave when a pair of familiar faces caught my attention and had me stopping in my tracks. The man and woman were so into their conversation that they didn't feel me staring at them for what seemed like twenty minutes. They sat and laughed at each other as if they were they only two in the restaurant. When the woman reached out and caressed his face in a familiar way, my stomach dropped to the floor. He didn't pull away or anything. It was as if he was in a trance and couldn't stop smiling and looking into this woman's eyes if he wanted to.

"Audri, why are you just standing there like that?" I heard my mom's voice say. "What are you looking . . ." Her voice trailed off when her eyes traveled over to where mine were looking. Finally taking my sight away from the scene in front of me, I turned to my mother and tried to read the expression on her face. Besides seeing her constantly blink her eyes to stop the tears from falling, I couldn't really tell what she was feeling.

"Mom, it's probably not what it—"

She held her hand up, cutting me off, and she sat back down in her seat. My mind was telling me to go over to the table and confront my father and that Erika chick, but my heart was with my mother. Even though I basically just wrote her off, I was all too familiar with how she must've been feeling right now. I sat back down in my seat but kept my eyes trained on the table my father was sitting at.

"You wanna know the reason I used to talk about your weight so much when you were younger?" When I didn't answer, she kept on going. "Because, as funny as it seemed, I didn't want you to end up like me."

I was confused. From the pictures I'd seen of my mother in her younger days, she'd never been fat, so I didn't know what she was talking about. "End up like you?"

She took a sip of her wine, then set it down. "Being in love with a man whose heart belongs to someone else. When I first met your father, he didn't see me in the way that I saw him. I was in love with that man from the second my eyes landed on that tall, dark, and handsome frame." She laughed. "There were so many days where I would try to get him to notice me, but with everything I did, changing the way I dressed, looked, what I majored in college, I was just his good friend Diana from economics class. Your father and his frat brothers were always around those real pretty women with those real curvy bodies and model-like walks. I mean, I was never a hefty girl, but I didn't look like the women they were always messing around with.

"Well, during our sophomore year, I ended up growing a couple inches, and my body started to fill out in all the right places. The boys on campus started to notice me a lot more, even some of your father's frat brothers too. But I wouldn't give any of them the time of day because I was saving myself for your dad. None of that stuff mattered, though, because that year he had reconnected with his childhood girlfriend, and when that happened, I knew I didn't have a chance, so I ended up dating this upperclassman named Douglas Woods.

"He was studying law, and he would always say he would be a Supreme Court justice and that he wanted me to be his wife. We dated for a few years, and it got pretty heavy. Heavy to the point where he actually asked me to marry him. I said yes, even though I didn't fully love him, and we started planning for a winter wedding after I graduated that summer. Well, a few months after he proposed, my aunt died and left me a large amount of money. Now, I was going to use that money to pay for this extravagant wedding that would be featured in every wedding magazine you could think of. Around the same time, your father came upon some hard times and lost a lot of his family's and friends' money in a dumb business move. Me seeing the man I was truly in love with being backed into a corner, I offered to help him out, but only if he agreed to a few things."

"Like marry you for the money."

"Yes."

"Daddy and Nana already told me this story."

"Did they tell you that I gave your father the option to not go through with it, too?"

I shook my head no because that was a part of the story that Nana and my father did neglect to tell me.

"The day before we got married, I told your father if marrying me wasn't what he really wanted to do that we could call the whole thing off, and I would just loan him the money. I told him that I believed in and loved him so much that I would be happy just helping him out. The day of the wedding, I was dragging the whole day because I didn't expect for your father or anyone from his family to show up. I had a speech ready for my family and friends who were already in attendance and everything, but as I got ready to make my way into the church to make the announcement, my cousin told me that your father was standing at the altar waiting for me to walk down the aisle. Long story short, we got married, I gave him the money to pay all of those people back, and we've been together ever since then."

"But Nana told me that Daddy left you like two years into the marriage."

She nodded. "We were arguing a lot. Especially behind Erika." She slightly turned her head and looked toward my father's table, then turned back to me. "For some reason, he couldn't let her go. Even after he found out she was engaged to another man. He was so angry. We argued so bad one time behind her that I threw a lamp at his head. That was the night he left and stayed gone for a few months. In the time that he was gone, though, I found out that I was pregnant with you. I wasn't going to tell him at first, either. It was just going to be my baby and me, but your Nana dropped by the house one evening to pick up some of his things and heard me throwing up in the bathroom like crazy. For the first time since knowing your Nana, I got to see her nurturing side that night. She stayed with me and took care of me until your father got off of work and came over. We talked about some things and eventually apologized to each other. I took a pregnancy test the next day to confirm that I was actually carrying you and, when the test came back positive, your father went and got his things from your Nana's and moved back in."

I was still looking in the direction of my father when I saw him say something to this Erika chick that caused her smile to turn into a frown. Whatever he had just told her obviously had her feeling some type of way.

"Should we go over there and say something? I mean, I know our relationship is rocky, but that still doesn't mean I would want to see my father disrespect you like this."

She drank the last of her wine and looked at me. "There's no need to disturb your father. I already knew who he was with."

"What do you mean you knew who was with?"

"I've been with your father so long that anything he tries to hide I always find out about. Besides, while he was in the bathroom last night, I went through his phone."

My mother and I shared a laugh that for some reason felt natural and good. I didn't like the situation that opened this feeling or line of communication, but I liked the end result.

"Do you always go through Dad's phone?"

She shook her head. "I don't, but the day he came from having breakfast with you and the twins, his whole attitude was kind of different. It seemed as if he was real happy. I don't know if it was what he ate that day but, whatever it is, he needs to do it again."

I didn't wanna add insult to injury by telling my mother that my father's good mood was probably from the fact that he'd run into the same woman he was having lunch with right now. My eyes went back over to my father's table, and I watched as he and Erika were having a deep conversation. What I wouldn't have given to be a fly on the wall next to them right now. My mom turned her head and looked over there too.

"If you want to go, Mom, we can." I looked down at my plate. "I'm done eating, and so are you."

She waved me off. "If you're ever going to be a good wife to Cairo, you need to take some pointers."

"Pointers? Like what? Not tripping on seeing my husband at a restaurant with his ex-girlfriend because I'm possibly cheating with someone myself?" I didn't mean for it to come out like that, but I wanted to know what was up with her not being angry with seeing my father here with another woman. The only logical explanation I could come up with was she was cheating too. Cairo witnessed her indiscretion with his eyes, and now I had the privilege of seeing my father's.

My mother grabbed the pearls around her neck and started to twirl them around her fingers. The pink Ralph Lauren pinstriped shirt she had on went with the light rosy makeup on her face. Her white slacks were fitted and pressed with a crease while her camel-colored peep-toe sling-backs matched her belt and purse. As always, her hair fell in those soft curls that framed her beautiful face, and her look was altogether flawless. However, looking into her eyes right now, I could see her on the verge of breaking down.

"So I see Cairo told you about seeing me at Crustaceans with another man?"

"He did." I paused for a minute. "He told me he saw you there while meeting with Alex. Is that why you're sitting here okay with seeing Dad out to lunch with another woman, at the place you've been begging him to bring you?"

"That was another reason why you and I didn't get along so much when you were little. You would always jump to conclusions and believe whatever you thought you saw or what someone told you without checking the facts."

"What do you—"

She held her hand up to cut me off. "The reason Cairo will be able to marry you in two weeks and not months from now is because of the man I was at lunch with that day. Douglas Woods didn't make it to the Supreme Court, but he did become a judge. I pulled a few strings and was able to expedite their divorce because of him. Did I sleep with him? No. Could I have? Yes. But my heart still yearns for your father to notice me."

A tear finally fell from her eye as she grabbed my hand into hers. "Audri, I wanna apologize for anything that I said or did to make you think or feel that I didn't love you. Understand that everything I did was to help you. I know how it feels to be in love with someone who never gave you their whole heart in return, and I didn't want you or Ariana to end up that way. I thought by me trying to make you look a certain way, you'd find a man who would love you unconditionally, but I was wrong. I was wrong about Eli, and I was wrong about Cairo. It was my own selfish thinking that wouldn't allow me to see the love that he really has for you. I want you to know now though that I see it, and

I must admit that I am a little jealous. Both of my daughters went after men I didn't approve of and ended up finding the love of their lives."

She looked over her shoulder. "Your father and I are going to be fine, so don't worry about that. You just focus on this wedding that's quickly approaching and being the best wife you can be for Cairo. You deserve it, and I feel like he's worthy of having your heart. I can see that you clearly already have his."

I didn't even know I was crying until the tears fell from my face and onto my chest. Reaching across the table, my mother wiped a few tears from my eyes. "I know we won't go to being best friends anytime soon, but I hope you can learn to forgive me for the things I've done in the past and be open to starting a new relationship between us."

I nodded and laughed. "I'm opened to that, Mom. It's all I've ever wanted for us." I got up from my side of the table and went to hug my mother. We sat there in our embrace for a few minutes before we finally released one another.

"I love you, Audrielle," my mother said with a tearstained face.

"I love you too, Mom."

We shared a laugh. "Now that we're on the road to being back on track, what do you want to do?"

I wanted to go confront my father and the Erika chick, but when I looked in the direction of their table they weren't there anymore.

"If you're looking for your father, he left already."

"How did you know that?"

"My dear child, you have a lot to learn. Especially if you're going to be married to that rich, fine-ass white man."

"What does that have to do with anything?"

My mother shook her head. "Do you remember me saying that I always wanted to come here, but your father always made an excuse?"

I nodded.

"Well, why do you think I picked this restaurant for us to meet? After I had gone through your father's phone last night, I asked his ass about it. When he told me that it was only going to be a friendly lunch, I told him that we could make this a double date because there was no way in the world he was going to be eating with his ex-girlfriend alone. Before you got here, I was at the table with them, but once you texted and told me you were on your way, I got us our own little spot because we didn't need any outsiders in our family business."

"But, you were sitting here damn near in tears. I thought you didn't know."

"Just because I knew about it doesn't mean that it doesn't make me feel some type of way seeing your father with the woman he's always had a thing for. She's a very beautiful woman and may still have a piece of your father's heart. However, I have the key to the kingdom, and if I take that away, your father's whole empire will crumble. You know as well as I do that your father is a very smart man. He knows how far to go with things."

"But they're gone, together."

"Who's gone? Because if you're talking about your father, he's standing right over there." She nodded toward the bar and, sure enough, my father was sitting there alone with a drink in his hand. "Now, as far as little Ms. Erika, her ass is gone. I gave your father forty-five minutes to get whatever he needed to get off his chest and part ways with her before I started to act a fool. He knows as well as anybody else that, behind all this proper dress and talking, I'm still a hood chick and I'll pull it out if I need to."

I couldn't do anything but laugh at my mother. Maybe this relationship of ours would be a good thing after all. I was seeing a side of my mother I'd never seen at all.

"Now that that's out of the way let's go walk down Rodeo Drive and put a dent in your father's credit cards for my grandbabies."

CHAPTER 17

CAIRO

It was the night before the twins' christening and the day Audri and I would start the rest of our lives as husband and wife. It'd been a stressful month with fittings, cake tastings, seat chart arrangements, and venue shopping, but with the help of Rima's party-planning friend Ijahn and everyone else pitching in, we were finally ready to embark on the next journey of our lives.

Surprisingly, I hadn't heard from Alex in the last couple weeks, and that was fine with me. Before that, she was calling my phone all day every day and leaving all kinds of crazy messages. So much so that I had to change my number a couple times. How she got those new numbers was still a mystery to me, but after I was advised by Chasin and Roderick to take out a restraining order against her, I had no other choice. Some of the things she would talk about doing to Audri prompted me enough to do something to ensure my family was protected. Yet, there was still this feeling in the pit of my stomach telling me that Alex was up to something.

"Why are you frowning?" Audri asked coming from the bathroom, dressed in a white sequined dress that stopped just above her knees and hugged her body like a glove. Her hair was pinned and smoothed down on one side while the other had a mountain of loose curls falling over her shoulder. She sat on the edge of the bed and slid her feet into the crystal-embellished Giuseppe heels her mother bought her as a "something new" gift. When she stood up and walked in front of the full-length mirror, I couldn't do nothing but lust after her reflection in the front and my tantalizing view of the back. She rose her arms above her head and started messing with her hair. "So you're not going to tell me what had you frowning like that?"

I stood up to button my shirt then sprayed a few spritzes of cologne. "It was nothing really. I just have this feeling that Alex is up to something."

Audri turned around to face me then slowly walked over to where I stood. "Stop worrying about her and her delusional ass. After that restraining order and the way my mother came at her, I doubt she'll even step one hundred feet within me, you, or the kids. At least, she won't if she knows what is best for her." Audri placed her hands on the collar of my shirt and turned it down before she smoothed her hands across my shoulders then my chest. Her eyes went to my dreads, which were half up and half down.

"When did you get your hair retwisted?"

"When I went to drop the twins off earlier at Mama Faye's. I didn't have time to go to the shop, so I asked her if she could hook me up."

She entangled her fingers in my hair, then started to massage my scalp. Closing my eyes, I embraced the chill that ran through my body the moment I felt her touch.

"You better behave yourself tonight at your brother's club. From what Niecey told me, Toby went all out for his baby brother's bachelor party."

"And from what Ness told me, Ariana and Rima did the same thing with your bachelorette party. So you better behave as well." I pulled her body closer to mine and nuzzled my face into the crook of her neck. "Do you think they would be mad if we skipped our parties and just stayed home?"

Audri moaned in my ear as she started to sway our bodies from side to side. "I don't think they'd be mad, but I do wanna go out and have a little fun tonight before I become Mrs. Cairo Broussard tomorrow."

"Ummm. I like the sound of that. Mrs. Audrielle Broussard," I said, placing light kisses down her neck. "You know I'll take a bullet for you, right?"

I could feel her nodding on my shoulder. "Yes, baby, and I would take one for you."

We stayed wrapped up in each other's embrace until both of our phones started ringing. It was Rima seeing where Audri was at and Finesse checking on my whereabouts.

"Did you call to check on the twins?" I asked Audri as we walked down the stairs and out of the house dressed in our all-white outfits. I made sure the security alarm was set and that everything was locked up before we left.

"They're fine, Cai. I just talked to Mama Faye a few minutes ago. She said Nana was laying Egypt down to sleep in the room while Cassius's and Nyles' little butts were in the living room with them watching movies."

I didn't know why I kept getting this urge to go check on my babies, but I knew that neither Mama Faye nor Nana would let anything happen to them. After kissing my beautiful fiancée one more time and promising her the world again,

I watched her drive off in the direction of her party before I hopped in my car and rolled in the direction of mine. Knowing the way Finesse got down and the way Toby liked to turn up, tonight was going to be one epic night.

AUDRIELLE

"There she goes!" Rima shouted as I walked into our VIP section at the Pentagon male strip club. Red plush couches surrounded us as our own private stripper pole sat in the middle of the floor. There were bachelorette party novelties hanging from everywhere and a big spread of food and top-shelf drinks scattered around the different tables courtesy of the sexy mixologist StarrTenders. I smiled as I saw some of my family and closest friends stand up to greet me with hugs and congratulations. When I finally made it to the table reserved especially for me, Ariana, Rima, Niecey, and Rima's party-planning friend, Ijahn, I couldn't hide the shocked expression on my face when I saw my mother and Rima's mother sitting to the side and enjoying a joint lap dance from one of the strippers.

"Please get your mother!" Ari shouted above the music. "She's been waving that same twenty around since he got over there."

I laughed. "Leave her alone. She's just having a little fun."

"A little too much fun if you ask me. I expect that type of fast behavior from my mama, but not Ms. Diana. I've never seen her smile so much in my life. Mr. Aaron better come get her ass before she gives that nigga dancing on her all of their money."

I watched as my mom's eyes went from low to wide after the stripper turned around to face them and pulled the front of his costume down. Her normally loose, curled hair was in a ponytail at the back of her head, which showed off her beautiful and youthful face a little more. As usual, her makeup was done flawlessly, and it matched the violet strapless silk jumpsuit she had on. Rima's mother Kenzie sat right next to her with a black low-cut dress on that she kept pulling down every time she moved. Her hair was flat-ironed straight with a part on the side. Both women were looking like party girls in their late twenties, instead of mothers who had daughters pushing close to thirty.

"Y'all leave them alone and let them have some fun. Truth be told, I'm going to be just like that the minute Typhoon brings his fine ass out here; and please don't let Magnificent be hosting this event. I might not make it through the night without having to change my panties at least once or twice after seeing them perform."

"Well, you might as well get a fresh pair out right now, because look who's coming this way."

As soon as I looked at the entrance to the private VIP section we were in, Typhoon's fine caramel-coated sexy ass was headed our way. The black leather vest he had on was open and displayed his eight-pack stomach, muscular tattooed arms, and forever-flexing, strong chest. The leather pants he wore hung low off of his waist, giving you a full view of that sexy-ass V shape he was rocking. I licked my lips the minute his hazel eyes connected with mine and zeroed in on me.

Lord, please forgive me for lusting over this man. And, Cairo, baby, I love you, I silently said to myself as I took a wad of cash out of my purse and started making it rain and pour all over our section.

CAIRO

Walking into the Lotus Bomb, I expected to see a small crowd of people vibing to the live music and enjoying the food and drinks, because that's what I told Finesse and Toby I wanted to do for my last night of being a single man. However, I should've known that the laidback atmosphere I wanted and expected would go totally different dealing with those two.

I walked through the front doors of Toby's club and had to do a double take.

"Welcome to Lotus Bomb. Are you a friend of the groom-to-be or are you family?" the young, blond hostess asked as her bright blue eyes scanned me from the top of my head to the bottom of my feet.

"I'm actually the groom-to-be."

Her eyes widened in shock then lowered back down to the little sexy squint she had when she first saw me. "What a lucky girl." She pursed her lips then smirked. "I'm Megan, by the way. Follow me."

I walked behind the scantily dressed hostess as she led me to the back area of the club that was curtained off from the rest of the main floor. Another waitress wearing a gold chain dress way more revealing than the one Megan had on walked up to us and handed me a glass with some brown liquor.

"It's a double shot of the Macallan 1824 Series single malt Scotch. Everybody who passes this part of the club is handed one. Compliments of Mr. Wright."

"Thank you," I simply said as I took the cool glass from her hands and entered the loud area behind the curtains.

Looking around at all the scantily clad women as I made my way deeper into the lounge had me wanting to run straight back home to Audri and go a few rounds. I knew we promised each other not to indulge in any sex until our wedding night, but being here around all these half-naked women wasn't helping my thoughts at all. I mean, my baby could give some of these girls a run for their money in the body department and was straight killing them all when it came to the looks. Hopefully, when I got back home later on tonight, she'd be lying naked in our bed and ready to give me what I wanted.

I walked up a few steps to the crowded VIP section in search of Toby, and I ended up running into more than a few familiar faces.

"When did you all get here?" I asked Roderick, Chasin, Finesse, Kong, Mr. Freeman, and a few other people I recognized from around the way. They were so into watching the girl-on-girl show in front of them that no one bothered to respond.

A hand identical to mine grabbed me on my shoulder while the other one handed me a Cuban cigar. "You gotta excuse them, bro. As you can see, they're being entertained by two of the baddest strippers on the West Coast, Roxy and Jewel."

My eyes went back to the two strippers who were feeling all over each other and damned near getting ready to have sex on the floor. Chasin's ass was so into the sight before him that he didn't feel his cigar fall out of his mouth until it started to burn a hole in his pants.

"What's all this anyway? I told you I wanted a chill night at your lounge, not no makeshift strip club."

Toby's smile widened as he puffed on his Cuban. "This, my dear brother, is what your bachelor party is supposed to look like." His eyes traveled to the dark-skinned stripper who was now grinding on Kong's lap. "You think Audri and the girls are being chill at the Pentagon with all those cocks swinging in their faces? We had to do it up for you, bro. Besides, since I wasn't able to send you off right for your first wedding, I made a few calls and arranged a few things just so I could do it right this time around."

"Damn, there's two of y'all," some Latin chick seductively said as she walked around Toby and me. Dressed only in a red thong and shiny red star pasties that barely covered her nipples, baby girl's body was a sight to see. "I've never danced for twins before. Would the two of you like a private show?" She winked her eye at me, then blew a kiss at Toby.

"If this were a couple years ago, I'd take you up on that offer. Unfortunately for us, this here is the man to be married tomorrow," Toby said shaking my shoulder. "And I'll be walking down that same aisle in a few months."

She pouted her ruby red lips. "Lucky ladies. Maybe next time."

"Maybe," Toby said, grinning like the Cheshire Cat as she turned to walk away. "Maaaaaaan, Niecey's ass is lucky I love her, or I would've taken Sofía Vergara Jr. up on that offer."

"And gotten your ass kicked the minute you got home.

"You may be right, but we're not going to worry about that tonight." Toby laughed. We walked over to a few vacant seats next to the fellas. "For right now, though, I want you to sit back, relax, and enjoy the show. By this time tomorrow, bro, you will officially be off the market, again."

AUDRIELLE

"Girl, I swear to God I'm about to go broke in this place. Can someone please tell me why we haven't come here before for one of our girls' nights out?"

"Because of what you just said. Between you and Audri, Toby and Cairo would probably have to file for chapter eight."

"Shut up, Ari, I didn't see you holding back on throwing a few dollars when Hangtime's ass came up here," I joked back to my sister.

"The keyword in your sentence was throwing a 'few' dollars. You two bitches probably just paid Typhoon's and Magnificent's mortgages for the next two years."

"Oh, lighten up, Ariana. Your sister is enjoying herself, just like you will be when you and Finesse finally set a date for your wedding," my mother said as she came to sit between us. "Now go do Mommy a favor and get me some change for these four hundred-dollar bills, while I refill your cup with some more of this Purple Haze Liqueur and put a few more pieces of cheese and fruit on your plate."

My mother tipped up the bottle with the Jimi Hendrix label, and she was about to pour it in Ari's glass when Ari placed her hand on the rim.

"I'm not drinking tonight, Mom."

"And why not?"

Her eyes looked around and connected with all of ours before she bowed her head and said, "I'm not drinking tonight because I'm pregnant."

"Whaaaaaaaaat!" The whole VIP area roared then cheered.

"Does Ness know?"

"How far along are you?"

"Why didn't you tell anybody?"

"My baby's having a baby?"

These were the questions being fired off at Ariana. She didn't know whether to laugh or try to answer everyone all at once.

"Well, first things first. Finesse knows. We found out about a week ago. As of today, I am officially nine weeks pregnant, and we didn't want to tell anybody because we were going to wait until after the twins' christening and your and Cairo's wedding."

"Oh, my God, Ari, you should've told me the minute you found out. I can't believe I'm going to be an auntie," I squealed as I gave my sister a hug.

"Hey, Audri, can I use your phone to check on the kids? Mine died thirty minutes ago," Rima said as she walked up behind me with her dead phone in her hand.

I reached in my clutch and pulled out my charger. "Here, plug that in over there and put some juice on your phone, then walk with me to the bathroom. We can call and check on the little minions after I release my bladder."

"Wait! Before you guys do that, let me get a picture of everybody together real quick," Niecey said. "I'll probably be gone by the time you guys get back. I promised my sister I would watch my niece while she goes to work tonight. Plus, I wanna beat Toby home so I can surprise him with a little something-something before we turn in for the night."

"You so nasty."

"Hey." She shrugged her shoulders. "After my man has been around those beautiful half-naked women for the majority of the night doing God knows what on them poles, I wanna remind him of the nasty freak he has at home who can do all of that and more."

We fell out laughing at Niecey's crazy ass, then straightened up for a few shots of everyone in attendance before Rima and I excused us to the bathroom.

"Um, you could've given me your phone before you went into the stall you know."

"Hold your horses, girl, it's not like the kids aren't doing anything but sleeping. It's past midnight, and you know Mama Faye and Nana don't play when it comes to kids going to bed. You remember all those times when Nana used to visit when we were younger? It was lights out at nine o'clock every night, regardless if homework was done or what show we wanted to watch on TV."

Rima laughed. "Yeah, those were the days. Now that I think about it, though, Nana's fast ass probably had us going to bed that early so she could have company sneak in and out without anyone seeing him."

We reminisced about old times as I handled my business then came out of the stall to wash and dry my hands. Pulling my phone out of my clutch, I noticed for the first time that I had a few missed texts from Cai and about twenty missed calls from Mama Faye and Nana.

"What's wrong, Audri? Your whole face just changed," Rima said after noticing my smile fade into a look of concern.

"Nothing. It's just that I have over twenty missed calls from Mama Faye and Nana. I hope everything is all right." My hands started to shake uncontrollably.

"Here," Rima said, reaching for my phone. "Let me call them back, and you try to calm down. I'm pretty sure everything is all right. One of the kids must be running a fever or something. You know how grannies tend to overreact at the littlest thing."

I nodded, then handed Rima the phone. She looked at me one last time before touching Nana's contact and putting the phone to her ear. Because the music from the club was kind of blocked out by the thick, heavy walls in the bathroom, I could hear every time Nana's phone rang on the other end. When someone finally picked up and screamed my name, I knew something was going on.

"Mama Faye? Mama Faye, I need you to calm down. I can't understand a word you're saying. Is everything all right with the kids?"

I could hear Mama Faye's deep Jamaican accent going a mile a minute. Rima's eyes connected with mine, but I could read her expression.

"What's going on?"

"I'm trying to find out, but Mama Faye's accent is too deep. All I can understand is her saying Egypt's name."

"Egypt? What's wrong with my baby?" I snatched the phone from Rima's hand and damned near put her eye out.

"Hello, Mama Faye! What's going on? Where are the kids?"

"She's gaan! Oh, Lawd, she's gaan! Mi tried to get har, but mi ena too slow."

My heart fell out of my chest. I didn't know who Mama Faye was talking about when she screamed, "She's gone." My mind automatically went to my Nana and tears started to fall from my eyes. Why else would Mama Faye be answering her phone when she and Nana were in the same place?

"Mama Faye, I need you to calm down and tell me what happened. What happened to my Nana?"

Her breathing slowed, but I could still tell she was frantic. "Yah Nana's in de front of mi house speaking tah de police. Oh, Lawd, mi sorry, Audri. Mi failed mi boi. Him will neva forgive mi."

At this point, my legs started moving as if they had a mind of their own. I walked out of the bathroom and was heading toward the exit of the club. I could hear Rima calling my name behind me, but I couldn't stop walking to my car. When I finally pushed out of the exit doors, I damn near knocked Niecey over.

"Audri, are you okay?" she asked as she braced her fall on the brick wall. "What wrong? Did something happen to the guys?"

"Mama Faye, why are the police there and where are the kids?"

"De boys are in de living room with Nana and de police. But . . . but . . ." She started to cry and talk in her deep Jamaican accent again.

"Mama Faye, where's Egypt?"

Her sobs became louder. "She's gaan, Audri! She's gaan!"

My body froze in the middle of the street. "She . . . she's gone? Where is my baby, Mama Faye? Where is my baby?"

"Mi don't know, Audri. I came tah check on her and de crib was empty. Mi so sorry!"

As soon as those words left her mouth, I felt my body get heavy and drop to the floor. The tiny rocks and gravel on the road roughly rolled against my chest as it began to heave rapidly up and down. Mama Faye started to scream my name again, but I didn't have the strength to lift the phone back up to my ear. The sounds of horns honking, heels running across the pavement, and my name being called were the last things I heard before my eyes closed and I completely blacked out.

CHAPTER 18

ALEXANDRIA

"Can you please shut them up! What was the point of you coming along for the ride if you weren't going to help with anything?"

"I came along because you said you needed someone to be the lookout."

"Well, we can both see that your lookout skills weren't of any use to me. Instead of coming out with both babies, I was only able to grab one. I thought you said everyone was asleep."

"I thought they were. Who gets up and checks on babies in the middle of the night?"

"Obviously not you."

"And you're one to talk. I'm surprised you have your son right now. What, the auntie must've been busy tonight?"

I rolled my eyes at Marjorie's high ass as I continued to head to the condo I had in Marina del Rey. Only one other person knew about it, and that was because he was living there. But after Sarah told me that Eli packed all of his things and hightailed it back to Seattle, I figured it would be the perfect place to keep Cairo and Audri's daughter until they paid the money for the ransom.

And yeah, I know what you all are thinking: how cliché, right? I felt that way too when Marjorie's ass came up with the idea, but after my surefire way to get that money went down the drain, I became desperate for anything. Now that I was thinking about it, this probably wasn't the best idea seeing as Marjorie's junkie ass was high as a kite and almost got our cover blown, but it was too late to turn around now. I was pretty sure the police and both Cairo and Audri were at Mama Faye's house trying to figure out who took their daughter.

As I drove to our destination, I thought about all of the crazy shit that happened tonight and how we almost got caught. Sneaking into the house was easy, only because I use to do it when Cairo and I were younger. Mama Faye didn't really care for me that much, so whenever Cairo wanted to see me, he'd have to sometimes sneak me in. I'd go through the backyard then climb through the back bathroom window. Cairo's room door was directly across from the bathroom, so once I was in, he'd act as if he was taking a shower, then minutes later check to make sure the coast was clear. Once there was no sign of Mama Faye, he'd hurry me into his room, lock the door, then sex me all night long. We could've easily avoided all of that by just going to my house. Cairo was more than welcome but, for some reason, he hated being around my father longer than he had to.

After I had crawled through the back window, I opened the door for Marjorie and had her stand to the side in the hallway where she had a clear view of the living room. Mama Faye was sitting up, asleep on one couch, while some other lady was laid out and snoring lightly on the other. Creeping into the first bedroom, I didn't see any babies, but I almost ended up pissing on myself when Marjorie snuck up behind me jumping up and down, talking about she had to use the bathroom.

"Hold that shit," I whispered between gritted teeth.

"But I can't," she whined. "I've been holding it ever since we left the house."

I angrily watched as she placed her hand between her legs and started to bounce from side to side like a little kid. "Ooooh, I'm going to pee on myself right now if I don't go." Her glossy eyes reflected the beam of moonlight coming from the semi-closed shade. Had this been an easy task for me to do by myself, I would've left her high ass at home.

"Go to the bathroom back down the hall across from the first bedroom we passed and don't flush the toilet."

"But that's so—"

"Marjorie!" I hissed her name a little louder than I intended. Closing my eyes, I counted to ten to try to calm my nerves down. After regaining some of my composure, I grabbed Marjorie by her shoulders and slowly explained to her, "If you flush the toilet, they will hear it, and if they hear it more than likely they will wake up. If we want to get out of here without being caught, we have to be quiet, right?"

She slowly nodded her head as if she was finally getting what I was saying.

"Okay, now that we're on the same page, go use the bathroom, don't flush the toilet or wash your hands, then go back to being the lookout. I have some sanitizer in the car you can use when we get back, okay?" She nodded again, then quietly walked down the hall and into the bathroom.

I stood at the end of the hall watching Mama Faye and her friend until Marjorie got back. When she returned to her post, I walked down the hallway to the next room where the door was slightly closed and pushed it open. There, lying on the king-sized bed all nice and cozy, were the twins and another little boy I assumed was Finesse's. The nightlight that was on illuminated the room just enough for me to see the pink footie the little girl had on and the sky blue footie the little boy had on. Picking up baby girl first, I cradled her in my arms and gently rocked her as she stirred. Her pouty pink lips were poked out and just begging to be kissed. Those curly blond locks that matched Cai's were soft to the touch and smelled like some kind of fruit.

"You are a beautiful little thing," I whispered as I inhaled her baby powder scent.

Holding her and staring into her angelic face really had me feeling some type of way. Cairo having a baby with a woman other than me was not how I pictured our future at all. It should've been me who he gave his heart to and me who should've blessed him with his first heirs, a set of twins. Be that as it may, I had to get over my little feelings and back into this criminal mindframe if we were going to get this money.

A loud thud from behind me had me looking over my shoulder in a panic. "What the hell are you doing?" I angrily asked Marjorie while making sure the babies were still asleep.

"She's up," she slurred.

"Who's up?" I whispered back.

"The darker one who was facing the TV." Marjorie pointed out of the room. "She's up."

The darker one was Mama Faye. "Where is she now?"

She shrugged her shoulders and started to cry. "I don't wanna go to jail, Alex. Maybe we should just forget about all this."

"It's a little too late for that," I snapped. "Now shut your wired ass up and come get the other baby."

She shook her head then quickly covered her mouth with both hands to muffle her cries when we heard the water faucet in the kitchen turn on.

"Come get this other baby now!" I mouthed to her, but just like the last time, she shook her head and started backing out of the room. "Come back in here! Do you want us to get caught?" I looked around. "We have to hide in the closet or under the bed until she goes back to the front of the house!"

The baby started to stir in my arms again, and when I looked down at her this time, she was looking directly at me. Eyes wide open and everything. Even in the dimly lit room, I could see that she shared the same eye color as her father. I could tell them eyes from anywhere. For a minute, I stood there lost in her bluish green irises. It was amazing how much she looked like Cai. Everything about her mirrored him, even the long and curly eyelashes. I was so into cooing over the small beauty that I momentarily forgot all about the task at hand.

When I looked back up to where Marjorie was standing, she wasn't there anymore. The bitch straight left me and didn't say a single word. I didn't know where Mama Faye was or if her friend had woken up too. For a split second, I thought about just putting the baby back on the bed and trying again some other time, but I'd already come this far and would more than likely not get this chance again if I were to get caught.

Sticking my head out of the room, I looked down the hall both ways. When I saw that the hallway was clear and that Mama Faye was still doing something in the kitchen, I quietly crept back into the direction of the back door with only one baby in tow. I was just passing Cai's old room when the swishing noise of Mama Faye's house shoes against the wood floor sounded as if they were coming out of the kitchen and in my direction. Quickening my steps, I damn near flew to the door trying to get away.

Finally reaching my exit, I breathed a sigh of relief when I noticed that the wooden door and the screen door were left wide open. "At least she had sense enough not to close them," I said to myself when I didn't see any sign of Marjorie waiting for me anywhere.

I reached behind me and closed the hard door, but left the screen door just like it was. As soon as my foot hit that bottom step, I took off running down the side of the house as I held baby girl tightly in my grip. When I got to the car Marjorie had already started it up and was in the back seat still crying her ass off. Her hair was all over the place and snot and smeared makeup were running down her face. All I could do was shake my head in annoyance before I handed her the baby, then hopped behind the wheel and pulled off.

Now, my son's ear piercing cry broke me from my thoughts.

"At least you stuck to one part of the plan," I said in reference to Marjorie having the car started and her sitting in the back. I looked in my rearview mirror and watched as she tried to get the babies to stop crying.

"I think they might need a bottle or their diapers changed or something. Did you happen to get a diaper bag?"

I looked back at her and rolled my eyes. This was going to be a long-ass couple of days.

Hopefully, Cairo would be able to get the money sometime tomorrow evening. Once he made the drop, I'd have someone pick it up for me, then get my ass out of dodge. I didn't think I was going to use any of that money to help out my father or the family business. His ass was still fucking up, and I didn't even think he cared anymore, especially after the FBI got involved. With them now reviewing the accounting books from the last ten years, I was sure saving the company would be the least of his worries. Maybe once I got my hands on the money, I could move to another state and really start over. Just me and my baby boy. Since his father didn't seem to want anything to do with him, there was really nothing or no one in L.A. to tie us there. Cairo had obviously moved on and would definitely not want anything to do with me once he found out it was me who took his daughter.

Getting off at our exit from the freeway, baby girl screamed at the top of her lungs again and almost blew my eardrum out. I held my ringing ear and shook my head. One thing I knew for sure was the next time I planned on kidnapping someone, I was going to most definitely pay somebody else to do it.

CHAPTER 19

CAIRO

Do you know what tonight is?
Boy it's all about you and me, all 'bout you and me

Teyana Taylor's sample of the Tony! Toni! Toné! hit "Anniversary" in her song "Tonight" was knocking through the speakers while the Sofía Vergara–looking stripper who'd approached Toby and me earlier worked her body around the pole. I watched as she climbed up to the top and spun around, then slowly slid her body down to the floor and into a split. The little pasties she had covering her nipples were gone, but the little red thong was still on her body, lost between the plump cheeks.

"Bruh, I swear Niecey is lucky I love her mean ass."

I laughed and shook my head. "You saying shit like that will still get your ass kicked, so you better stop."

He took a sip of whatever he'd been drinking majority of the night, and he hissed. "Yeah, you right. But still, you can't tell me that her little ass ain't sexy." Toby nodded toward the stripper who know had her attention trained on us as she rolled her hips and pinched her nipples.

"You're right, she's an attractive woman, but she still doesn't have anything on Audri. Hands down, my baby could give her and any other girl in here a run for their money. Body wise, look wise, and dancing wise."

"Man, shut your sprung ass up!" Toby hollered as he grabbed his stomach and laughed. "But I'll give you that: sis-in-law is bad. Plus, she's educated, career-minded, and about her money. You couldn't ask for a better mate, bruh. I'm happy for you and wish you and Audri nothing but the best in your future." He raised his glass to me. "Salute."

I clinked my glass with his. "Thanks, man, and salute."

We downed our shots then watched the rest of Sofia Jr.'s show. Once she was done, she picked up the thousands of bills spread across the floor then disappeared behind another set of curtains on the other side of the room.

Toby stood up and smoothed down the light blue shirt he had on over his gray slacks. He ran his hand through his short blond hair then let out a slow breath before gulping down the rest of his drink. "All right, twin, I'm about to go to the office and make a few calls. Do you want me to have one of the waitresses bring your phone? I'm pretty sure it's done charging by now."

I forgot to charge my phone up before I came out tonight fooling around with Audri. A little after I had gotten to the club I called Mama Faye to check on the twins, and it died on me in the middle of our call. I had to use Finesse's phone to call her back. Once she told me that my babies were fine and about to eat dinner, I told her I'd call her in a couple hours before she put them to bed. I then gave my dead phone to Toby to charge in his office since I didn't want to take it back to my car and leave it in there.

"Yeah. I was trying to hold off on checking on the twins since I know they are in good hands, but something keeps telling me to call Mama Faye and see how everything's going."

"Ain't no problem with checking on your shorties and whatnot. I'll have Trina bring you your phone. Did you want something else to eat or are you good?"

"I'm fine, man. The crab cakes, steak, and loaded potatoes were enough. You just take your sprung ass to the office and call Niecey." I laughed. Toby thought he was slick. I knew those phone calls he had to make were only to Niecey. They'd been sexting each other since I got here. After he laughed and flipped me off, Toby grabbed our empty tumbler glasses then turned and walked out of the VIP section.

I turned my attention to the empty stage with the shiny stripper pole. *Audri's ass would look sexy as fuck up there with nothing on but those purple pumps she bought the other day,* I thought as I played the erotic scene over and over again in my head.

"Ay, Cai, man, I'm about to head out," Chasin said, rudely breaking me from my freaky thoughts of Audri. He looked back at the stripper Jewel, whose arms were wrapped around his. Both smiling from ear to ear, I watched as they silently promised with their eyes what was in store for them later on tonight, before Chasin turned his attention back to me. "As you can see, I'm about to be busy for a few hours. We need to be at the church by twelve tomorrow, right?"

"By eleven. And you better be on time. You know Audri will have a fit if the twins' godfather is late to his own godkids' christening."

"Naw, you know I'm already there. We'll just have to skip breakfast in the morning." We dapped each other up and said our good-byes before he finally turned to leave.

I looked around the once crowded VIP area and saw that most of the faces that were once here were now gone or either still indulging in their surroundings. Kong was getting another lap dance from Jewel's partner Roxy, and Mr. Freeman was ducked off in the corner half asleep. Roderick was busy texting on his phone, and not paying attention to any of the dancers who were trying to get him to focus on them, while Finesse was MIA. A few of my partners from around the way were huddled up sipping on their drinks and talking, while the others were trying to get a few of the strippers to do something strange for a little piece of change.

"Ay, man, have you seen Finesse?" I asked Chasin, who came back to the VIP section get his green pea coat. I looked around the area once again and didn't see Ness anywhere. We had a few drinks and watched a few dances before he got up and said he needed to use the bathroom. That was twenty minutes ago.

"He wasn't outside. Come to think of it, I haven't seen him since he went to relieve himself. You know that nigga could never handle his liquor." We laughed because it was so true.

Finesse was always the designated driver whenever we used to go out in our college days. One glass of anything and he was torn up. That's why I was sort of surprised when I walked up into the VIP area and he had two drinks in his hands. "Oh, wait, here he comes right now. But what's wrong with him? That nigga looks pissed off."

At the same time Finesse was walking toward us with his phone to his ear and a screwed-up face, Toby was headed our way on the phone and looking the same way.

"We need to go now!" Finesse said as soon as he stepped in front of me.

My heart rate started to pick up when I noticed the look of concern flash across his face. "What's wrong? Is everything okay? Are the twins okay?"

"Cai, I got the valet pulling my car to the front right now. We need to get to Mama Faye's house, then the hospital."

"Mama Faye's house? The hospital?" I jumped out of my seat and ended up knocking the brown liquor that was sitting on the table beside me all over my white Pierre Balmain jeans. "Did Mama Faye relapse or something?"

From the corner of my eye, I could see Roderick stand from where he was sitting and start pacing the floor. His hand was on his hip as he started barking orders into his phone.

"Is anyone going to tell me what going on?" Toby looked at me then to Finesse, who looked from Toby then to me.

"Look, bro, I don't know how to say this, but Ari just called me and said that the ambulance just had to come get Audri from the club they were at."

I could feel my throat close up, and my hands start to sweat. My heart rate increased to double, and I could feel it beating out of my chest. Was something happening to Audri the real reason I wasn't so into my own bachelor party anymore? I'd been feeling like leaving for the longest, but Audri's request for me to let loose and have a good time kept ringing in my head.

Roderick walked up to our little circle. "Cai, I already called in a few favors and got some of my best men handling the situation. I promise we will have Egypt back within the next couple of hours."

I swung my body toward him and walked into his space. "What the fuck are you talking about, Roderick? And what does my daughter have to do with any of the shit they just told me?"

"Look, man." He wiped his hand down his dark face. "Rima just called and said that when she and Audri were in the bathroom, they called Audri's Nana to check on the kids. Instead of Nana answering the phone Mama Faye did going crazy and talking in that heavy Patois shit. They couldn't understand anything she was saying until

Audri grabbed the phone from Rima and calmed her down." The expression of his face went from nervous to sympathetic. "When she was finally able to calm down, she told them that someone snuck into the house and . . . took Egypt."

"Took Egypt?" I knew Roderick didn't have anything to do with my daughter disappearing, but that didn't stop me from charging at him. It took Finesse, Chasin, and Kong to pull me off of him and hold me back.

"Yo, Cai, I know you in your feelings right now, but this isn't the way. Rod didn't have anything to do with what's going on, so you taking your anger out on him isn't going to help the situation," Finesse said to me, trying to calm me down.

I bit my bottom lip and nodded. When Chasin and Kong felt that I was placid enough to stand on my own without going after Roderick again, they let me go.

"My bad, Rod, man. I didn't mean to come at you like that." I stuck my hand out, and he accepted it, bringing me in for a one-armed hug.

"I understand. If it were me, I'd probably be the same way. But we need to head out and get to Mama Faye's house and check some things out. I'll make a few more calls to see if we have any leads. Can you think of anyone who would want to hurt you in any way by taking your kids?"

It didn't take me but a second to respond to his question. "Alex. It was Alex. My gut is telling me that it was her. She's been too quiet for my liking and this type of shit has her name written all over it."

"Well, let me call—"

Roderick didn't even get a chance to finish his statement because I turned around and bolted out of the club. I could hear Chasin, Kong, and Mr. Freeman yelling my name, but I wasn't trying to hear that shit. I needed to find my daughter and wasn't no one going to stop that.

"Wait up, bro, I'm coming with you," I heard Finesse say as soon as I hopped into the car Toby said he had already called to the front. "I know you want to get to Egypt, but I think we should go check on Audri first, then handle whatever it is you got planned after that. If it was Alex who kidnapped Egypt, you know she's going to make some sort of contact with you, whether it's for some kind of ransom or her crazy ass using my niece to get you to fuck her one last time. Roderick and Mr. Freeman said they will meet us at Mama Faye's house after we leave from checking on Audri and Toby said he'll be over once he closes up the club."

I nodded then pressed the gas all the way down to the floor, causing the wheels of Toby's Jaguar XJ to leave skid marks as we sped down the street.

"Text Chasin and tell him to have that paperwork ready and to be on standby, because if I reach this bitch Alex before the police do, I'm going to kill her."

"Hi, I'm looking for my fiancée, Audrielle Freeman. I was told she was brought to this hospital about an hour ago."

The nurse typed Audri's name into the computer and waited for the information to come up. "I see that she was brought to the hospital, but as of five minutes ago, the system is showing that there was an AMA form filled out."

"An AMA form?" Finesse asked.

"What does that mean?"

The nurse closed out of the computer then looked at Finesse and me. I could tell by the bored look on her face that she was starting to become annoyed, but I didn't give a fuck. If she didn't like helping or answering questions pertaining to anything going on in the hospital she chose to work at, then she needed to quit.

She continued to chew and pop her gum before she rolled her eyes and finally decided to answer our questions. "AMA means against medical advice. It's a form we have the patients sign when the medical risks and benefits have been explained to them by a member of the medical staff and they still want to leave. It releases the medical center, its administration, personnel, and the patient's attending and/or resident physician from any responsibility for all consequences, which may result by him or her leaving under these circumstances."

"Well, could you at least tell me what was wrong with her and if it was something she didn't necessarily have to stay in the hospital for?"

"You are asking way too much now. I already did enough looking up the girl's name and telling you that she left. How do I know if you're really who you say you are to her?" She looked at Finesse. "Now if he would've said that he was her fiancé, I probably would've believed it. But you?" She turned back to me and looked me up and down. "Even with your dreads and semi-hood style, you look like you'd be engaged to or date them girls who look like Taylor Swift or Carrie Underwood."

I had to laugh to stop myself from grabbing this dumb chick by her Mickey Mouse scrubs shirt and choking the life out of her. I didn't have time to even go back and forth with her. Making sure Audri was good then going to find my daughter were the only things I was focused on.

Turning and walking back out of the emergency room, I left Finesse to try to get some more questions answered while I pulled my phone out of my pocket and called Roderick. After he had informed me that Egypt was still gone, I released the call with him and was getting ready to try Audri's phone again when I see Rima's BMW coming to a stop in front of the lowered gate.

"Rima!" I screamed out, causing the few people who were visibly shaken by my outburst to either hurry into the lobby doors, or look around curiously. I ran over to Rima's car and banged on her side window before she was able to let it down and give the machine her parking ticket.

"Damn it, Cairo, you scared the shit out of me."

When I looked over into her empty passenger seat, my breath hitched in my throat. "Where's Audri?"

She didn't even answer my question. Instead, she let down the back window on the driver side and unlocked the door. "I made her get in the back seat to lie down for a minute. She was still a little dizzy from her head hitting the concrete when she fell. I tried to get her to stay at the hospital, but she said she had to be there for when they brought Egypt back."

The cars that were waiting behind Rima's started to honk their horns as I opened the back door and took Audri's face in my hand and started placing soft kisses all around it. Besides the few cuts across her chest and the right side of her face being a little swollen, she didn't look too bad.

"Baby, can you hear me? Audrielle, wake up, baby. I'm here."

"Maybe you should let me pull over, Cairo," Rima said as she watched some of the cars behind her hop into the other exit lines, talking shit.

"We good. I need to make sure my baby is okay first. Audri, can you hear me?"

"Cai . . . Cairo," she said just above a whisper.

"Yeah, baby, it's me. I'm here, and I promise I'm going to bring our baby girl back to us in one piece." She tried to sit up but fell back down to the seat. "Maybe you should let Rima take you back to the hospital. You know I'm about to tear the streets up looking for Egypt, and I won't stop until she's back in our arms."

Audri slowly nodded. "No, I . . . I'm good. Wherever you go, I'm going too."

"But, Audri, you're in no shape to—"

She cut me off. "I'm not about to sit in nobody's hospital while some crazy muthafucka has my baby somewhere." Tears started to roll from her eyes. "Now you can either let me go with you, or I'll make Rima take me to my own car, and I'll go looking myself."

This time when she tried to sit up, she actually was able to sit straight up. Her body swayed a little before she grabbed the front of her head with her hand, then rested it on the back of Rima's headrest.

"Excuse me, sir, I'm going to need you to move out of the way. There are people behind you who are trying to exit as well."

I closed my eyes and counted to ten trying to control my anger. I knew the rent-a-cop was only doing his job, but I was getting tired of people interrupting our conversation.

"It's okay, Cai," Audri said, placing her hand on my cheek, instantly calming me down. "We're sorry for the holdup, sir. We're about to go." Audri slid her body from Rima's car while holding on to my shoulders to steady herself. "If you're ready to go, then let's go get your car and be on our way. If not, I'll get back in the car with Rima and do what I told you I would do."

Not wanting to argue with her anymore, I grabbed Audri's hand and started to walk toward the parking lot where I parked Toby's car. "Do you need me to carry you to the car? I don't want you falling out before we get there."

She shook her head. "Naw, I'm good, but I'll be better once we find our baby."

No other words were spoken as we finally reached the Jag and hopped in. I sent a quick text to Finesse telling him to meet us at the exit before he got his ass left. I knew going to Mama Faye's house should've been our next destination, but I needed to pay someone a visit real quick if I wanted to have any chance of finding Alex's psycho ass.

CHAPTER 20

ALEXANDRIA

We'd been at my condo for about three hours now, and both of the babies were still getting on my last nerve. I gave Elijah a warm bottle of milk and changed his diaper twice, yet his little ass still wasn't satisfied. Cairo's daughter, on the other hand, did stop for a minute after I fed and changed her, but as soon as I picked her ass up and put her in the playpen with Elijah, she started crying again.

"Marjorie!" I yelled. Her ass went to the bathroom twenty minutes ago and still hadn't come back. "Marjorie!"

"What do you want?" she yelled back as she stumbled into my living room with the craziest look on her face. She walked past the crying babies as if they weren't there and plopped down on my couch. You could tell she fingered through her messy hair a little bit, but it was still all over her head. Lines of dried mascara streaks made her face look like a raccoon. She looked at me look at her then sniffed her nose.

"How the hell do you expect to help me with these babies if you keep snorting that shit up your nose every twenty minutes?"

She laid her head back on the couch. "I need something to help me stay calm."

"Calm! Your ass has been freaking out ever since I picked you up and you were high off of something then."

She waved me off, then laid her whole body down on my suede couch. I wanted to say something, but I decided against it. I knew she wasn't going to get her ass on the floor, and she most definitely wasn't going to lay her high ass in any of my beds.

"At least take those damn boots off. I don't even know why you would come dressed like G.I. Jane. I told you to wear all black, not no army fatigues."

She raised her head up a bit and looked down at her outfit. "You act as if I've committed crimes before. You told me to dress comfortable, and this was the first thing that popped up in my head."

"So some black pants and a black shirt was totally out of the question?" I sarcastically asked.

"Instead, you wear some fatigue pants with a matching T-shirt and some eleven hundred dollar combat boots?"

She lifted her leg into the air and waved her foot around. "What, you don't like my Burberry military boots? I assumed you would think that they were very fashionable." She busted out with the loudest laugh, which amazingly had both of the babies quiet down and look at her.

"Oh, my God. Do that again!" I told her when Elijah's bottom lip poked out, and his eyes became misty. Marjorie laughed out loud again. This time, she actually got a smile from the both of them. Who would've ever thought Marjorie's loud-ass cackle would be entertainment to them? While she continued to make the babies laugh, I went in search of my phone and went through my missed calls and texts.

Sarah called a few times, but I was sure she didn't want anything but to check on Elijah. I tried to get her to watch him tonight, but she said that she couldn't because her husband planned some type of romantic dinner for them. That night she came to my house and saw Elijah for the first time, she immediately broke down crying. When I asked her what was wrong, she said that Elijah reminded her so much of Eli when he was first born. She told me that Elijah looked identical to his father at that age. I thought everything was good until Elijah smiled at her and she started crying again. When I asked her what was wrong that time, she said that the dimple in Elijah's right cheek was what got her. Something about their deceased father having that same dimple in the exact same place. Needless to say, that was all it took for Sarah to fall in love with her nephew and agree to help me out with learning how to take care of him for a whole week. I even let her take Elijah back to her house for a couple nights. I asked her if she would tell Eli about his son since I hadn't been able to get in contact with him, and she said yes, but he had yet to call me back and attempt to see his son.

I shook my head and, for the moment, dismissed any thoughts of a family reunion with Eli and Elijah. I needed to concentrate on the task at hand if I wanted to pull this thing off and get that money.

I walked back into the living room where Marjorie and the babies were. They were still quiet, so I figured she must've found another way to entertain them. When I looked over to where they were, Marjorie was still by the playpen on her knees, but her ass was leaning against the top bar, fast asleep. Elijah and baby girl both had a death grip on her hair and were tugging at it as hard as they could and Marjorie's ass wasn't feeling shit.

As long as that kept them quiet and busy while I went into the kitchen and made me something to eat, I wasn't about to wake her ass up at all.

Walking into my kitchen, I couldn't decide if I wanted to make a sandwich or heat up some soup. Being that I had a taste for both, I opted to go with half and half. Midway through making my snack, the sound of keys jingling at my front door caught my attention. The sound was so faint that I couldn't tell if the person was coming to my house or if it was the neighbors across the hall trying to go into theirs. When my locks didn't turn after a few seconds, I figured the couple across the way had returned home. I was so caught up in seeing if my front door was about to open that I ended up cutting my finger with the knife I was slicing the tomatoes with.

"Shit!" I hissed to myself, putting my finger in my mouth. I needed a bandage, but I didn't know if I had any here. Taking my bowl of soup out of the microwave, I set it on the plate with my sandwich and went in search of a bandage. I was just about to go to the bathroom to check on a first aid kit when a tall figure standing over the playpen caught my attention.

"Eli? What the fuck! You scared me half to death! When did you get in here anyways?"

He turned his brown eyes toward me. Even though we slept together only once, I wouldn't have minded doing it again. Eli was fine as hell, but not as fine as Cairo. It burned me up on the inside how Audri's fat ass had both of these men caught up in whatever it was they saw in her.

"So this is my son?" he asked, reaching in the playpen and lifting Elijah up.

I slowly nodded. "Elijah Christopher Blake."

"We slept together only one time, Alex."

"And one time was all it took," I snapped. I wasn't trying to be nasty, but what was he trying to say?

Ignoring me, he smoothed his big hand over Elijah's curly hair, then kissed his chubby little face. "I only came back from Seattle to get my son. We both know you're not mother material and, from what my sister tells me, you don't know the first thing about taking care of a baby."

Wait. Did he just say he was here to take my son? My heart started to beat fast as hell. I mean, I knew at first I didn't want anything to do with a baby, but now that I'd gotten the hang of handling him, I didn't think I could just give him away like that.

"Eli, I don't know about all of that."

He kissed Elijah on the cheek again, then placed him back in the playpen. When Eli turned back around, I had to clench my thighs together to stop my pussy from pounding so hard. My eyes scanned his fit body from head to toe. The night we used each other to get over our own heartbreaks and had sex started to replay vividly in my mind. Maybe he wouldn't have minded giving me one for the road. I mean, that was, after I told him he wasn't taking my son anywhere.

"Look, Alex, this right here isn't up for discussion. From what Sarah has told me and what I've read in the papers, you and your father are looking at some serious time."

"See, now that's where you're wrong. I'm not looking at no time. All of those charges are going to fall on my father. Everything that the FBI is looking into has his name and signatures on it; none of them are mine."

Eli laughed. "You sound dumb as hell right now, Alex. You and your father headed the investment brokerage firm that participated in a securities-fraud scheme involving racketeering and physical violence, and cost investors fifty million dollars. And that doesn't even include the charges of sexual harassment that are being brought up against your company, either."

"That doesn't have anything to do with me, like I said. I already talked to the FBI, and as long as I'm willing to testify against my father, then I'm good to go."

"You really think it's that easy? You really think once your father finds out that you're working against him that he's just going to sit there and not implicate you? How are you going to explain your houses, your cars, your lifestyle, shit, the one and a half million dollars you gave me to try to break Audri and Cairo up?"

"My ex-husband, that's how. Cairo and I were married around the time I bought this condo and got my new car. All I will say is that they were gifts from him. He did give me five million dollars a couple weeks after we got married."

Eli walked over to one of my barstools and sat down. He looked at me, then laughed again. "You really are crazy if you think that man is going to go along with anything you have to say after all of the bullshit you put him through."

I shrugged my shoulders. "It really doesn't matter if he does or doesn't. Once Cairo gives me this money I'm asking for, Elijah and I will be long gone before anyone can come knocking on my door."

"What money? From what the papers say, your finances and assets are all frozen. How are you providing for my son properly if you don't have access to any money?"

Eli was really working my nerves with all of these questions. Was he working for the FBI or something? Naw, I doubted it. With all of his gambling problems, I didn't believe he'd even say hello to an FBI agent, let alone work for one. I walked over to the playpen and looked at my son and smiled. I knew some of the things I'd done in the past were fucked up, but I promised myself that once we were out of California, I would go on the straight and narrow. My eyes shifted over to Cairo's baby girl, whose big blue eyes were focused on me. I watched as she gnawed on her little fist something terrible and I smiled.

"You hungry, baby girl?" I cooed, tickling her little chin. "I'll be right back." Ignoring Eli's stare, I went into the kitchen and grabbed one of Elijah's bottles from the cabinet. After mixing the warm water and Enfamil, I returned to the living room. I picked the baby girl up from the playpen, sat on the couch, and put the bottle in her mouth. At first, she wouldn't take it; she kept spitting it out. But after I had squirted a few drops of milk in her mouth, she latched on to the nipple.

"Whose baby is that?"

I froze at the question Eli just asked. How was I going to explain that I had his ex-girlfriend's baby and why? He knew as much as anyone else did that I hated Audri, so me having her baby for any reason would not make sense. Then again, if I was able to get Eli to help me out again for a small fee, this show would probably go by a lot faster.

"How would you like to make some more money, Eli? I'm pretty sure you have a few debts you need to pay off."

"How much you talking about?"

"Way more than I gave you last time."

"Bullshit! You don't have access to that type of money anymore."

"But I will."

He watched me finish feeding baby girl then put her on my shoulder to burp.

"How will you get that type of money, Alex?"

I looked at him and bit my bottom lip. It was now or never. If I wanted him to help me out, I had to tell him the truth. Marjorie's ass wasn't going to be of any use if she kept getting high. I needed someone whose whole head would be in the game.

"Well?" he asked, waiting for my answer.

I blew out a breath then told Eli everything. I told him everything from the beginning, to why I married Cairo, to why I now had his baby. When I finished telling him the story, we sat there in silence. Baby girl had fallen asleep on my shoulder, so I got up from the couch and took her to my bedroom and laid her in the middle of my king-sized bed. After making sure some of the pillows surrounded her at a safe distance, I walked back to the living room. Marjorie's ass was now seated on the couch looking like she was about to cry and Eli was nowhere in sight.

"Where did Eli go?"

"Who's Eli?"

"The dude who was just sitting right there on the barstool in the black jeans and striped shirt. You didn't see Elijah father when you got up?"

Just when she shook her head no, Eli walked back into the house from the balcony. His phone was in his hand, and he was looking at his screen.

"Who the fuck was you on the phone with?"

"Calm your ass down, Alex. I was just calling my boy in Seattle to let him know that I would have his money that I owe him in a week."

"So you're going to help me out?" On the inside, I was jumping for joy, but I didn't want him to know.

"Only on one condition."

"What's that?"

"After we get this money, you move to Seattle with my son so I can be a part of his life."

Shit! I wasn't trying to stay anywhere in the States, just in case the FBI did try to charge me with some of the things they had against my father. Then again, with the amount of money I was going to get from Cairo, I was pretty sure I could stay off of the radar for a while, and just have Eli put everything in his name or just pay for everything in cash. I thought about it for a few more minutes, then gave him my answer.

"Okay. Deal."

Eli nodded. "That's what's up. Do the babies need anything while we're here, like some more diapers, milk, food?"

"We are running low on diapers. The ones I have for Elijah don't fit Cai's baby. I had to tape two of Elijah's together to put on her," Marjorie said.

"Well, I'm about to run to the store and pick up some more diapers and a few other things for Elijah and myself. If we're going to be here for the next couple days, I need to be comfortable. Did you two want me to pick you up anything while I'm out?"

Marjorie's dumb ass rattled off a list of things that she really didn't need while I shook my head.

When Eli left, a weird feeling came over me. Something wasn't right about what all just went down. Could I really trust Eli not to rat me out? He helped me once before, but would he be willing to risk his life to help me once again? Shit, what was I thinking? Eli's ass was a gambler. With ten million dollars on the line, he'd be a crazy muthafucka to pass this easy money up.

CHAPTER 21

AUDRIELLE

I stood in the foyer of Alex's parents' home and watched as Cairo damn near beat Alex father to death.

"Come on, man, that's enough," Finesse said, grabbing his arm. "He obviously doesn't know where his daughter is, or I'm sure he would've told you. You see he pissed in his pants the minute you pushed yourself through the door."

Cairo had his arm in the air, about to strike Alex's father again, when he put it down, then threw him to the ground. "If I find out you knew this whole time where your crazy-ass daughter was keeping my baby girl, I'm going to come back and finish you off. It's going to take more than the hand of God to pull me off of you."

"I'm sorry, Thad . . . I mean, Cairo," Alex's dad cried. Blood was pouring from the gash over his right eye covering most of his chiseled face. The neatly trimmed salt-and-pepper beard was now a full crimson red. His white T-shirt was ripped right down the middle, exposing his pale chest, while his pajama pants were soaked from top to bottom with the urine he frightfully released. "I promise you, things were not supposed to get this far. It was all Marjorie's idea. She's the one who gave Alex the kidnapping idea in the first place."

"Marjorie? As in my stepmother Marjorie?" Cairo asked.

He quickly nodded and wiped away some of the blood obstructing his vision.

"Why would she even be involved? What Alex and I had going on didn't have anything to do with her."

Alex's dad's head turned in the direction of his wife, who was standing on the spiral staircase with a glass of wine in her hand. We didn't even know she was standing there until he turned to look at her.

"Ms. Lydia, I apologize for disrespecting your house and all, but—"

She cut Cairo off, waving her free hand. "You don't have to explain anything to me, Cairo, darling," Lydia slurred then took a sip of her wine. "I knew Matthew's philandering ways would catch up to him sooner or later. I'm just surprised it took this long. What he do this time?" Her eyes shifted over to me. "Try to hit on this beautiful young woman right here?" I didn't know why I blushed, but there was something about the way her smile reached her eyes when she said that that made my cheeks heat up in embarrassment.

"This really doesn't have anything to do with him. It's more your daughter. Your husband here claims not to know where Alex is hiding out with my baby girl, but I think he's lying."

Lydia's hand flew to her chest, dropping her glass of red wine. "Matthew! Now you want to add kidnapping to the list of charges the FBI is already trying to hit you with?"

"I don't, Lydia. I swear to you, I don't. This was all Alex and Marjorie's idea. I told them to leave it alone and just let it go, but Alex just won't leave well enough alone."

Alex's mom walked down the stairs, careful not to step on the spilled wine and broken glass. When she got over to her husband, I assumed she was going to check on the cut above his eye that was still bleeding, but when she passed him up and grabbed a hold of Cairo's bloody hands and started to sob, I looked at Finesse with pure confusion written all over my face.

"Cairo, honey, I'm so sorry for even allowing this mess to go on for as long as it has. Had I known what Alexandria and her father were up

to, I would've been put a stop to it, but somewhere along the way, I checked out on my life
and started to let alcohol control me. It was the
only way I could be at peace being in a marriage
full of lies and giving birth to a daughter whose
heart is as cold as ice. When you and Alexandria
were dating in college, I could tell then that you
two weren't meant for each other. I don't know
if anyone has ever told you this or if you've ever
noticed this yourself, but your eyes give you
away. You've never looked at my daughter the
way you look at this young lady."

She turned and pointed at me. "The way you
look at her is totally different from the way
you ever looked at Alexandria. I've never met
this beautiful woman before a day in my life, and
it only took me a few seconds of watching you
two from those stairs to see the love you have for
one another." She smiled at Cai then let go of his
hands and walked over to her husband.

"Matthew, I'm only going to tell you this one
time, so you better hear me good. Whatever it
is that Cairo and his guests need to know about
Alexandria and where she has their baby, you
better talk now, because if not I'm going to make
sure the FBI knows about all of the clients whose
money you've supposedly invested and lost."

"I promise you that I don't know where Alex is keeping your daughter. I've been calling her since last night, and she hasn't returned any of my calls. Neither has Marjorie."

"You never told us why or how Marjorie got involved. I've never done anything to her, so why would she want to kidnap my daughter?"

Alex's dad looked around nervously before he put his head down in shame. "Marjorie and I have been sleeping together for the last three years. She was in my office the day Alex came to me and told me that you were not going to give her any money for the baby until there was a DNA test done. At first, Marjorie was going to have one of her friends switch the DNA out, but we had to nix that idea the minute we saw Alex's baby for the first time. When that plan went down the drain, she brought up the idea to kidnap both of your kids for ransom. I told Alex not to do it, especially when we were just subpoenaed by the FBI to turn in all of our accounting books; but, like always, the girl never listens. I do remember her mentioning that she would probably lie low at a motel outside of the city before she makes the call, but other than that, I don't know where she could be."

My phone which was in my hand started to vibrate. Eli's number popped up on the screen, but I ignored the call.

"Cai, I think he's telling the truth," Finesse said. "Maybe we should call Rod and tell him everything he just told us; that way they can try to track Alex's phone if she still has it on or put out something in the news in surrounding areas. You beating the shit out of him isn't going to get us any closer to finding Egypt."

"What do you think?" Cairo asked, turning his attention back to me. His white button-down was covered in blood. Bloody handprints from where Alex's dad tried to grab a hold of Cai decorated the length of his pants leg. I watched him ball and release his fist as if he was trying to relax his muscles. I could see his bruised knuckles from where I stood.

"I agree with Ness. We need to go back to Mama Faye's house, tell Rod everything we got from them, then just wait and see what happens from there."

Cairo shook his head. "I can't do that." Tears began to fall from his eyes and my heart broke. "I can't just sit around waiting for someone to find my daughter. I'm her father. I'm her protector. I should be out there searching these streets for her. I'm sure if we put our heads together we can come up with some other ideas. I don't wanna go just sit down and wait for this crazy bitch to contact me. I'm the reason why this is happening. I can't let my baby down. I can't let you down. I have to find my baby and bring her back home, Audri. I have to."

I walked up to Cairo and wrapped him in my arms. When his head fell onto my shoulders, his sobs became louder and louder. At that instance, my heart broke. Everything Cai was feeling right now I could feel too, but one of us had to be strong just in case a worst-case scenario happened. I didn't think that Alex would harm Egypt in any kind of way, but you never knew where people's mental was at when their back started to be pushed against the wall.

While still in our embrace, I felt my phone start to vibrate again.

"Who's calling you, Audri? You should answer it. It might be Alex." The hope in his voice almost brought me to tears.

Wiping the tears on his face away, I shook my head then stepped back out of Cairo's space. "It's not Alex calling me. It's Eli. He's been calling back to back since we've been here." I looked down at my screen and noticed that, instead of leaving a voicemail, he left a text message.

"What the fuck does he want?"

I shrugged my shoulders. "I'm not sure, but he left me a text message this time." I opened my phone and went to my messages. When I pulled up the one Eli just left, I didn't know what to think.

"What does it say?" Finesse asked. I almost forgot he was here with us. He had been so quiet.

"It's just an address. 4635 Marina City Drive in Marina del Rey."

"Who do you know who lives there?"

"I know this muthafucka better not be hitting you up on no 'let's get back together' type shit when he knows you with me and ain't going nowhere."

"I doubt that's what this means."

"What's that address again?" Alex's father asked, finally standing back on his feet with the help of his wife.

"Somewhere in Marina del Rey," Ness said.

"4635 Marina City Drive?"

Alex's dad looked up to the sky and closed his working eye as he recited the address over and over again. "I could be wrong, but I think I remember seeing that address somewhere in Alex's house before. When I went to go drop off some important paperwork while she was at a doctor's appointment one day, I went by her house. The mailman had just run, so I picked up her mail and put it on her dining room table. The first envelope on top of the pile was addressed to her at a Marina del Rey address. She must've put a change of address in with the post office, though, because they forwarded the mail from that house to Alex's home address."

"Ness, call Roderick and tell him what's going on and that we're headed that way. Audri, call Rima and tell her to make sure she stays with Mama Faye and everybody else at the house." Cairo barked as he headed for the front door.

"Cairo, honey, please be careful. I doubt my daughter will do anything to hurt you or the baby, but just in case, be careful." Lydia said as we made our way out of her home rushing to the car.

"Thanks, Lydia, you just make sure that husband of yours doesn't do anything like call and tip Alex off. If we get to this address, and there's no sign of my daughter, I will be back first thing in the morning and, this time, I'm not going to stop until I beat the living shit out of him."

"Don't worry about him. He's told you everything he knows, and I'm going to make sure he doesn't call our daughter or anyone else for that matter."

As soon as we all got into the car, Cairo plugged the address that was sent to me in the navigation system. We had about a fifty-minute drive until we arrived at our destination. For Alex's sake, I hoped my baby was there and not a blond curly lock was missing or even tampered with on her head. *If Cairo thought he did something with Alex's dad when he beat his ass, just wait until I get my hands on that daughter of his.*

CAIRO

"I think that's it right there."

"Naw, that says 4625. We need to go down a few houses."

We drove down the quiet street a couple more houses until I spotted a familiar car. "Isn't that Alex's car right there?"

Sure enough, her silver Maserati Kubang was parked in the driveway, next to an all-black sedan that had those rental car barcode stickers in the back window. I passed up her condo and parked a few houses down. I didn't want to alert her that we were there and coming in.

"Maybe you should text Eli to see if he's still there," I told Audri. I figured if he was willing to tell us where to find our daughter, he was willing to let us in to get her.

"He said he left but should be back in a few minutes. He had to go pick up some things from the store right quick." Audri laughed. "This nigga is a joke. How you walk into the middle of a kidnapping then leave to go to the store? I don't know what I ever saw in him."

I wanted to tell her that he was probably picking up his baby some things, but she'd find that out in a minute. We got out of the car and walked back down the street. Roderick told us to wait until he and the police got here, but I wasn't about to wait for shit. If my baby was in there, I was going to be the first one to take her from the arms of this crazy bitch, and then let Audri stomp a hole in her ass.

"Do you think she has security cameras around here?" Finesse asked as we walked up the long hallway to the steps.

"I don't think so. Alex always prided herself on living in areas with little to no crime rates at all. If there are any security cameras in here, the previous people must've had them installed. Even then, I doubt that she checks the footage."

"Eli just texted again and said that he told Alex to have the door unlocked for him, so we should be good."

I nodded then motioned for Finesse to get behind me. "Okay, me and Ness will walk in first, just in case there are any problems. Once I'm sure Alex doesn't have any weapons and that Egypt is safe, then you come in, okay?" I looked at Audri, waiting for her to respond. When she still didn't say anything that told me that her ass was already thinking about being hardheaded. What I needed her to understand was I meant what I said when I told her that I'd take a bullet for her every night before we went to sleep. If Alex even thought about attempting to harm Audri in any way, she would have to go through me first.

"Audri? Come on, babe, don't try anything stupid. Once we get Egypt back, then you got the green light to handle your business, okay?"

She pouted her lips. "All right, Cai."

"That's my girl." I pulled her to me and kissed her forehead then her lips. "You already know—"

"You'd take a bullet for me."

I nodded, then turned to walk up the flight of steps with Finesse right behind me. When I reached the top, I placed my ear against the door to see if I could hear any type of noise or movement on the other side. The TV was blaring loudly but still couldn't block the sound of a baby crying. Before we made it up here, I made it up in my mind that I would try to talk Alex down in order to make sure that Egypt was safe, but with those baby cries growing louder and louder, I threw caution to the wind and opened the door hard as hell, sending it crashing into the flat screen that was behind it. Marjorie's high ass froze up on the couch with her hands raised high above her head. When her glossy eyes focused on me, her body started to shake.

"It wasn't my idea!" she screamed as she shook her head from side to side. "I tried to stop her, but she wouldn't listen. I'm so sorry. Please don't kill me or call the police. I don't want to die or go to jail."

"Where's my daughter at?"

"I don't know. Alex took her to the back, and that's the last I saw her."

"Then who's that crying in the playpen?" Finesse asked as I walked over to where I could hear what sounded like a baby whimpering.

"That's Alex's son. I've been trying to get him to be quiet ever since Alex went to take a shower, but nothing works."

I looked at little man lying in the playpen crying for his mother's attention and my heart broke for him. After seeing the way Audri loved Nyles, I could never imagine a mother not really caring about her son. Nyles was a mama's boy, and I was pretty sure this child would be if Alex was willing to be a mother to him instead of a money-hungry bitch. Even though I didn't have any feelings for Alex, I still felt bad for her son. Hopefully, Elijah was really on his way back to take him away from the life his son would more than likely grow to hate if he has to stay with Alex.

"Marjorie, who are you talking to? Is Eli baaaaaa . . ." Alex's voice trailed off when she walked from the back of her condo and saw Finesse and me standing in her living room. Her eyes went from me then to Finesse, then back to me. When she looked down at my bloody shirt and pants, she finally swallowed the lump that was in her throat.

"What did you do to my baby?"

Her lips started to tremble as her eyes kept darting to the blood on my shirt. Had I known any better, I would've thought she really cared, then again, this was Alex I was talking to. Her crying could only be an act to get some sympathy. Unfortunately for her, she wasn't about to get any of that from me.

"Bitch, don't even try it. Now tell me where my daughter is so we can go."

She held her hands up and started to walk backward as I stalked toward her. "Cairo, wait. Just listen for a second. I can explain."

"Save your explanation for someone who cares. And before you even fix your mouth to spit out some more lies, know that your father already told us everything you two have been up to." I pointed to her, and Marjorie. "The police are already on their way, and I'm pretty sure the FBI has been informed to add kidnapping to the long list of charges that they have against you and your father. I don't want to hear shit else you have to say. All I want is my daughter and that's it."

"The police!" Marjorie shouted. "Alex, you didn't say the police would be involved. You said we would keep the baby for a few days, call for the ransom, get the money, then give the baby back. Where in that plan did the police come up?"

"Shut the hell up, Marjorie."

"No, I will not shut the hell up. I told you when we broke into his mama's house that this wasn't a good idea."

"You're the one who gave me the idea in the first place."

"Yeah, when I was still high after sucking your father's dick," she screamed, getting up from her position on the couch and walking over to Alex. "I didn't think you'd really go through with it. Do you know what those women in prison will do to a woman like me?"

"It's not like I put a gun to your head. You yourself kept saying how much you wanted to hurt your husband's bastard son the same way he and your sister hurt you."

Marjorie looked at me as tears started to fall from her eyes. "I did say that, but I really didn't mean any of it, Cairo. You have to believe me. These drugs, they make me into this nasty, vindictive person I don't even recognize. Come tomorrow morning, when my high has come down, I won't remember any of this. But right now, while my mind is running in a million directions, I want you know that I am so sorry, and it was never my intention to take your baby from you."

The sound of hands clapping came from behind us. When I turned around, Audri's ass was standing in the doorway leaning against the frame. "Had this been in the movie theaters, I know your ass would've for sure won the Oscar for the best supporting actress."

Marjorie started to talk, but Audri cut her off. "I don't wanna hear shit else you have to say. You still have an ass whipping coming from the way you spoke to me that night at the family dinner."

"Audri, what are you doing in here? I thought I told you to wait until I gave you the green light." I was angry with her ass for not waiting, but I already knew in the back of my mind that she wasn't going to listen.

"I was going to wait, but y'all was taking too long. You said you were going to come in, make sure there wasn't any weapons, get Egypt, then be on our way." Her eyes scanned the living room again. "Where is my baby?"

The fear that was once in Alex's eyes was replaced by a smirk. "She's not here."

"She's not here?" Audri questioned, walking farther into the condo. "But Eli said she was."

Marjorie started to say something again, but Alex cut her off this time. "Eli is the one who took her. He said that we were going about this kidnapping thing all wrong. He said I shouldn't have kept her somewhere that you guys could've easily found, so he came to pick her up and took her to another location."

"Cairo, is she telling the truth? Where is my daughter?" Audri's eyes started to become misty. I watched as she pulled her phone out of her pocket and started to dial what I assumed was the number Eli called and texted her from. "Eli!" she shouted into the phone. "Where the fuck is my baby? You said she was here, and now this bitch is saying that you have her. Somebody better start talking or I'm about to start killing muthafuckas in here."

"You ain't 'bout to kill shit."

I didn't know why Alex wanted to test Audri's patience, because as soon as the words left her mouth, Audri hopped over the couch and tackled Alex down to the floor. From where I was standing, all I could see was Audri's fist going from left to right as she beat the shit out of Alex's face.

"Awwwww, Cai! Get her off me! Get her off me!"

"Ay, man," Finesse said, "maybe we should stop her. Looks like sis is going for blood." He laughed. "Her dress is about to match your shirt and pants in a minute."

Movement from the corner of my eye caught my attention. When I looked up, Marjorie was stumbling over to a big black purse that was sitting on top of the table.

"What the hell is she doing?"

"Probably about to get her next fix," I responded. "Help me pull Audri off of Alex. I think she's done enough damage. Plus, I don't need her going to jail for murder."

Finesse and I walked over to the hall where Audri was still going at Alex. When I went to pull her off, she pulled from my grasp and stood up herself.

"This is all of your fault, Cairo! Everything that has happened bad to me in the last year is all because of you!" she cried.

"Baby—"

"No, Cai! Had you not brought this bitch into my life, none of this would be happening. I wouldn't be out here beating anybody half to death, my baby would be safe at home with me, and my heart would've never been broken the way you broke it. This is just too much. I just want my baby, Cai. I just want my baby, and I just wanna go home. We're supposed to be celebrating us getting married tomorrow and our babies being christened. Not running all over town trying to find this bitch. Every time we are enjoying life, her ass always finds a way to come and corrupt it. Well, I'm tired, Cai. No more. I can't do it no more. No more drama, no more crazy bitches, no more pretending like we're going to live happily ever after." She looked down at a bloody and bruised Alex with pure disgust. "As long as this bitch is somewhere lurking around, I don't think my heart and mind will ever feel safe enough to go on with you."

"Audri—"

Before I could say how I felt, Alex jumped up from the ground and pushed Audri face first into the wall. "You stupid bitch!" Alex roared as she climbed onto Audri back. "Look at my face!"

Before Alex could land her first hit to Audri, I hopped over the couch, grabbed the back of the robe she had on, and flung her across the room. Her body crashed into the TV and then fell into the glass table on the floor.

"Audri, baby, talk to me. Can you hear me, baby? Say something." I turned Audri over on her back and cradled her in my arms, and I tried to make her open her eyes.

She whispered something to me, but I couldn't make out what she was saying.

"Say that again, baby. I didn't hear you. What did you say?"

She moaned and moved her head to the side. "My baby. I hear my baby."

It was at that moment I could hear Egypt's cries coming from behind one of the closed doors.

Gently laying Audri back on the ground, I got up and went toward the cries. Opening the door, my heart fluttered at the sight of my baby girl lying in the middle of the bed rapidly kicking her legs and swinging her arms and crying her eyes out.

"Shhhhhhhhh," I whispered as soon as I picked her up and cradled her in my arms. The minute her eyes connected to mine, her cries stopped. "That's Daddy's baby. Daddy's got you. Mommy and I promise never to let anything happen to you again."

Placing her back on the bed, I unzipped her little outfit and checked her out from head to toe, making sure there wasn't a scratch on her or a hair out of place. Once I was done with my inspection, I closed the pink footie back up and headed back up to the front of the condo. I nuzzled my nose into Egypt's neck and shoulder and inhaled her powder fresh scent. You never knew how much you missed the smell of something until it was gone.

With a smile on my face and a burden being lifted off of my shoulders, I walked back toward the living room ready to grab Audri and Ness then be on our way; however, as soon as I rounded the corner, I froze at the scene before me.

Finesse was holding Audri up on one side of the room while Alex stood on the other side with a gun pointed directly at my heartbeat.

"Nice of you to join us again, Cairo. Now how this is going to work, since you messed up my plan to get some ransom money, is you have two choices to make. Either leave now and go get the ten million dollars I was going to ask for, or watch me kill the bitch you can't seem to live without."

"Let her kill me, Cai. Don't give this bitch any of your money," Audri slurred. I could tell by the way her eyes kept opening and closing that she was going in and out of consciousness. The hit Alex gave her when she slammed her against the wall and the hit to the head she got earlier when she blacked out were both working against her.

"So what is it going to be, Cairo?" Alex wiped the blood falling from her nose with her arm. The robe that she had on was pulled halfway over her body, and I could see the cuts and gashes from when she fell into the glass table. Blood was dripping from every inch of her body. "Do you see this, Marjorie? Even with his so-called bitch here, he still can't keep his eyes off of my body."

Marjorie, who I just noticed, was sitting on the couch rocking back and forth hugging herself as she cried.

"Look, Alex, just put the gun down and we can talk about this like adults. I'm pretty sure we can come to some sort of resolution," I said as I moved over toward Audri and Finesse. If I could make it over to them in time, I could hand Egypt off to Ness then shield Audri with my body.

"Move another inch and I'll shoot her right now."

I held my hand up. "Okay, okay. Just let me put my daughter down in the playpen so we can talk. I won't be able to concentrate on anything you have to say with you swinging that gun back and forth, and she's in my arms."

She thought about it for a minute, then motioned her head for me to place Egypt in the playpen with little man.

"Now that your precious little baby is out of harm's way let's talk about this money and how you're going to give it to me."

I walked back over to where Finesse and Audri were standing but didn't get too close. I made sure that there was enough room though for me to jump in front of the gun if Alex's psycho ass decided to pull the trigger anyway.

Before she could start with this new plan, the front door was slowly pushed open.

"Alex, what the fuck are you doing?" Eli asked as he looked at the scene before him.

Alex turned and pointed the gun at him. "You got some nerve showing your face back here after you tipped this bitch off about our plan. I thought you wanted me and Elijah to come to Seattle with you. How can we do that now if I go down for kidnapping?"

While she was going off on Eli, I made it over to Audri and took her other arm and wrapped it around my neck. At any moment now Roderick and the police should have been there, and I wanted to get her out of here as quickly as possible.

Alex's attention turned back to me. "What the fuck are you doing, Cai? Didn't I tell you to stay your ass over there away from this bitch?" Her brown eyes went black. "You love this fat bitch that much that you are willing to die for her?" I could hear the anger and hurt in her voice. "You've never loved me in that way. Why, Cai? What does she have that I don't?"

Audri started to laugh. It was low at first but then started to get louder and louder. "The one thing I have that you never did is his heart." Audri looked up to me with a tear in her eye. "I'll take a bullet for you," she whispered. Before I could even ask her what she was doing, Audri released the hold she had around me and Finesse's neck and charged toward Alex.

Pow! Pow! Pow!

Three gunshots rang out as my body crashed into Audri's and my eyes were consumed with darkness.

EPILOGUE

One Year Later

AUDRIELLE

*I worship the rain that falls on the grass
that you walk on
and the sun that shines on it to help it
grow . . .*

In my custom-made Pnina Tornai wedding dress, I walked down the aisle lined with purple rose petals with my eyes focused on nobody but my handsome groom. Those bluish green eyes, which I fell in love with the very first day I saw them, bore into mine as Toby sat behind the white baby grand piano and serenaded us with R.L.'s song "As Long as U Know." A small smile spread across my lips behind the one-tier cathedral veil that covered my face. I was so in love with this man that I couldn't wait to become his for the rest of my life. Who would've thought a year after everything went down the way it did that Cairo and I would finally have our day to become husband and wife?

For a minute, I thought that we would never make it here, because after all that happened Cairo and I were in a weird space. I blamed him for a lot of the shit that happened, and he was mad at me for putting my life in danger. It took my mother sitting me down and talking to me to help me finally see that I was pushing out of my life what I could describe as the greatest thing that ever happened to me. And, before you even ask, I questioned the advice coming from my mother seeing as she and my father were having their little quarrels about that Erika woman. But after she confirmed that her son did not belong to my father and that she was very much in love with her own husband, my mother and father were now trying to work on their marriage. After all, they had been married almost thirty years, and I was sure in that amount of time my father must've developed some kind of love for my mother. Why else would he have stayed?

My chest started to heave up and down as we got closer to my soon-to-be husband. I blew short breaths with every step that I took. Smiling at Nana and Mama Faye as I passed them, I nodded. The both had their hands clasped together and raised to their chests. Happiness for their children could be seen in their eyes. My bridesmaids, who consisted of Ariana, Rima, Niecey, and Chasin's friend Jewel, stood to the left while Finesse, Roderick, Kong, and Chasin stood to the right behind Cairo.

I focused my attention back on my groom, and I began to take short breaths again. My palms, which were just fine a few seconds ago, became sweaty and started to shake. I could feel the tears welling in my eyes and threatening to fall. I looked up to the sky to try to stop them from falling, but that didn't help at all. My father, who was walking me down the aisle, stopped a few inches from the front of the church and placed his strong hand on top of my shaky one.

"Are you sure you're ready for this?" he leaned into me and whispered in my ear. I looked at my father, then to Cairo, and nodded. "Then what are you so nervous for?"

It took me a second to answer, but I did. "I don't know."

"Do you love him?"

I nodded again, with my eyes still focused on those bluish green ones.

"Then let's not keep the man waiting," my father said as we began to continue our walk to the awaiting bridal party.

When we finally made it to the front of the church, I started to cry again because of the tears I saw running down my groom's handsome face. As soon as my father gave me away, Cairo wiped the few tears from his eyes then walked down the two steps before him and took my hand in his.

"If anyone here objects to the union of these two people, let them speak now or forever hold their peace."

We turned to face our guests in attendance and looked at each one of them. When no one spoke up, Cairo and I both started to turn around but stopped when an ear-piercing scream filled the church.

"Now, either that young lady doesn't want her parents to get hitched, or she needs her diaper changed," the preacher joked, causing the guests to laugh.

"No, she's just spoiled. Cairo, come get this little girl before we don't make it through this wedding at all," my mother hissed, rolling her eyes. She was looking just like Diahann Carroll's character on *A Different World* when Whitley was supposed to marry that cat Byron: big, floppy hat on her head, pearls around her neck and all. I laughed as she hurriedly handed the baby over to Cairo and waved her off. I thought Grandma was a little mad her granddaughter didn't want to sit with her.

Cairo walked down the steps again in his black one-button formal three-piece Armani tuxedo looking good from the front and the back. His dreads were on the top of his head in a neat man bun, and his face was trimmed and looking right. He grabbed Aniya from my mother and walked back to where I was standing.

Just in case you were wondering, yes, Cairo and I welcomed another baby girl into the world three months ago, and just like Egypt, she was a daddy's girl 100 percent. Couldn't nobody hold her for longer than ten minutes without her crying for her father, not even me. The night I fainted in the street when I rushed out of my bachelorette party, the doctor at the hospital told me that I was pregnant then. That's why he wanted me to stay overnight to make sure the baby was okay. But I couldn't sit still not knowing where my first baby was. Then to find out it was that crazy bitch Alex who had her. Let me woosah a few times before I start to get mad at my own wedding.

Woooooooooosah.

Okay, that's better, now where was I? Oh, yeah, another reason why I was going in and out of consciousness after I beat Alex's ass in her apartment that night was because of Aniya's little butt. My blood pressure was sky high, and my body was trying to tell me to sit my ass down before I lost my and my baby's lives. It wasn't until we ended up back at the hospital the following morning that they were able to get my blood pressure back down to normal.

I shook my head as I looked at Aniya snuggle deeper into Cairo's arm. Her curly dark brown hair was being held back by a lace white bow. Her little dress resembled her big sister's purple flower girl dress, just in a smaller size. She turned her head and looked at me, her little tongue sticking out with those spit bubbles bubbling over. If I didn't know any better, I would've thought she did that on purpose; then again, you could never tell with these new-age kids nowadays.

Once we got her settled, the preacher continued with the wedding without further interruption. And after exchanging our own vows and placing our rings on each other's fingers, we finally became Mr. and Mrs. Cairo Deval Broussard.

The guests cheered as we sealed our marriage with a kiss and walked back down the aisle and out of the church.

"So how does it feel to finally be Mrs. Broussard?" Cairo asked once we got into the back of the limo that was waiting outside for us.

"Honestly, I feel like I just died and gone to heaven," I said taking in that moment. "I can't wait until we go on our familymoon to Jamaica." Yeah, you read it right. We would be going on a familymoon instead of a honeymoon. Since Mama Faye hadn't been to her homeland in so long, we decided to bring her along for the trip. When she told Nana that she was coming with us, you know Nana had to come along too.

"All those fine young men out there," was Nana's excuse when I asked her why she needed to go. It wasn't long before Ness found out and bought him, Ari, Cass, and their newest addition, Cree, tickets too. Because Cairo didn't want to leave my parents out, he ended up buying them tickets too. The only two who couldn't come were Rima and Roderick because they both couldn't get off of work.

I felt Cairo's hand slip around my waist and he scooted me over closer to him. I laid my head on his shoulder and inhaled his scent. A tingly feeling shot through my body and warmed me all over.

"You know I'll take a bullet for you right?"

I nodded. "And I'll take one for you."

CAIRO

The Caribbean's warm sun, soft sand, and beautiful blue water greeted me as I walked barefoot off of the patio that was connected to the six-bedroom, five-bathroom beachfront villa that I rented for the family in Ocho Rios. I'd just finished my morning workout and decided to go for a nice walk while everyone was still asleep.

I waved hello and said good morning to some of the natives and tourists who decided to enjoy the breezy morning just like me. Finding a shaded spot underneath a palm tree, I sat down and looked out at the ocean. It's crazy how life turns out sometimes. Had it not been for Eli's quick thinking around this time last year, neither I nor Audri would be alive today.

As much as I hated to admit it, I was glad Eli walked into Alex's condo the moment he did. When Audri took it upon herself to try to get the gun out of Alex's hands, my whole life flashed before my eyes the second she took that first step. It took everything in me to jump in front of her when I did and tackle her to the ground. Her life was all that I cared about at the moment and all that I was focused on saving at that second.

When the first gunshot went off, I felt when it flew past my ear, missing my head by a few inches. When the second gunshot sounded, I had already hit the ground and rolled on top of Audri to shield her from whatever Alex tried to do next. It wasn't until the third gunshot went off and I heard Eli grunt and Alex fall to the ground that I finally looked up. Eli was bleeding profusely from his right shoulder as he held the 9 mm Alex had in his hand. No words were spoken as I silently thanked him for what he'd done with a simple nod.

Three minutes later, Roderick and some of his police buddies burst through the door with their guns drawn and they took in the scene. Eli dropped the gun he had in his hands and got on the ground as instructed. Once they did a sweep of the house and saw that there were no other threats, we were allowed to get up. Ambulances were called for Eli, Audri, and a distraught Marjorie while Alex was read her rights and taken downtown.

I threw a flat rock into the crystal clear water and watched as the ripple of circles became bigger and bigger then finally disappeared. I was so mad at Audri for putting her life in danger like that, especially after I found out in the hospital later that morning that she was carrying another one of my seeds. For a couple weeks, I wouldn't allow myself to speak to her, let alone be in the same room with her. I couldn't get why she would willingly try to leave me and her kids like that. I knew whenever I would say, "I would take a bullet for you," she would turn around and say it in return. But I didn't think that she would literally do it. It was my job to protect her and our family at all costs, even if it meant me losing my life in the process. Eventually, after having Nana, Mama Faye, Ari, Rima, and even Ms. Diana get on my ass about the way I'd been treating Audri, we finally had a talk about everything and hashed it all out.

The warm Caribbean breeze slid across my bare chest and had me closing my eyes. The moment was so serene and almost had me lost in time. It wasn't until I felt a familiar touch massage my shoulders then envelope me into its hold from behind that I opened them.

"What are you doing out here this early?" I asked Audri.

"I was looking for you. When I didn't feel your body next to mine, I couldn't go back to sleep. So after checking on the kids, I came out here to find you." Her lips kissed the part of my back between my shoulders and made my dick jump.

"Don't do that unless you want me to fuck you right here on this beach and put another baby inside of you."

She laughed as she released me from her hold then stood up and walked in front of me. My eyes took in the beauty of the woman who had made me the happiest man in this world. The gold two-piece she had on complemented her caramel skin and left very little to the imagination. Since she'd had Aniya, Audri had been shedding that baby weight and regular weight like crazy. She went from a size twenty-four while pregnant with Aniya down to a size sixteen. The little tortilla flap that was once above her coochie was gone and everything. Changing her diet and working out with me every morning helped her to achieve her new look. When she asked me which did I prefer, bigger Audri or smaller Audri, I told her whichever one she was happy being. I fell in love with her when she was bigger and was still in love with her being smaller.

"Nana and Mama Faye are going to take the kids with them to see the city Mama Faye grew up in, so they are going to be gone for a few hours. Ari and Ness are taking their kids on the banana boat, and my mother and father are going to scope out places to renew their vows next year on their anniversary; so, if you want, we can head back to the villa, eat some breakfast, see them off, then fuck in all the places we haven't fucked yet," Audri said as she straddled my lap and kissed my lip. I placed my hand on her thick hips and held her still so that she could feel my dick grow another two inches.

"Let me slide your bikini bottoms over real quick and slide up in my favorite place on earth."

She looked around. "Cai, there are people out here."

"So you gonna deny me my early morning fix? I mean, that's the real reason why you came to find me, isn't it?" I smirked. "Your spoiled ass done got used to me beating down your walls every morning before we go work out, huh?"

She bit her bottom lip, and I groaned. Sometimes it was the simplest shit Audri did that drove me crazy.

"If I give you a sample out here, you got to promise to let me sit on your face when we go in the house."

"Shiiiiit. That's all you want? Go on and slide them thangs to the side. I'll let you sit on my face for the rest of the week if you want."

Audri squealed and did her little happy dance, then rose up to let me in. I already knew she was wet and ready for me by the heat that was radiating from between her thighs. Pulling my dick out, I positioned it at her opening and watched her slowly slide down inch by inch, until I filled her all the way up. A low groan escaped from my mouth, and a sexy-ass moan escaped from hers.

"You know you mine forever, right?"

She nodded. "Until death do we part."

"You gon' give me more babies?"

"A whole fucking village if you want."

She started to roll her hips, and my eyes rolled to the back of my head. Audri's pussy was golden, and I would never get enough of spilling my seeds into her wet, tight, and warm insides. I grabbed a handful of her hair and brought her lips down to mine.

"You know I'll take a bullet for you," I said against her lips after I pulled away from our kiss.

She looked me in my eyes as she came all over my dick. "And I'll take one for you."

ALEXANDRIA

A tear slid down my face as I looked at the picture of Elijah that Sarah sent me in the mail today. My baby was going to be two years old in a few months, and I wouldn't be there to celebrate another year of his birth.

I looked at his handsome little face and saw nothing but his daddy. Even with the little dimple showing, he was Eli up and down. The curly hair that used to be on top of his head was cut low, his brown eyes were bright, and his mocha skin was smooth, just like his daddy. The way Eli dressed him reminded me of him as well. My baby had to be one of the most fashion forward one-and-a-half-year-olds I'd ever seen.

I kissed my baby's picture, then put it, along with the update letter Sarah sent me every month, in my little shoebox under my cot. Not feeling like going out for rec, I lay on my hard-ass bed and thought about everything I'd done in my life. There were so many things I would change if I could go back in time. One being ever meeting Cairo and doing him the way that I did. Sometimes I wondered if my father never found out about that inheritance money and planned the little scheme we had going on, would my life have turned out differently. I mean, we were doing pretty good back then, so I really didn't see my father's need for that money; then again, he was running through receptionists back then the same way he was a year ago. Maybe that's one of the reasons why he started stealing money from our clients: to make sure me and my mother still lived in the lifestyle we were accustomed to and to pay off the girls who threatened him with harassment lawsuits. Whatever it was, it didn't matter now; our beds had been made, and we were literally lying in them.

My mind drifted off to that night my life actually turned for the worse. Had I known Eli was going to text Audri and tell her where I had her baby, I would've just let him take Elijah, then gone and got my son back once I had my hands on that money. That's what I got for trusting the father of my child and, even worse, trusting a junkie who had a fear of going to jail. It was Marjorie's testimony at my trial that had me sitting in this cell for the next twenty years of my life. Breaking and entering, kidnapping, and attempted murder were all the charges brought up against me individually. I was still waiting to see what the FBI decided to do with the fraud, money laundering, and racketeering charges they implicated my father with. If my father signed the plea deal, then everything that went on in the company as far as the charges went would fall on him. If he decided to go to trial, then I would be brought up on those same charges since I signed off on some of the transactions.

"Tate! You have a visitor!" The CO yelled from outside of my cell. I climbed out of my cot and put my shoes back on. Only one person came to visit me, and that was my lawyer, so I didn't bother with fixing my hair or anything.

I walked down the long hallway toward the visiting room in my tan jumpsuit ignoring the other inmates who were talking shit and throwing things at me. I had the slightest idea of why they didn't like me, but I wasn't trying to be anyone's prison bitch, so I kept quiet and only spoke when spoken to.

Entering into the visitor room, my eyes scanned all the tables for the lawyer I managed to pay for before I actually came to jail. When I didn't spot him sitting in any of the blue chairs, I started to turn around but stopped when my eyes landed on the last person I expected to see.

"Mom?"

My mother sat at a table in the corner of the room looking way different than the last time I saw her. Her auburn hair was in a low ponytail to the back. Her makeup was light and fresh. The silk blouse she had on matched the brown slacks she wore, and the nude pumps went with the nude purse she had sitting on the table. My mother looked like the woman she used to be when she and my father first got married. The woman who would never touch a drink if her life depended on it.

I slowly walked over to the table and took a seat in front of my mother. I watched her look at me for what felt like twenty minutes before a tear fell from her eye and she quickly wiped it away.

"Mom, what are you doing here?"

She licked her lips then responded, "I came to see how you were doing, Alexandria, and to update you on your father's case."

I nodded. "Okay."

She took a deep breath then blew it out. "Well, first things first, how's everything? Are they treating you right in here?"

"I'm good, Mom, and they're treating me like any other inmate."

She looked down at the table then back up at me. "Well, your brother says hello. He and Oliver are vacationing in Europe for a couple weeks. He says he's going to come visit you as soon as he gets back."

"Mom, it's been over a year. I doubt Matt will be coming to see me anytime soon." My brother hadn't even written me a letter, let alone called me, so I wasn't going to hold my breath waiting for him to come up here.

My mother drummed her fingers on the table as she tried to find something else to talk about. "I saw my handsome little grandson last week." That was news to me. Sarah didn't say anything about Elijah being out here in her update letter.

"Was he with his father?" She nodded. "Why were they out here?"

My mom hesitated for a minute before she finally opened her mouth. "Cairo and Audrielle got married last week, and Eli and Elijah were invited to the wedding."

I didn't know how I felt about that. Cairo and Audri hated my guts, but they didn't hate Eli's. I understood he somewhat saved their lives when he tried to take the gun from me, but that still didn't change the fact that he was a part of the plan to break them up.

"However you're feeling right now, Alex, you need to get over it," my mother said as if she were reading my mind. "You and your father tried everything to break those two up, and nothing happened. It's been a year, honey. Someday you just need to let it go and move on. Maybe while you're here for the next nineteen years, that day will come to you."

I let out a small laugh and shook my head. This was why my mother and I never got along. I was done with hearing about how happy everyone else's life was going outside of these walls, so I asked my mother about my father.

"Well, your father signed the plea deal, so there won't be any trial."

I jumped for joy on the inside. I knew twenty years was a long time, but adding whatever the feds would've given me on top of that, I would've died.

"Wow. I guess that's a good thing." My eyes locked on hers. "But where does that leave you?

Aren't they going to sell all the stuff they seized to make up for the money that was stolen?"

My mom nodded. "They will, but I'm not worried about any of that."

"Why not, Mom? How will you live? Where will you live?" All of the money that I had in my shoeboxes at my house, I gave to Sarah for my son. I knew she would put it to good use and not gamble it off like his father. It wasn't a lot, but if my mother needed some money, I had no problem sending her to Sarah to get some.

"I'm not worried about it because I've been seeing somebody for the last nine months, and he takes good care of me. So much so that he asked me to move in a couple months ago and I did."

"So you moved from Calabasas?"

She shook her head.

"Then this man you're dating must have some money. Is it somebody I know?"

She nodded.

"Who is it?" I needed to know who my mother was seeing who lived in Calabasas to make sure it wasn't anyone my father stole money from and was just dating my mother to get back at him.

My mom was looking everywhere in this visiting room but me before she answered. "It's Greyson."

"Greyson?" I asked going through my mental Rolodex.

"Greyson Wright."

"Greyson Wright. Cairo's father?"

"Visitation over, inmate. Back to your cell. Let's go!" the CO shouted.

I stood up from my seat. "Wait, Mom! When did this happen?"

"A couple months after Marjorie was sent to the rehab center in Utah and he divorced her. And, before you ask, yes, I was at the wedding. I was Greyson's plus one."

"Let's go, inmate!" the CO shouted again. "Before I put you in the hole!"

"I'll put some money on your commissary, Alexandria, and I'll try to come see you after I get back from the trip Greyson and I are taking to Hawaii. Keep your head up, sweetie, and remember, you already have one year down. There's only nineteen more to go," was the last thing my mother said before she blew me a kiss and disappeared through the gray double doors and I was escorted back to my cell.

Nineteen more years to go. This was some bullshit!

THE END!

CONTACT ME

Facebook:
www.facebook.com/thebeginning616

Instagram:
@six2cutie

Twitter:
@thebeginning616